FRANK BALER FINDS T.H.

An abbreviated Mystical Novel

By Frank Baler

Frank Baler Finds T.H.

Frank Baler Finds T.H.

Frank Baler Finds T.H.

Copyright © 2024 Frank Baler. All rights reserved.

No part of this publication may be reproduced, distributed, or transmitted in any form or by any means, including photocopying, recording, or other electronic or mechanical methods, without the prior written permission of the publisher, and the author, except in the case of brief quotations embodied in reviews and certain other non-commercial uses permitted by copyright law.

This is a work of fiction.

This book is not intended as a substitute for the medical advice of physicians and/or psychologists. The reader should regularly consult a physician in matters relating to his/her health and particularly with respect to any symptoms that may require diagnosis or medical attention. Mental health problems should be addressed with a duly qualified professional.

This book does not promote or endorse any particular spiritual doctrine. Any resemblance between any character in this book and a real person, living or dead, is a mere coincidence. All statements made herein represent only the author's personal opinions, not medical or psychological advice.

All figures, logos and marks are registered and copyrighted by the author and publisher. No image shown in this book may be copied or used in any way without written permission from the author and publisher of this book.

ISBN: 979-8-9905845-0-1

3C7D15F565C54C0E2839671B61040D509E3A4BECA0

A4D65B073A37BFA21107B0

Frank Baler Finds T.H.

DEDICATION

This book is dedicated to you, if you lost hope, if you feel broken, if you feel that nothing makes sense in your life. If you feel that the forces of darkness got to you, or if you feel deeply betrayed, read this book.

I wish I could sit with you and tell you that you will be okay, for I have been there, and I found better than okay; I found joy and so can you.

There is a lot I could not tell you in this brief account you are about to read. I can tell you, however, that you are loved immensely.

Please know that each of you is deeply loved by God.

Despite searching for a higher truth all my life, I still carry many flaws as a man. What I found though, and what I hope each of you finds as well, is that God's plan for our lives is always perfect, even when we do not believe we can go on… I can now assure you that God is at work in our lives, and that all things bring us closer to the Light.

May your awareness of God's blessings bring each of you eternal joy.

Frank Baler

YOUR PERSONAL PORTAL

---○---

In your personal portal, you will find some of the guided meditations that I used while regenerating my own life. There are other resources in your personal portal that can enhance your reading and life experience.

I thank you for purchasing this book and hope you will visit your personal portal at: www.frankbaler.com.

I would also appreciate a useful review of this book. Thank you!

Frank Baler

Frank Baler Finds T.H.

CONTENTS

———◯———

DEDICATION 5
YOUR PERSONAL PORTAL 6
CONTENTS 7

ADVENTURES IN DUALITY 9

ACKNOWLEDGEMENT 11
THE BEGINNING OF THE END 12
AND SO IT CAME TO PASS 16

THE UNDERWORLD 19

THE JOURNEY AHEAD 21
THE ASSEMBLY OF MASTERS 76
STRANGE ENCOUNTERS 93
THOU SHALL LIVE 151
DISLODGING GRUDGE 173
THE END OF MAGIC 194
A WARRIOR IS BORN 221
SHE IS ASLEEP 266
IT IS ALL OVER, FINALLY 301

ONENESS AT LAST 321

WAKING UP 323
CLARITY 335
THE MOUNTAINTOP 386

WHAT NOW? 403

THE AFTERMATH 405

Frank Baler Finds T.H.

PART 1

ADVENTURES IN DUALITY

Frank Baler Finds T.H.

ACKNOWLEDGEMENT

I wrote this book in 33 days.

Then it sat in the computer for two years, untouched.

It took three months to edit the manuscript when I got to it. The changes during editing were minimal. Two professional editors then reviewed the manuscript thoroughly. They made only minor changes. Then two more years passed, with the manuscript untouched.

Could I have written this book in 33 days? Clearly not.

I believe we are all capable of tapping into a higher wisdom, and I believe that higher wisdom wrote this book. I just typed it into the computer.

I want to acknowledge, therefore, that higher wisdom for having chosen me to type its book.

THE BEGINNING OF THE END

———○———

My name is Frank. I have always been interested in mysteries. When I was six years old, I loved hosing down the driveway and the sidewalk in front of the house where we lived. I would look at the stream of water emanating from the hose and the effect it had on the gravel and pebbles on the sidewalk. The experience was mesmerizing to me.

One night I had a dream in which my father told me not to dig too deep into anything, referring in the dream to the water and the crevices between the rocks I wanted to clean with the water that emanated from the end of the hose. The more I dug in, my father said in the dream, the more stuff would come out, and there would be no end to it.

Years later as a hypnotherapist I often thought of that dream. I dug in as deep as possible with anyone who came to see me. In some cases, I dug so deep that people felt hurt. I would never stop; 'there is more there, and we are going to get to the bottom of it,' I often thought.

The same thing happened in my personal life. I dug into people as though our lives depended on it. To be honest, I do believe our lives depend on it because to me, digging into ourselves while looking at the mirror of our relationships is the best way to grow; and growth, to me, is the only reason and purpose for life itself.

Naturally, I hurt everyone in my life, I mean everyone. I alienated myself and became miserable. Yet, even in my darkest hour, which you will read about later, I never stopped digging into myself and into the Mysteries. I later discovered what one of my Mentors would call a divine paradox: the worst things that happened in my life turned out to be the best things, and the best things, in some cases, turned out to be the worst. I have certainly lived both branches of the paradox.

I hurt beautiful people who did not deserve to be hurt by me or by anyone else. When I owned what I had done, I determined never to hurt others again. That determination came with a challenge to myself: I would never hurt others again or I would die. Hurting myself was out of the question, but I would find a way to remove myself from this world, which I came to believe would be better off without me in it.

Once I issued the challenge to myself, I had to unravel the origin of the offensive behaviors that were so natural to me. Psychological explanations relating childhood events to adult behavior made no sense to me because I knew I had chosen those parents and circumstances for my birth. No, I was like that before birth, and I had to own who I really was, that would be the only way to heal for real. It was time to dig deep into the Mysteries I had been dabbling in from the surface.

What follows is an account of my journey; a journey filled with bright and dark moments, finally ending in profound joy.

I will tell you about the out of this world experience as honestly and accurately as I possibly can. I will tell you a little about the events that brought me to that point, then I will tell you about this amazing journey that I could not have imagined or dreamt even if I wanted to. I will tell you exactly what happened, and how it happened.

It is true that writing the original manuscript took thirty-three days. I barely slept at the time, and I was not working at my usual load, so I spent much time typing on a small laptop. The original manuscript, however, contained close to one hundred and fifty thousand words. There were three problems with the original manuscript that caused its publication to be delayed by four years.

The first problem had to do with the protection of identity. I did not want any of the characters mentioned here to seem related to people outside of this account. That problem was solved, and the book was then edited by two professional writers who loved the work.

The second problem was the length of the book. The complete story tells two stories intertwined into one. How could I abbreviate it? What is non-essential? That problem was also solved.

The third problem was the most complicated for me. I continued experiencing a personal problem, even after everything that you will read about here happened. I did not know how to feel good about this narrative while at the same time still struggling with a personal problem. The third literary problem was solved, and here you have its product.

I Hope that reading this book brings you healing and joy.

AND SO IT CAME TO PASS

I sat on the white couch in the fifth-floor apartment where I lived. The couch faced north through panoramic windows.

Across the street from the building, there was a yard the telephone company used to park service trucks. On the other side of that yard there was another road.

A white truck driving on that road, about one third of a mile away, caught my attention. The driver had been going east but pulled into the yard across from the building and stopped the truck.

The driver climbed down from the cab and paced back and forth next to the truck. I felt drawn toward him. Quite suddenly, I found myself standing next to the African American man who a moment ago was driving the truck. No words were possible or necessary, for I understood him, and he did not seem to perceive my 'presence'.

Frank Baler Finds T.H.

This man was about sixty years of age. He was hungry, but he only had five dollars in his pocket. He was not mad or angry, but he felt very sad. I walked up to him, close, and talked as I would have talked to a client in hypnosis at the office. Then I turned around, took a few steps, turned back to him, and 'said':

"I am impressed by you driving that huge truck around town."

As soon as said that last phrase I found myself back on the white couch, still looking out of the panoramic windows, at a white truck on the yard across from the building.

The driver ran back into the truck with a spring in his step and drove away.

I smiled quietly, knowing what so many before me had discovered. My awareness was no longer limited to the immediacy of my physical body.

I thought of a past life in France. I had already visited a few key events in that lifetime, but now I wondered what that man, I after all, felt as he was dying; what the end was like that time around.

My belly was huge. I laid on a small bed by myself. A friend sat close by, we talked periodically. I was sad. My wife had died several years earlier alone in a different country. I was a doctor and had immigrated to work with the understanding that I would hurry back to her. I got caught up in one issue after another, and by the time I came home it was to dispose of her assets. She had already been dead. I felt sad that I never enjoyed her or the marriage; work was all I ever thought about.

Back on the white couch, I noticed that my ability to travel in space and time, without my physical body, was expanded and enhanced.

A sense of relaxed freedom filled me with joy. I was able to discern a difference in the way it felt to me, to exist. Knowing that my awareness, experience, and presence were not tied to a physical body, knowing and experiencing that viscerally, produced the greatest sense of freedom and joy I have ever felt on this planet.

Regressions and projections are not important, freedom and joy are. You are important.

I just told you the result of a series of experiences that I could not have imagined or created on my own. It was not always that way, however. In fact, come with me and I will tell what happened. I will tell you a very unlikely story. The true story of how I went from devastation to profound joy.

I believe you will find your own freedom and joy as well as you embark on this adventure with me.

PART 2

THE UNDERWORLD

Frank Baler Finds T.H.

Frank Baler Finds T.H.

THE JOURNEY AHEAD

———O———

One afternoon I paced the hallway outside the office where I lived at the time. Back and forth I paced, clutching my phone in my hand, as if waiting for something to happen or someone to call. Suddenly, and quite impulsively, I called Mercy, a friend of mine. Mercy was also a therapist; we had known one another for about thirty years.

This was the first time I asked for help.

"Look, I'm desperate, I need help now." I said. She knew what was going on in my life, so I didn't have to explain.

"Let me call you back," she said.

A moment later my phone buzzed.

"I made an appointment for you to see a friend of mine," she said. "Frank, the waiting list for him is three months long. As a special favor to me, he said he can see you tomorrow. Four o'clock in the afternoon. Are you going to be there?"

"Sure, Mercy, of course."

The next day at four o'clock I walked into a particular women's clothing store and introduced myself to the impeccable-looking woman manager, just as I had been instructed.

"Please take a seat," she replied.

From what Mercy had told me, for several reasons the couple I had come to see worked clandestinely. Defining their practice was not easy; they did a combination of astrology, psychic readings, psychology, and life coaching. I'm not sure what licenses they operated under, and they chose to stay out of sight of regulatory agencies. And because they cast out demons, literally and metaphorically, they chose to work only with people who had been referred by previous satisfied clients who could be counted on for their discretion.

Behind the manager's counter in this fine boutique was a small opening, not quite a door, but a small opening covered by an olive-green curtain. When she ushered me through that opening, I entered a huge space, well appointed, clean and

Frank Baler Finds T.H.

pleasant. She showed me two right turns and I faced a small desk with two comfortable sitting chairs in front of it.

Behind the desk was a couple. She was visibly older than him, but they seemed to enjoy a great deal of respect and chemistry together. John was Hispanic; his face was very bright, even though his taut skin was darker. John's hair was white, with some gray strands, pulled back with a short ponytail tied in the back. Each time I saw John he wore a white linen shirt with a small opening under his neck, no buttons. John was impeccably clean and well groomed. His round gold-rimmed eyeglasses were spotless. John only spoke in Spanish with me.

John's wife, Priscilla, spoke only in English with me. She would often explain, in English, what he had just explained in Spanish, often with a twist of her own that made it easier for me to understand them. Priscilla was beautiful, a bit taller than John, with a beautiful full head of long blond hair. As I looked at them from across the desk, she was on my right, John to my left.

In front of John was one laptop computer. Behind the desk was one large stainless-steel floor lamp. The walls were white. The space felt clean, safe and cozy at the same time.

They welcomed me warmly, no hand shaking or kissing, just a heart-felt, compassionate, welcome with a typical namaste salute. Without wasting time, he asked me for my astrological data: place, time and date of birth. John entered the data into his laptop and soon had a chart on the screen. He turned the laptop around so I could see the screen and began:

"This is your natal chart; it represents a picture of the sky taken at the time and place you were born. The positions of the planets and stars at that instant, viewed from where you were born, represent a code that can be read. The information encoded into that picture, represented here in this chart, tells us everything about you."

"Does this change over time?" I asked.

"No, this particular chart is fixed because it represents a picture of the sky when you were born," John explained.

Then he casually told me not to take my life. He said that he knew, based on what he was looking at, that my life was in danger.

I remembered that when I was in graduate school the first time, in my twenties, before my first marriage, after a particularly intense Initiation, I had a dream. In the dream, I died in the laboratory where I worked at the university. I was all alone, had no one in my personal life, and it took days for the body to be found in the lab, because no one ever went there. I had died of a heart attack, medically speaking, but it was really a broken heart. In the dream, I clearly remember being 52 years old at the time of my death.

Soon after that dream I left the university to practice hypnotherapy. For years I enjoyed helping clients and students, always surrounded by people and basically keeping busy all day.

As the years went by, I got deeper into my spiritual practices. I eventually recognized that what I had experienced that night was not a dream, but a clear vision of my eventual future. I dug deep into the Mysteries and developed the idea that I could change my destiny through service to others.

The hypnotherapy practice served several purposes: I made a living; I felt as though I was engaged in my spiritual mission of spreading the Light; I was learning more about life than I could in any other job; and I felt that by helping enough other people I was changing my destiny from certain death at the age of 52 to a blissful long life.

When I got married the second time at the age of 47, I thought I had defeated early death as I had seen in my earlier dream. I would build an awesome life with my wife and have a long, happy life… that is what I thought.

By the time I went to see John and his wife, I lived at the office and had just come back from a near death experience.

Frank Baler Finds T.H.

I was not able to sleep at that time, felt horrible anxiety and constant panic, cried non-stop, and really wanted to die. I actually blamed myself for wanting to come back from the NDE instead of moving into the light and letting go of this lifetime of pain and suffering. I was 52 years of age at the time.

"I am listening." I said to John. Whatever this drawing is showing you is true so far, I thought.

Then he told me when I got married the first time. He kept showing me little marks on the drawing on the laptop and telling me:

"You have two daughters here, your marriage ended here..." John would say pointing to little marks on the chart.

Everything was true and exact, just as he was saying. Then he told me there was a second marriage, two daughters, and the end of that marriage soon after the second baby was born. A third woman showed up on my chart. Although that other relationship had been extremely passionate, it was also very destructive, ending abruptly, and badly, John said.

My second wife, Hana, and I constantly talked about being together forever. She frequently talked about our unending love as something that would transcend this lifetime. She loved me immensely, she said, and I felt the same way toward her. Then she broke up with me soon after

Frank Baler Finds T.H.

our second daughter was born, quite unexpectedly. So far, John was right on the mark.

The third woman who showed up on the chart after Hana was clearly Liaran.

Liaran had three marriages before our relationship. One gift to our union was the one-year-old daughter she had with her second husband.

Soon after Liaran and I united, we had a fateful photoshoot with the whole family and Liaran's daughter that did not go well. The night of the photoshoot she gave me a severe beating and left the house with the baby. I waited three days for her to come back; when she did not, I went to get her. When we finally spoke, the condition for her to return to the house was that I apologized to her and to her father for her beating upon me. I wanted the family, I loved her. I apologized to her and to her father. I sealed my fate.

Then we went for a weekend trip to Bush Gardens in Tampa, Florida, and had a horrific car accident. The accident was so horrible that, when we went to pick up a suitcase left in the trunk of the crashed car, the attendant at the junk yard said that she thought everyone had died in that car at the time of the accident the day before. It was really eerie.

The night of accident, after the kids were in bed at the hotel, I asked Liaran for a talk. I told Liaran that I thought

Frank Baler Finds T.H.

the accident was an omen, that we should make peace and have a good relationship. She agreed that the accident was indeed an omen, but that, to her, it meant that the relationship was over.

The day of her daughter's birthday in August we separated again. Although the relationship did not officially end in August of 2018, as John claimed to see in the chart, it was pretty much hell at home from August to November 2018.

John told me many details of my life with incredible accuracy. According to the figure he had on his laptop, there was another woman in my life after my second wife, who would be heavily influenced by the forces of darkness, and who would just about destroy me. He said that, again according to the chart, I was a good man, with a good heart, and therefore I would not succumb to that woman's malicious plan, and would eventually meet the real love of my life, in this lifetime.

One thing John emphasized several times was that the real love of my life was not Liaran. The woman who caused so much pain, after my second wife, the one I thought of as the love of my life, he said, was simply a decoy, someone sent to me to burn away a whole lot of karma in a short time. She would be gone from my system soon, and would be irrelevant to my future, according to John. Then he provided interesting astrological details about an upcoming love.

John closed the laptop. His wife got involved in the conversation. They both looked at me intensely for what seemed like a long time. I was crying and in constant panic.

"Frank," she started, "you must be strong, for you have strong trials and tribulations ahead. You must stay true to your essence."

"It cannot get worse than this," I said.

"Oh dear, it has not started yet," she replied firmly.

"You know you are a Seeker of the Higher Truth," John said. True seekers undergo similar processes, call them Initiations if you will, but they all go through similar processes.

I had to admit that was true. My Mentor lived through similar circumstances, and most mystics I had studied were completely broken at one point in their lives.

"There is a purpose for everything," the wife said. "You must develop your five superpowers, that is why this is happening *for you*."

"For me?" I asked showing frustration. John looked at me as if saying, 'don't be silly, you know better than that'.

"Frank," she continued, "what do you know about the biblical Samson?"

"Oh, he fell for a hot woman and she betrayed him," I said, mostly expressing my own pain.

"Actually, that story has nothing to do with the man/woman issue," John interjected. "Go home, read the stories of Joseph, Moses, Samson, David and Daniel. Come back when you have something novel to say about these characters."

"I am familiar with these stories, what are you trying to tell me?" I asked with an air of petulance.

"Frank, my dear, it is enough for today. Read the stories and call us in the morning," Priscilla said.

"Okay," I answered without much of a choice.

I stood up, offered them each the namaste salute, lowered my hands and walked out.

"John will see you tomorrow at four o'clock," the store manager said to me unceremoniously. The discrepancy between what they told me inside and what the manager said did not bother me.

"Thank you, madam," I said as I laid out the agreed amount of money on the counter and walked out.

Once safe in my car I began to cry. Again, not a gentle sob, but a profound catharsis. Little did I know at the time that these profound cathartic events would continue for a long time; there was so much accumulated pain to heal, and so much to learn.

For various reasons at the time, I had lost the ability to read. For a good two months I could not extract meaning from written words. Now this mysterious man, who seemed to know details of my personal life, was asking me to read five biblical accounts in one day. I knew I could not do it; but there was something else I could do.

I went back to the office, washed my face, pulled out blank sheets of paper from the printer tray and began to write. I wrote about the biblical characters, allowing only memory and intuition to guide me.

I wrote for a few hours, sheet after sheet, one side only. Nighttime visited us; I stood up to turn the lights on and continued writing. I wrote stuff I never knew, but I never paused to read it.

The battle within me was unbearable, it hurt more than I thought I could stand, but at the same time I understood what was happening. One part of me wished so much to die, as a way out of the extreme pain, the other part of me felt that life would actually start once I got through this process.

Somehow, I felt, not quite knowing what it meant, I must go through what Joseph, Moses, Samson, David, and Daniel

Frank Baler Finds T.H.

went through. I would find what I had been looking for, for centuries, on the other side of this ordeal.

I was awake all night, as usual at that time in my life. At about 3 in the morning, I usually went for a walk at a local park, sometimes a jog. I dozed off for a few minutes at times, but immediately jumped up startled, in a panic. I was happy to go back and talk to John and Priscilla that afternoon.

I looked over all the scribbles I had written the day and night before. I decided to summarize it all in a way that would make sense to John, in case he asked me for a report on the homework assigned.

What I wrote was a poor summary of the biblical accounts. I later found these notes:

Joseph, book of Genesis: sold into slavery by his brothers. Ended up in Egypt. Eventually the headmaster at Potiphar's house. Potiphar's wife attempts to seduce him, he is loyal to his boss and refuses her. She feels disgruntled and accuses him of misconduct. He is sent to jail where he heals many, primarily through dream interpretation (hypnotherapy?). Eventually Pharaoh has a dream no magician can interpret. Joseph is called from jail and Pharaoh ups the ante by asking Joseph to tell him his dream, and then interpret it. Joseph says only God can do that, so he comes back the next day with the dream and its interpretation. Pharaoh makes Joseph second in command of Egypt. Later Joseph saves Israel because he is in charge of the food supply.

Moses, book of Exodus: found in a river by an Egyptian princess. Raised as an Egyptian, but of Hebrew origin. Kills an Egyptian and flees to the desert. God asks him a favor; he offers God several excuses why not him. God teaches him magic, he outperforms the Pharaohs' magicians, and eventually splits the red sea to free his people. He climbs a mountain, where God gives him the 10 commandments, but when he comes back, many built a golden god. Moses never makes it to the promised land after 40 years wondering in the desert.

Samson, book of Judges: a nazarite, son of a barren mother. Archangel Gabriel intervened in her pregnancy, same with Sarah and Mary. Strong man; has several affairs. Eventually is seduced by Dalila who betrays him. His eyes are gouged out, I think his tongue was cut out. he was tied to a millstone – going around in circles, lost. His hair grows back, he regains his strength and destroys the Philistine palace, killing the philistines who enslaved him, and himself.

David, I Samuel: young boy volunteers to defeat a giant warrior. He throws a stone killing the giant. Really represents the ability to overcome major obstacles.

Frank Baler Finds T.H.

Daniel, book of Daniel: refuses to bow down to the king, only bows down to God. The king punishes him by feeding him to the hungry lions. In the morning, the lions are laying down next to Daniel. The hungry lions represent the bestiality of human ignorance. The spirit of God prevails over ignorance always.

The next day at four o'clock, I walked in to see John and Priscilla and handed him the sheet of paper. John, as usual, surprised me. He never looked at the paper, he simply tossed it in the garbage bin next to him.

"That means nothing," he said sternly.

"Well, I can't quite read right now, and you asked me to read…"

"Yes, I asked you to read, but I did not ask you to read a book. I was hoping you would have read your soul and come up with something better than that crap! In fact, I asked you to come back when you had something novel to say. That is not novel, that is memorized crap" he said as he stood up.

"Oh Margarita, your manager, told me to come back…" I said defensively.

"Frank, have you heard of the kabbalah?" The lovely wife asked, rescuing me from John's apparent fury.

"Well, yes," I said.

Frank Baler Finds T.H.

"What have you heard about kabbalah, dear?" This woman was wise, I thought. Adding the word 'dear' at the end of the question melted a lot of tension away. I mentally thanked her for that gesture.

"Well, I have been studying kabbalah since the early 90's. In the mid-nineties I received three Initiations into the kabbalah, in America, Israel and Egypt. When I turned 40 years of age, according to Tradition, I started teaching kabbalah. Have been teaching and studying it ever since."

My answer did not impress anybody, in fact, they each seemed to look at me as an impostor. Perhaps it was my own inner misery and self-judgement speaking, but inside, in my mind, it felt as though they were asking: if you are a kabbalist, how come you are so devastated? The craziest part of the story is that I felt like answering aloud: it is *because* of kabbalah that I am suffering so much!

"Okay," John said now sitting down and much calmer. "So, you know that the desire to receive cannot be eliminated, only converted from the desire to receive for the self alone to the desire to receive to share. We all want to receive and have everything we like; that cannot be changed. Changing that which cannot be changed cannot be our goal." John paused, then continued.

"The goal" John said slowly, "is to learn to share; to receive what you want, not only to have it, but to share it with others as well."

"Yes Sir," I said while nodding my head, but a little dizzy having no idea how this talk would take my pain away.

John was on a roll, not about to stop.

"Biblical writers of the Old Testament sometimes represented the desire to receive for the self alone through the figure of a woman, since the female energy is the receptive one."

"Are you saying then, that Dalila represents Samson's indulgence in his desire to receive for the self alone? Are you saying that the mighty Samson was immature mystically and squandered his strength by being selfish?" I asked to be sure of what he was saying, while following up on the question asked the previous day.

"That is one way to put it," John said. "As a kabbalist, you must keep in mind that all of the Old Testament must be understood symbolically, according to the teachings of kabbalah. The truth is that none of those characters I asked you to read about even existed, they are just personifications of lessons we must all learn."

"Frank," his wife joined in seamlessly, "the story of each character we are going to talk about hides a secret message that, when you get it, awakens in you a superpower. A true mystic must have all five superpowers awakened, developed, and at the service of the community."

"A true mystic?" I said crying. "I am nothing. I am dying. I failed my wife and family, I failed my Mentor, I failed all my Initiations, I failed the Masters. I am a failure!" I said almost shouting. "Please either take this pain away or show me how to die."

Neither of them was impressed by my immature rant. I heard what came out of my mouth, however, and I was astonished.

"What do you want?" John asked. "If you want to die you take care of that away from here." He continued. "By the way, what exactly do you think happens the moment after you destroy your body? Anyway... let me know right now what you will do, so we don't waste time on the dying."

This was one of those moments when everything seems to slow down. 'Either the mind speeds up quite a lot, or time actually slows down' was the first of a series of thoughts that occurred to me during the gap between John's last words, and the wife's next phrase.

The inner voice that we call 'thinking' continued:

'What John told me was almost word-for-word what I told clients who came to see me expressing a desire to die.

Frank Baler Finds T.H.

Do we all tap into the same ideas? I thought while at the same time feeling the pain of his apparent cruelty. I was truly suffering, and he simply did not get it. I must have been a cruel therapist all these years, I thought, for people have come to me in pain, and I did tell them that killing themselves would only make the pain worse. First of all, I would say, there is no death. The moment after you destroy your body you will feel more alive than before, except that now you have one more problem to deal with. In addition to the pain that caused you to kill yourself in the first place, there will be the additional pain of no longer having the means to heal the actual problem, which is the use of your body.

'I never lost a client to suicide in 24 years of therapy,' the mind continued. While the explanation above is good, what dissuades people from killing themselves, I thought, is knowing that it is not necessary to take their lives in order to take the pain away. People actually want to live, as I do, I kept thinking. What we need when we suffer is a way of truly ending the pain; a way out of misery and into joy.

I must have become distracted because Priscilla's next words jolted me a little:

"Let the dead care of the dead…" she added, quoting Jesus.

Frank Baler Finds T.H.

"Guys, obviously I am not going to hurt myself. I am hurting to the point that I am not sure the body can continue functioning, but I know there is nowhere to go. What I really want is to cure the pain, and death itself is not a cure, it only adds to the pain, because there will be one more regret to deal with later."

"Cure the pain?" John asked. "Just run back to Liaran and beg her to take you back once again."

"I wish it was that simple John. Even if she took me back, the problem would only get worse; my pain is not for lack of her, therefore, her presence in my life cannot take the pain away."

There were brief moments, sometimes in the middle of the night, sometimes while working or teaching a class, sometimes while jogging, when I had clarity. During those moments, I understood that I had placed myself in a tight spot from which I could not escape; there would be nowhere to run to, no physical solution to the inner pain, I would have no choice but to seek more Light or face my extinction. My soul had made this choice a long time ago, and this woman agreed to play her part in my plan. The plan was perfect and effective. It just hurt like crazy, and I had no idea how to proceed forward at that juncture.

Frank Baler Finds T.H.

How I felt reminded me of a magician I had once seen on television who had placed himself inside of a safe, handcuffed, then had the safe thrown into a river. The challenge for the magician was to get out alive, and the cost of not getting out was his life.

It occurred to me how all Masters, at anything, eventually voluntarily place themselves in situations that can cost their lives if they fail. The lion's den, the battle against goliath, the devil in the desert, the safe under water were all analogous, for a therapist, to finding joy after losing not only the desire to live, but the very desire to fight for one's life; the very survival instinct that therapists pinch in their clients to jolt them out of their own misery was missing within me. I actually wondered how a person could heal if the very core of the being that actually heals the person is no longer there.

I felt like that magician, handcuffed, inside of a locked safe, under water. I placed myself in that awful situation by accepting absolutely unacceptable behaviors from Liaran: the constant lies, the physical violence, the 'little' betrayals, affairs… it was all there, in plain sight. I was aware of the transgressions, I commented on them, I wrote notes about them, I asked her for dialogue and change, but, I kept accepting the unacceptable.

Frank Baler Finds T.H.

"Frank, it is normal to want your woman back..." she said nodding.

"I would love to have my family and relationship restored, but only if it did not interfere with my Path. My Path and my relationship with God come first, the marital relation is second. I told Liaran that much quite clearly, since day one, she knew that, and tested me each day on this. I never wavered. God first, relationship second. I put my life on the line for this principle."

"Okay, you got it. Good enough for now. We meet soon." John said as he stood up again.

When I came back the next day at four in the afternoon, the wife started, as John smiled discreetly.

"We did not tell you about Abraham yesterday quite intentionally. But the first superpower on the Path is hidden in the story of Abraham. By the way, she continued, you will awaken all of the superpowers soon... not just the five we mentioned."

"How many are there?" I asked.

"That depends on the student, John added." You discovered and mastered the first superpower on your own, so we know you will awaken at least seven superpowers, but perhaps as many as the nine, in this lifetime, that enlightened Grand-Masters have available for service."

It is all so symbolic, I thought, one superpower for each month of gestation. No wonder they call these guys 'born again' or enlightened. Then I came back to room awareness:

"Yeah, Abraham had two boys later in life, I had two girls late as well, what is the lesson there?" I asked half knowing the answer.

"Frank, dear, it is time for you to own yourself. You are more than you attempt to appear. For instance, how about you tell me what the lesson hidden in the Abraham story really is," the wise lady said.

It was true. I saw myself as an eternal student and disciple. I did not own my personal power. What I called a 'miserable life' was a consequence of that mindset that was beginning to feel really antiquated. So, I took a deep breath, reminded myself that I have the right to be where I am at in my personal journey, adjusted my position on the chair, cleared my throat, dried my tears, and spoke:

"Abraham asked God for a son. God provides abundantly and gave him two, not one son, because that is what Abraham wanted the most. I wanted to marry my soul mate more than anything. God provided me with heaven through her; more than I could imagine, including two precious babies. When she was not happy, God gave me a true love forever, Liaran. Abraham loved his son so much that he doubted his ability to love God as much. That inner struggle was captured in the biblical story where God asks Abraham to sacrifice his son, what he loved the most. I loved Liaran so much that I feared losing myself in her and forgetting my mission and relationship with the divine. My struggle was manifested in constant strife and the eventual need to make a choice. Abraham raised the knife to sacrifice his son, and I left the home. Abraham loves God more than anything on the earth, so do I."

Then I added, "I needed to test myself on that last one, now I know for sure."

"That is correct," John said. "All things on the earth are good, for God creates all things. The moment we become attached to one thing, however, we forget where it comes from. When we realize that we forgot the source, we learn to remember. But before we can live in full grace, we need to test ourselves. You planed on this test yourself, long before your birth. And you proved to yourself what is really important to you."

Priscilla continued seamlessly "Your first superpower, my dear Frank, comes from knowing what really matters to you, and from your willingness and readiness to let go of anything else," She said wisely. "All mystics who preceded you had to walk away from the love of their lives, whatever that was at the time, for the glory of God."

This couple was wise, and I felt we had a lot of growth to accomplish together, but I was uneasy with the religious terminology and symbology. The whole notion of sacrifice had nearly cost me my life, again, I thought. I have been sacrificing in the name of God for about six hundred years that I can remember. Somehow, the Father, the Abba, the true God cannot be about more sacrifice.

"You are correct," John said.

Was he reading my mind, I asked myself, or am I so deranged that I spoke my thoughts aloud not realizing it?

It did not matter because he continued: "Joseph was second in command of Egypt, he was joyous serving the community, and he saved Israel from famine."

"Yes, but not before he was humiliated, betrayed and jailed," Priscilla added, again seamlessly.

"Humiliation through betrayal seems to follow all mystics," I added. "Is that the mechanism whereby the power of the ego over the inner self is defeated?" I asked quizzically.

Frank Baler Finds T.H.

"Well yes, some mystics need to break that bond, so they choose humiliation as a mechanism. Betrayal is simply the tool that creates humiliation most effectively." John said.

"I see it…" I continued. "And jail is analogous to the desert where Jesus prayed. An embryonic period, hidden from public view, so that the new man can be made. It is an opportunity to purify oneself, such as what Mandela chose."

"I would not say publically that Nelson Mandela chose jail because you will be misunderstood. Mr. Mandela was unjustly incarcerated in the physical plane, but his soul needed that experience to purify the man so he could accomplish his mission of unification later." She said.

"And I am in a metaphorical jail cell now," I continued. Just like Papini's character[3], I built my own cell to find myself. My pain, suffering, and loneliness are the bars on the cell. My sentence will be over when I forgive myself, and I will have forgiven myself when I can feel joy independently of external circumstances. Wow," I said.

"Now you know why you were betrayed where it hurt you the most," she said, "you know why the humiliation of calumny, you get why the injustice of false accusations from

---

[3] His Own Jailer, by Giovanni Papini (1881-1956). December 9, 1922

the person you loved the most. It was the only way to put yourself in that embryonic state of purification and rebirth. I like that you mentioned Nelson, because the example applies, but we are talking about Joseph, who did become second in command."

Then she fired the question:

"And why would the biblical writers not represent Joseph's triumph by putting him in charge as number one in the story?" She asked to see if her student was paying attention, I thought.

"Ah, Abraham can answer that," I started. "It is a matter of what is number one in your life; religiously, God would not tolerate a human being who thought of himself as number 1. Kabballistically, God is the first principle, therefore represented by the number 1; that leaves number 2 for great mortals. Joseph's greatness, as Jesus would say, came from his father, from God, in this case represented by Pharaoh. All great mystics are number two in command; never number one." This time I answered with no hesitation.

"Tomorrow at four o'clock we will talk about what we can learn from the story of Moses," John said as he stood up and showed me out.

I went back to the office, where I still lived. There was only one thought on my mind: maybe, if I learn enough, if I

Frank Baler Finds T.H.

heal enough, if I become a good man, Liaran and I can be happy together; our relationship can be restored. It was clear to me that all the problems we ever had were because of my stupidity and inability to be a good man. She had always been right, and she was right then. I did see how I had forced her to beat me severely and repeatedly; after all, I drove her crazy. Obviously, I drove her into an affair, since I was not a good enough man, she needed support from someone else. Of course, I was responsible for the pregnancy that resulted from that affair; after all, somehow, I must have had something to do with her not being on birth control. And obviously the abortion was my fault. I told her I would raise the kid as our own, but she most likely felt that I would use the kid's existence to judge her later for the infidelity. An abortion was her only remedy; and I pushed her into it.

I cried and cried, not quite able to process how stupid I had been. God had given me a perfect woman, and I had corrupted her to the point of beating me, having affairs, and having at least one abortion that I knew of. She told me I was 'garbage' and not a good man, and she was right.

A good man, I was sure, would have started with the woman I ended up with (in pain), and converted her into the woman I started off with (awesome). Considering that

Frank Baler Finds T.H.

Liaran went from awesome to awful with me, I was indeed garbage, as she repeatedly and correctly pointed out to me.

My newly discovered flaw, together with the desire to make Liaran happy gave me the impetus to work hard. Tomorrow, John had told me, we would talk about Moses. Reading was almost impossible for me at the time, but I made an effort; I worked for several hours well into the night. I started by reading a summary online, then I was able to read the biblical account of Moses. Finally, I wrote several pages of notes. At the top of the page I wrote, and circled the following:

All mystics who preceded you had to walk away from the love of their lives, whatever that was at the time, for the glory of God.

When I walked in to see John and Priscilla the next day, they both looked at me serenely for a moment. They were quiet, just looking at me. Then she broke the silence:

"Tell us Frank, what did you learn from Joseph?"

I had forgotten all about Joseph; I prepared for a talk about Moses. As it often happened back at that time in my life, I cried of sadness. Where was the brilliant student I used to be? The brilliant talker? The Maestro? I could not find

Frank Baler Finds T.H.

him. I felt dead, and severely anxious to the point of panic. Yet, I started talking, not quite certain of where the strength or words were coming from.

"Well," I said hesitantly, and mostly waiting for something to say, "the writers talk about three, not one, injustices against Joseph. He was sold as a slave by his brothers; he was accused of rape he did not commit; and a man the cured in prison forgot about him. That's three injustices. The number three points to stability and completeness, such as in a three-legged stool that is always stable even on uneven ground; the number three refers to the law of triangles, cause, manifestation and effect. Because the number three is associated with completeness and totality, it also points to a full expression of divinity, such as in father son and holy spirit."

"So, what did you learn from Joseph?" John asked this time.

"Having three injustices perpetrated against the character in the story shows us that what happened to him was really unjust, as in an effect without a cause. Had there been a karmatic reason for the so-called injustice, we would not have a true injustice, and the writers would have mentioned one, two or four events, but never three.

"What do you mean?" The wife nudged me on patiently.

Frank Baler Finds T.H.

"Well, an intentional action from us is called a *cause* because it will set into motion an eventual *effect*. When something just happens unexpectedly, we think of it as the effect of a prior cause. In our conception of reality, we claim that effects follow causes temporally; we also say that there is no cause which does not generate an effect, and there is no effect that does not result from a prior cause.

"Wait," she said, "is that 4 things?"

"No, actually 5 lemmas that amount to what we call the Law of Cause and Effect." I answered.

"Can you state those lemmas for me please? This is interesting," she said.

"Sure." I admit I loved that she thought what I was saying was interesting.

- Every intentional action constitutes a cause.
- Unintentional happenings are effects.
- Every cause is followed in time by an effect.
- There is no cause that does not generate an effect.
- There is no effect without a prior cause.

"Okay, thank you for that lesson. It is nice to see the teacher in action… I admit I heard great things about your classes." Priscilla was generous, I thought.

"Oh, from Mercy? She is just kind. My Mentor taught some impressive classes!" I said shyly.

"Frank," she got back on track, "people come in here every day asking us why things happen to them. They do not know why it happened, therefore there is no cause?"

"Oh no," I reflexively jumped. "Human awareness of something is quite distinct from the thing's actual existence. A cause may exist, yet I may be unaware of it... or unconscious of it as we hypnotists say. In fact, our job is to help people uncover unconscious causes so that they may mitigate them, thus turning off the effect, which is the problem they came to the therapist to solve."

"Nobody explained therapy to me quite that way, but what does that have to do with the notion of justice?" She asked while John seemed to be deep in thought.

"Ok," I started again, not quite believing they were listening to me. "When something happens to us, we automatically ask ourselves what we may have done to cause or deserve it. The very word 'deserve' implies that a cause exists and we either found it, or may find it. When we do not find a cause, we call the unexpected event an 'injustice'. An effect without a cause would violate the Law of Cause and Effect. We believe it is just that an effect follows a cause, but if an effect happens without a cause, we believe a 'true injustice' has taken place."

"Interesting, what do you mean by 'true injustice', Frank?" she asked. Now I seemed to feel more relaxed, so I continued:

"If a cause exists but I just cannot find it, we have an 'apparent injustice', not a true one. It would be up to me, in that case, to work harder at uncovering causes, so I can repair them in order to eliminate the effect. A true injustice would be an effect without a true cause."

"Frank, this is interesting stuff, but what does that have to do with Joseph?" Priscilla re-focused the conversation, I obliged:

"Of course, had Joseph betrayed his brothers, and consequently was sold as a slave, there would be no injustice. Had Joseph violated Potiphar's wife, ending in jail, again, there would be no injustice. Had he refused to cure a man in prison, the man forgetting to put in a good word for Joseph would be just. The Biblical account, however, portrays the story as a sequence of three true injustices. There was no human cause for the effects observed; that is the first kabbalistic clue that a divine process is under way. Second, it just so happens that the number of injustices was three, again a kabbalistic clue that points to a divine process."

"So," John finally jumped in, "the fact that the injustices are truly unjust, and number of injustices being three, points to a divine intervention, as in the so-called injustices being a part of God's plan. God had a plan to save the Israelites from famine; for that he needed an Israeli in charge of the food supply in Egypt, for that all the other events had to happen as they did. It was a perfect plan with a purpose, for a purpose."

"Okay," now Pricilla intervened. "I see where you are going. But what about the poor man, Joseph, what can you learn from him?" She asked me. Somehow an answer came out of my mouth:

"Patience and righteousness. Joseph waited patiently for God's plan to unfold, never lost sight of the fact that he played a part in a much greater plan of God, and rather than being bitter about the injustices, he served all he could with love and devotion."

"What do you mean?" She asked.

"Well, had he raped Potiphar's wife, we would have understood his criminality on the grounds of his anger for being unjustly sold into slavery by his own brothers. Our culture almost glorifies bad present behavior on the grounds of an unjust past. Joseph, however, was loyal to Potiphar, to the lady, to himself, and ultimately to God. Then he goes to jail. He would be justified in being mischievous in jail, considering that he got there as a result of calumny. He took the time to heal others and interpret dreams, however. When Pharaoh called him in, he could have been upset and uncooperative, after all he had just come out of a 10-year unfair jail sentence. He cooperated with Pharaoh to the best of his ability, however. His ultimate show of righteousness was toward God; despite all the misery he endured throughout his life. When Joseph had the opportunity of a meeting with Pharaoh, he did not complain, but praised God instead."

John was brilliant and talented; he was a good teacher, but he sometimes surprised me, such as when he changed the subject and brought up something totally unrelated to the conversation, as he did next with a question that made no sense to me because it was so out of place:

"And how many injustices did you say happened to you?" John asked. A bit irritated by his distraction, I answered:

"Liaran accused me of crime I did not commit. She was having an affair, while telling me she loved me and blaming me for everything that went wrong in our lives. And the worst of all: there was no break-up talk, ever; so, I was left

Frank Baler Finds T.H.

hanging, not knowing where anything stood, and waiting for closure."

To be honest, I felt irritated by his distraction. We had been talking about something important, such as how Joseph manifested God's love, and he asked me an unrelated question that brought me back to my misery. Furthermore, as I recounted what I thought were the injustices, John sat there, almost smiling faintly. Thankfully, the wife continued:

"John," Priscilla said, "I think we can talk about Moses now."

"Yes, but please bring him some water first," John responded as he handed me a box of tissues. I was crying again, and I had no idea why. Tears just gushed out of my eyes, for no reason.

As I dried my eyes and sipped on the water, Margarita, the store manager, walked in holding a tray. On the tray were three small cups of expresso and a small plate with several cookies. I reflexively gulped down one cup of expresso, and only then said "Thank you." A few minutes later it was time to get back to work.

"What were you telling me about Moses?" John asked casually, as if we had been talking about last night's game on TV.

Frank Baler Finds T.H.

"Yes," I said fueled by the hot expresso, "Moses was the Egyptian he killed; more accurately, Moses killed the Egyptian in him so he could find God, again, after some time in the desert."

This time they both shifted on their chairs, and perked their ears, as if saying: continue. I did continue:

"Moses was Israeli but raised as an Egyptian. He had to kill the Egyptian in him to become the liberator of the Israeli. The story is about childhood, social and religious indoctrination. We must kill all that slime out of our system so the authentic inner self can emerge. In essence, we must save the inner self from the slavery of social indoctrination represented by the outer self."

"Wow, back up a little Frank. Tell me the story from the beginning," she said.

"Sure. Moses' mother was Hebrew, according to the bible, but Pharaoh had ordered all newborn Hebrew boys to be killed in order to reduce the Hebrew population and decrease the threat to Pharaoh. Moses' mother hides him in a basket and sends him down the Nile River. An Egyptian princess, daughter of Pharaoh, finds the baby boy and raises him. Two maids try to dissuade the princess from defying her father's order, but the archangel Gabriel kills them. Moses, therefore, is Hebrew, but is raised by the royal

Frank Baler Finds T.H.

Egyptian family as an Egyptian. There are many parallels with the story of Jesus; the threat to his life as a newborn, the flight to Egypt, and the intervention by archangel Gabriel. Moses grows up and eventually kills an Egyptian who is mistreating a Hebrew, the bible says. He flees to the desert, across the red sea, and meets God, who orders him back to Egypt to deliver the Hebrew nation from Pharaoh." Then I stopped to wait for their feedback.

"Please go on," John said.

"This part of the story is so human," I said. "It is hard to remember we are talking about the great Moses."

"What do you mean?" Priscilla asked.

"Well, Moses gives God five reasons why he cannot do the job, and why God should send someone else."

At that time, I could only remember the number of excuses as five, and two of them, namely that no one would believe that God had sent him, and that he was not an eloquent speaker. I did mention that the story was in the book of Exodus. Later I looked up the excuses:

1. Who am I? exodus 3:11
2. I don't have answers. Exodus 3:13
3. They will not believe me. Exodus 4:1
4. I cannot speak well. Exodus 4:10

Frank Baler Finds T.H.

5. I am not qualified. Exodus 4:13

"The point is," I continued, "that God answered all objections and equipped Moses for the job. God taught Moses magic, which Pharaoh' magicians duplicated. Eventually, however, Moses performed one trick that Pharaoh's magicians could not duplicate, then Pharaoh believed Moses was sent by God. God also appointed Aaron, Moses's brother, as his spokesperson. All objections presented by Moses were addressed by God."

"Frank, that is an interesting analysis of the narrative," the wise woman said. Somehow, however, that comment in that context did not seem like a compliment, I thought. She continued:

"Can you tell us what you learned from the story?"

I had been waiting for that question all day. The academic in me prepared for this question, so I fired off the following answer, literally with bullet numbers:

1. Your mission is to rescue and free your inner most identity by freeing others.

2. You must let go of all social norms and cultural impositions in order to reclaim your true inner nature and 'speak to God'.

Frank Baler Finds T.H.

3. You must improve upon your culture, up them one, show them what they cannot do, and do it yourself. The power to do that comes from God.

4. All the resources you need for your mission will be provided once you get on your mission.

5. Know that some people will follow you to defy you. There will be people who build golden calves while you prepare to serve them more. Those are the swine Jesus warns you against. Bless them and let them go. Do not look back.

These lessons, as written above, were copied from my notes written in preparation for that session. As I tell you the story, however, I am flabbergasted by the realization that she asked me what I had learned from the story, and the lessons I told her I learned were all written in second person.

Still, when I finished reciting the lessons learned, I reached for the box of tissues. My eyes were swollen from crying so much and not sleeping. I was not eating either, resulting in a twenty pound weight loss, and my face looking really strange to me. I had lost the ability to meditate and read. I felt isolated and devastated. I was suffering and sacrificing my life. Looking back, I guess I really needed some sort of applause for doing what I thought was my homework. Instead, John looked at his wife and asked her:

Frank Baler Finds T.H.

"Do we see him tomorrow?" She responded non-ceremoniously:

"Yap, four pm."

They lowered their heads. There was no namaste salute, no good-bye. They simply looked down. I knew that was my cue to stand up and exit. Margarita collected the fee outside and reminded me: "Tomorrow, same time."

When I returned the next day at four o'clock, Priscilla wasted no time:

"Frank, last time we mentioned Samson, and you described Dalilah as a hot woman who betrayed him. Do I remember that correctly?"

"I believe I said something like that, yes madam." I said.

"Do you think of 'hot' women as prone to betrayal?" She insisted.

"Well," I said, "that is a long discussion. First, we would have to talk about what actually constitutes 'betrayal'. Then we may discover that betrayal has more to do with lack of personal sincerity than with the attractiveness of the physical body." Priscilla would not allow me to dodge the question with a philosophical dissertation; she continued:

"Do you like hot women, Frank?" She asked the question while squinting her eyes, lowering her voice, tilting her head

Frank Baler Finds T.H.

to my right, and the ultimate clue: she actually adjusted her hair! Was I dreaming this? Was she flirting with me, in front of her husband? What is this? I thought.

"Do you?" She actually insisted in a low voice.

"Well, I like women, if that is what you are asking; and, other things being equal, sure, hot women are awesome," I said trembling because I could not even sleep, let alone think of women or sex. Mostly I felt confused by this line of inquiry in this context.

"But you are afraid of hot women." It was a statement, not a question. "You fear what you desire," she was on a roll, "hence your troubles with women. This is rooted in your fear of your mother, whom you loved, but was violent toward you as a child."

"So, Sansom had a problem with his mother?" I figured the smart-alecky comment would spare me from the conversation about my mother and childhood.

"It is better than that," John intervened. "We all have this same conflict, in one way or another."

"Why is that Frank?" She asked more normally, I thought.

I stared at the box of tissues motionless; tears literally dripped on the table under my chin. Then a thought popped into my mind. At first, I dismissed it, thinking that I was distracted from the important conversation about childhood abuse that was sure to follow. Words, however, came out of my mouth as if I had nothing to do with them; I could not have said them, or prevented them from being said:

"We are all aliens in a foreign world. We are divine souls suffering the pain of separation from what we call God. As long as we feel separated from God, we are separated from ourselves, we hurt immensely."

They both looked at me as if I was about to have a breakthrough. I also felt that I needed to get the words out on my own, with no nudging from either of them. So, I continued:

"We all intuitively know that the only solution to the pain, which takes many forms, is to reunite with God. We fear that God will reject us for having left in the first place, though. So, we don't go back, and we suffer." After a brief pause to clean my nose, I said:

"The desire is to unite, the fear is of punishment for having ventured out. So, yes, you are right," I said looking at her, "we fear what we desire."

"What gives, man?" John asked jovially for the first time.

"I guess we must learn that we never ventured out. Separation is an impossible illusion." I said quietly, knowing that my personal reality was impossibly far and removed from that concept. I felt not only separated from it all; I actually felt abandoned.

Margarita walked in with a tray at that moment. John motioned to her, asking her to come back later with his hand. They both remained silent, as if knowing that I needed time to absorb the words that had just come out of my own mouth.

"You are close Frank; you are very close. Be strong now." Priscilla said looking straight into my eyes and breaking the silence. "Samson's initial strength," she continued, "represents God's gift of youth and good fortune. Youthful good fortune is reminiscent of paradise, of pre-incarnation, of the original state of the human soul."

"Yes, but remember the bread of shame, my dear kabbalist," John added. "The soul wants to earn its divinity. We recognize that we must share to own what we never lost. Sansom's desire to receive for the self is only an amnestic mechanism, meaning that we need to forget our divine identity to then learn it on our own, by the sweat of our brow."

"Oh, that's what the writers meant!" I said as if suddenly illuminated. "In the book of Genesis, when Adam is expelled from paradise, God punishes him with a curse: he will live off of the sweat of his brow. Now it made sense, we first work on forgetting our true identity just so we can go

Frank Baler Finds T.H.

through the motion of working hard to remember it. When we work hard to remember, we never forget. Which, of course, is exactly what Jesus meant by the parable of the prodigal son. Wow, it all connects," I said.

"What else have you connected, Frank?" John asked.

"Yeah, I see it now. Sansom's desire to receive for himself causes him to forget his divine identity, represented by his eyes being gouged out and being tied to a milling stone. The writers just meant that when we forget who we are, we lose our vision and go through life in circles, never getting anywhere. But now I see why Jesus constantly quoted the scriptures," I continued. "The New Testament is the same as the Old, just interpreted based on the grace, as opposed to the wrath, of God."

"Why do you say that?" Priscilla asked.

"The prodigal son that Jesus talks about in the New Testament also left his father's house demanding his inheritance, a detail that points to the desire to receive for the self alone. He also loses his power and ends up eating with the swine, as Samson ended up with no vision and going around in circles. Finally, both redeem themselves by their own means, but aided by God. Samson grows his hair back and destroys the Philistine temple during a banquet; and the prodigal son returns home, but the father meets him halfway and celebrates a banquet in his honor. They are the same story."

"Frank, I heard from Mercy that you were also a powerful man before your crisis." She said. "And dude, I love you, but right now you look worse than trash." She continued. "Are you relating yourself to Samson and the prodigal son?"

"Yes, I see what you are saying," I said hesitantly, uncertain of where she was going.

"Decision time honey!" John said sternly. "What are you going to do? You are welcome to throw in the towel, just raise your hand and angels will come to your rescue. You will be restored, I guarantee you will heal in three weeks, but you are off the Path. The Mystical Path is for giants such as David and Daniel." John paused, then continued. "If you don't think you can put this beast down, if you cannot tame this hungry lion, you are better off quitting now Frank. You can have a normal, comfortable life man, or you can grow up and serve." He paused again, then said chilling words: "But it will get way worse before it gets any better."

Suddenly I stood up with such force and determination that even I was startled. Then I heard some words pronounced with deep determination. The man who said those words was not kidding. The strange thing was that the words came through, and out of, my own mouth:

Frank Baler Finds T.H.

"My body, mind and soul are at the service of humanity, for the Glory of God!"

They just looked at me motionless. My body was trembling slightly but rigid. It had assumed a pose reserved for certain Initiates within certain rituals. John waited patiently for the enormity of the moment to sink in, then asked:

"In closing, tell me what's up with the hair thing… Sansom's hair?"

"Oh," I said, calming and sitting down, "hair is just a way of saying that the power that allows us to remember our identity comes from within ourselves. In a sense, the God we seek is within." I said almost trivially, then I lowered my head.

When I looked up, Margarita was serving us a cup of expresso and cookies. A couple of minutes later John stood up and, for the first time, shook my hand saying:

"I will see you at four, tomorrow."

When I walked in the next day, they smiled ever so slightly, as if thinking that their project had some hope of working out. I felt devastated; another night without sleep, and barely able to stop crying. John got right into it, asking, "Talk to me about David…"

I started:

"At first glance, as presented, the story of David seems like an improbable one. A boy, unarmed, against a giant, experienced warrior. Scholars question this depiction of Goliath, claiming that, according to the biblical description provided, Goliath suffered from acromegaly, a consequence of a pituitary tumor that actually made him weak. But this discussion is part of the literal, not the kabalistic interpretation of the story." I blew my nose, then continued:

"The point is that David feels small as compared to the size of the task before him. David's depiction as a boy, is symbolic of our feeling of impotency and inadequacy in the face of many issues in life. We often feel small when dealing with the big issues of life that do not seem to have easy answers. Goliath, of course, simply represents those problems we don't think we can overcome. Rage, jealousy, grief, for instance, for the person who feels these feelings, while they feel them, seem unsurmountable. They feel like a giant we cannot overcome. Death itself seems to be the ultimate giant none of us can tame." I needed some water, then I continued:

Frank Baler Finds T.H.

"Now, Goliath is described as an infantry soldier, skilled in hand-to hand combat. The king offers David equipment necessary only for infantry battle. David changes the domain of the battle, however. David is a slinger, he uses artillery tactics, he sends a projectile from a distance and eliminates the mighty warrior on the ground." At this point I asked for permission to use the restroom. When I came back, I continued:

"We learn from David that all demons, all major problems in life are goliaths. When we step aside and raise above our problems, we can eliminate them. Send stones of love and forgiveness down to our goliaths from above, don't get bogged down in battle with an infantry soldier. Stay away from danger but send out projectiles of forgiveness and you will be delivered from your worst enemies. The key lesson from David is to switch the domain of the battle. A physical problem requires a mental solution, and a mental problem requires a spiritual solution. A spiritual problem requires divine intervention."

"A spiritual problem?" They both started laughing, really laughing. "Frank, what do you mean by 'a spiritual problem'?"

I knew that some problems have no solution until we seek divine intervention, so it seemed to fit my hierarchical narrative to have a category called 'spiritual problem'. John continued, laughing again:

"You must mean like Job... Job had a spiritual problem, right?"

The book of Job is probably the most controversial in all of the Old Testament, because in it, God is described as running a bet with the devil. When the movie 'Trading Places' came out in the early eighties's I related it to the book of Job. I was so impressed by the movie that I wrote a college paper based on that movie. From the perspective presented in the book of Job, I could see why John was laughing.

"Yes, the writers present the same theme in Job that they do through all the other narratives we have been talking about. The difference, I continued, is that in the account of Job the story is written from the unconscious perspective."

"What do you mean Frank?" She asked me sweetly.

"Well, in all the accounts we have discussed, the person is victimized in some way, loses it all, or risks losing it all, remains faithful, and is restored to greatness. In Job's case, the writers mention the number seven, as in seven times greater than before the ordeal, clearly indicating enlightenment. In the story of Job, however, we are introduced to a dialogue between God and the devil. That dialogue reflects the soul's deliberation of what that incarnation will be about. The spiritual part of us decides on the mechanism whereby we can finally return home, while incarnated. That decision is made prior to birth, leading some mystics to the idea of a 'soul contract'." This time Priscilla asked:

"Frank, are you saying that both God and the devil in the book of Job represent parts of Job's soul? Wait, Job does not even exist," she continued, "are you saying that we are all God and the devil? Ourselves?"

"I am saying that madam, because that is the truth." I said calmly.

"Wow," she said, "that gives a whole different meaning to the notion that 'the devil made me do it'…"

I sat in silence, since I had not been asked a question. Soon John spoke:

"Tell me about Daniel…" he said. I straightened myself on the chair and spoke quietly:

"The story of Daniel encompasses the lessons we have discussed so far. Like Abraham, God is number one to Daniel, as he refuses to bow down to the King. Like Joseph, Daniel has the fortitude and patience to allow God's plan to unfold. Like Moses, Daniel also surpasses the magicians of the king, so we know he is a High Initiate. Like Samson, he is defeated when thrown into the lion's pit, but restores his

Frank Baler Finds T.H.

glory by taming the beasts. And like David, he is the epitome of defeating giants."

"So, what is Daniel about?" John pressed on.

"Daniel is the consummate Initiate. In the entire biblical record, only Jesus is greater." My voice was firmer, somehow.

"Why do you say that Frank?" Priscilla now nudged me along.

"Daniel encompasses all the previous Initiates mentioned. Jesus does what Daniel did, the lions in the den being the devil in the desert, and then some: Jesus restores life; his own as well as that of others."

"Frank, you describe eloquently 8 out of the 9 superpowers enlightened Grand Masters have at the service of humanity. We can tell that you mastered the first one in your body, quite viscerally. The others you seem to know a whole lot about, but we are not sure that you have embodied them." The wife said, and John continued:

"You are a young man; astrologically and genetically you are poised to have a long life. We know from previous experience, we mentioned that to you several days ago, remember? that those who master the first superpower on their own before getting to us also master at least six more superpowers in this incarnation. Having seven superpowers at the service of humanity makes you an awesome man; maybe next time you can reach enlightenment." John talked about enlightenment in the next lifetime as if mentioning purchasing bananas at a different grocery store.

"I am curious John, you told me that I discovered the key number one, the first superpower as you put it, in Abraham's story on my own. Why did you not mention that key? When you mentioned the superpowers, you told me about Joseph, Moses, Samson, David and Daniel. You did not mention Abraham, Job or Jesus." I inquired, actually very concerned.

"Oh, that was the test, we needed to know who we had in front of us," John said.

"So, what would have happened if I had not gotten that key?" I pressed on.

"Nothing. We would not have worked with you," he said. Then he continued: "Frank, the Path is hard enough when God is number one in your life. Remember, we are not talking about words here; we are talking about a test, a visceral reaction where one actually walks away from what one loves the most, if it gets in the way of his Path. Very few people pass that test when it comes right down to it. Many people talk about God being number one, but few are as committed." Then he got to the point: "I was saying that the Path is hard enough when it is the most important thing in a person's life, and there are absolutely no guarantees of anything. Now, can you imagine working with a person who is not totally, entirely, viscerally, committed? It would be like pearls to the swine, and we don't do that here," he concluded.

Wow, I thought, we never know how close we come to total loss or total victory sometimes. A very small omission, had I not mentioned something that day, and my destiny would be very different.

As John opened his laptop to start writing something, the wife and I jumped in almost at the same time:

"You first," she insisted.

"Well, you told me that each story we discussed hides a key that, when found, awakens a superpower within us. You told me there are nine superpowers, but we only discussed eight characters. What is the ninth superpower?"

"We cannot discuss that here!" John said quite sternly, leaving no room for further conversation. I acquiesced and the lovely lady spoke softly again:

"Before we are done, we will play one final game. It is not a test; it is a game; I will mention a name and you say one phrase to describe the lesson learned from that character. I will go slow at first, then I will speed up the tempo. Finally, I will scramble the names. Just say what comes to your mind

Frank Baler Finds T.H.

once you hear each name." Then she said, "max 3 or 4 words per name, okay?"

"Abraham?" "God is number 1."

"Joseph?" "God's plan is perfect. Allow it to unfold."

"Moses?" "Become yourself, God empowers you for the mission."

"Samson?" "True power comes from within."

"David?" "Switch domains, elevate your perspective to win."

"Daniel?" "Total love and devotion to the truth tames any beast."

"Job?" "Greatness is always restored seven times over."

"Jesus?" "Life restoration, or resurrection, through total forgiveness."

We went through a few rounds of that game. Then, she said I was a good student, but that I needed to embody those lessons.

"Simply trust that you will be guided," she said. "There will be lots of pain ahead because there is still much rigidity in your mind. You must let go of a lot, but as you do, you will feel great; your greatness will be restored seven times over, as was Job's."

Frank Baler Finds T.H.

I saluted each of them reverentially, my heart so full of gratitude, and pain as well. Working with John and his wife Priscilla dressed my pain with a map through which I could understand causes of the pain and also the pathway to healing. The actual pain, however, was as intense as ever. I was not sure at the time whether there would be a tomorrow for me.

I said 'thank you' to Margarita as I handed her the bills, forced myself to smile while tears ran out of my eyes, and walked to the car.

As I sat in the hot seat of a car that had been parked for a couple of hours, even during the winter in South Florida, it occurred to me that no matter what happened in my life, or to my life, my priorities were clear: my first love is for God and the divine. In some way, I felt as though I had indeed met Abraham.

Frank Baler Finds T.H.

THE ASSEMBLY OF MASTERS

———◯———

The annual hypnotherapy conference was fast approaching. I had applied to deliver a paper at the conference, which was accepted. The application, however, was submitted the year before, months before the crisis I then faced. To be honest, I did not even remember what the supposed paper was about. Something was different within me, however: I looked forward to the conference.

When I caught myself feeling the desire to see fellow therapists, and actually deliver a good paper at the conference, I realized that I was healing; suddenly, my life mattered to me; I wanted to live.

I still barely slept. Thinking, reading, and working, were still challenging to me. I am still not sure whether the latter difficulties came from lack of sleep alone, or if all these other

Frank Baler Finds T.H.

functions broke down as well as a result of another cause that also created sleep deprivation.

I went to the conference as scheduled. When I got there, I got a conference brochure and read the short description of my talk. I was determined to be real, instead of academic or intellectual. It really did not matter to me if I was ever invited or accepted as a speaker again; I wanted to speak from my heart. I had no notes, no visual aids, no speech prepared, no opening or closing lines memorized. When called to the podium, I simply stood up and shared with the other therapists there what I could about my experience applying concepts from *A Course in Miracles* to my clinical practice.

A large gathering formed around me at the lobby after the talk; there were enthusiastic questions and comments. Later, they sent me written feedback forms and a score: 10/10. All respondents to their survey wanted me back the following year, and several requested longer talks. I made several new friends.

There were several social gatherings throughout the days I was there. One afternoon, a bunch of us talked by the pool and ocean; there was a fire pit and some s'mores. I started talking to Arturo, who enthusiastically commented on my talk, and on what he was hearing from many other therapists about the talk I delivered. I changed the subject and told

Frank Baler Finds T.H.

Arturo that I was still broken, not quite back, despite many moments of apparent normal function. Arturo, a fantastic therapist after all, shared with me a part of his life I did not know. He had been married to a woman who broke him years earlier, but he had healed, he said. He told me about an exercise he uses at his office to help clients in situations such as the one I was experiencing.

I asked for his help, and Arturo graciously obliged. We left the gathering and found a small empty classroom. Other conference participants, and staff members, were walking around the hotel, instead of enjoying the pool party, thus Arturo locked the door from the inside so we would not be interrupted. We sat down and talked for a while. He started:

"Now that we here alone, and in the spirit of therapeutic confidentiality, tell me what really bothers you."

I started crying violently. "Why did you do it?" I was asking Liaran in my mind, but aloud.

Arturo let me cry without interruptions. He then asked me to explain what I meant.

"Man, I started, it was not just the betrayal in terms of an extra-marital affair; it was a betrayal of everything we shared, the entire meaning our relationship had. She stole 2 SD cards from my laptop with all kinds of notes and outlines for courses; she copied my notes verbatim in a book she

Frank Baler Finds T.H.

published. She stole a proposal I had written for the company she worked for, and now did that job. She accused me of crimes, including against a child. She did her best to get me to jail. The betrayal was meticulously planned and executed. She wanted me out of her life forever and planned this 'termination' carefully. Throughout all that, we made love passionately every night, she told me she loved me forever. I don't get this…"

"What else Frank?", Arturo asked.

"Well, there has never been a breakup. I left the house, as I often did to sleep at the office one night, and we never spoke again. I need to break up with her… but we cannot talk."

"If you could talk to her, what would you say?" Arturo asked, ever so wisely.

"I would ask her why she did all that, particularly when I had offered her on several occasions to leave in case she was not happy with me."

Then Arturo said something similar to what I would say to a client at the office:

"Yeah, but the guy in there, what would he say to her?"

I cried and cried. Then I cried some more. Then I said softly:

Frank Baler Finds T.H.

"Why didn't you love me Liaran? What was it about me that was so unlovable? You seem to hate me, to want me destroyed. Why do you hate me?"

Therapy is tough work. It is hard to explain to a non-therapist how tough our job is. I felt for Arturo as I noticed him swallowing saliva that was not in his mouth. When a client expresses something deep and heartfelt, it is as if something comes out of the person. The therapist must absorb that something, otherwise it goes right back into the person. The trick for the therapist who lasts in the profession is to discharge it later, but accepting the energy the client releases is tough work indeed. I mentally blessed Arturo, because I knew he was serving me that way right now. He understood and accepted my question to Liaran as an expression of my deepest childhood wound. Yet, he continued with the process:

"Okay," Arturo summarized, "you want to understand what happened, presumably from a causal perspective, since you already know what happened from a phenomenological one, and you need closure. Is there anything else Frank?"

"Man, God bless you and your entire profession," is all I could say, still blowing my nose and wiping away tears.

"Thank you, professor," Arturo said smiling.

Frank Baler Finds T.H.

Arturo then explained to me what we were going to do. We would enter a deep hypnotic state, using a quick induction followed by a fractionation deepening. When ready, he would offer my subconscious mind the suggestion to enter the Assembly of Masters. That was all he said before asking:

"Is this what you want?"

"Yes, please," I responded.

"Do you agree with the process I described?"

"Yes sir," I said.

"Do you have any questions or concerns?"

"No man; may the Light of God be with you," I said.

"All right, please take a deep breath and relax gently…" I was hearing words I pronounced several times each day, for the previous 22 years… How interesting it was to be on 'this chair', I thought.

Arturo asked my being to go into the Assembly of Masters and present all of my pain and doubts to them.

I saw the Masters for the first time in a long time. To my human relief they did not seem upset or disappointed with me. Apparently, I had not failed the Masters by suffering so much, by being so weak, and by taking so long in the dark night of my soul.

Frank Baler Finds T.H.

The Masters 'listened' to me, or more accurately, understood my plight, apparently by some sort of telepathy, and then One 'spoke':

"You knew from day one that you would have to choose between the relationship and your spiritual Path." The Master said. "You told her yourself she would betray you; you told her that when you first met. You could have worked out your human relationship with her, but it would have taken you away from your Path. You were free to choose, and you chose the Path."

"But I thought she was a gift from You… I thought that I had to work out the union between us to carry out the Path. I thought she was a part of the Path, and that she and I were on this Path together," I said.

"She was a part of the Path. So are your four girls, who will be very important in the near future. You had to be their Father; it is all a part of the Path. Only she could have put you in a position of having to choose, and you had to choose!"

I knew what the Master meant. Any other woman in my life would not have touched me that way. In the past, if any type of relationship got in the way of what I called the Path, there was no choice to be made, she was out of my life. My two wives had no chance in that regard. Liaran brought me to a choice I never made before.

Then I projected a word I was constantly called during the previous two years. I projected the word with a question mark:

"Bazura?"

'Bazura' is Spanish for garbage. Liaran is Eastern European, brought up under communism. Being Brazilian, my native tongue is Portuguese, not Spanish. We lived in Miami, where you hear a lot of Spanish being spoken all over, so we both speak Spanish fluently. The point is that often Liaran spoke in Spanish, thinking that she could dig deeper into me that way. Liaran constantly called me "bazura" to the point that I seriously questioned whether I was garbage. One year prior to this encounter, I actually consulted my Mentor's widower on this topic. "Soy bazura?", I asked her at the time, really not knowing the answer to the question.

The Master did not repeat or honor the word 'bazura'. He said instead:

"Your relationship was improbable from the beginning. We are surprised by your tenacity, and by how hard you worked to keep it. You have cared deeply, you have loved honestly, you have made serious and severe corrections and improvements to your person. You surpassed our expectations for what you could achieve personally during this opportunity (I understood lifetime, but maybe it was meant as 'relationship'). You still have much to learn, but your heart is good," He said.

At that point, I still felt deeply responsible for her well-being, so I projected the concern.

"She will be fine." That is all The Master 'said'.

Perhaps I did not want to leave their presence, plus I had so many questions, so I tried again, at the risk of overstaying my welcome:

"But why am I such a weak man?" I asked referring to the intense pain I was experiencing.

"You are not weak!" His voice sounded stern for the first time. "A weak man would have walked away much earlier. You believed in an ideal, you worked hard and honestly toward that ideal. You loved with innocence and sincerity. You gave yourself to what you believed to be important and real. You constantly made corrections; you sacrificed your joy and goals, and always put the relationship before your wishes. There was no weakness. The pain your body is feeling now is not a sign of weakness, it is a sign of your spiritual fortitude."

Frank Baler Finds T.H.

Then I 'heard' something that I both totally understood, and also had difficulty with:

"We made it difficult for you" he 'said' almost as an afterthought.

I was aware at the time of how God had empowered Moses to talk to Pharaoh, but simultaneously hardened Pharaoh's heart against Moses' request to let the Hebrew people go. This is a topic I had worked quite a bit on with Students on the Path over years past. I did not like it, but I understood it.

Then I 'said' one more thing that in retrospect reminds me of my 2-year-old baby:

"Well, I don't know if I will make it..."

I was complaining about the pain, which was simply a reflection of my own resistance to becoming what I had requested years earlier to become. By 'making it', of course, I meant, advancing on the Path, but I was bargaining with the Masters for a 'better deal'. Yes, it was pathetic. The answer I 'heard' was loving yet dispassionate:

"You don't have to... we can leave."

With that the experience came to a close. I opened my eyes and looked at Arturo. He seemed so brightly lit that my eyes almost hurt. I told him a part of what had happened, to which

Frank Baler Finds T.H.

he replied 'I know'. We had been in that room for more than three hours, so we said 'later' and went to get ready for dinner.

As I showered, a couple of phrases were on my mind:

'The pain your body is feeling now is not a sign of weakness, it is a sign of your spiritual fortitude.' And, 'We made it difficult for you.'

I was almost afraid to unpack those phrases, but like a song a teenager hears at the dance club when meeting a pretty girl for the first time, the phrases kept 'playing' in my head.

Before getting dressed for dinner, I tried to meditate a little, something that had been nearly impossible for a few months by then. This was not a full and regular meditation, but rather a moment to reflect on the earlier experience with the Masters. Somehow, I thought, those two phrases that kept playing in my mind must be important; so, I figured I would at least begin to unpack them, no matter how uncomfortable it felt. I also knew by then in my Mystical journey that the help from the Masters was not limited to the session with Arturo. The Masters would accompany me on that hotel room couch just as they always had in previous years.

Frank Baler Finds T.H.

Meditation is one of those topics that can mean whatever a person wants it to mean. I have seen people who insist that you can only meditate in one particular position, facing one particular cardinal point, or wearing a certain garb. There is no singular accepted definition of 'meditation' that applies to all. Usually, you can trace a person's understanding of meditation to the definition used by the person who first introduced them to the idea.

My understanding of meditation comes from the word itself: to me, meditation is the action of tuning into the center, 'medi' of my being. The very center, or core, is devoid of mind, although we enter that state through the mind. I think of a human as having 4 parts: body, conscious mind, unconscious mind, and soul. The idea is to identify completely with the soul, to be the soul. In true meditation, according to my understanding of it, there is no awareness of the body or mind.

Hence my difficulty with meditation while in pain, for pain brings awareness to the body, making meditation nearly impossible.

Still shirtless, fresh out of the shower, I sat on the couch, placed my hands on top of my thighs and took several deep, slow breaths. I focused on my feet and relaxed them, then the lower legs, and relaxed them too. I went through each

Frank Baler Finds T.H.

part of the body, from the tips of my toes to the top of my head relaxing, physically relaxing, as much as possible. I did that a few times, always starting at the tips of the toes, and always ending at the top of my head.

Once I felt the body pretty limp, I begun to relax the mind by using affirmations. The affirmation I use typically is 'relax and sleep' or 'sleep and relax'. I repeated that phrase several times, sometimes in my mind, sometimes aloud, in a soft voice, until my eye lids felt so relaxed that it did not seem that I could open my eyes.

I then imagined a 'magical stairway' with 10 steps, going down. I counted the numbers as I slowly went down the stairs in my mind all the way down into the core of my being. The ability to vividly imagine and experience a stairway that is not physically there is a function of the unconscious mind. The next step to meditate is critical, and the most difficult. I simply let go completely. I let go of what I think should be, or not be… let go of mental images, thoughts, and feelings. Initially it feels as though I fell asleep, but it is not sleep, it is a profound disconnection from the mind, or the mental realm. It is the beginning of the identification with the soul.

It is very difficult to explain what happened next precisely because it happened outside of the mind. A few minutes later the experience was over; my eyes were open and I could feel

Frank Baler Finds T.H.

the ocean just outside of my hotel room window. My first awareness was that the ocean itself is alive; in fact, everything around me felt alive.

I had an understanding of the two phrases that bothered me so much before the shower, so I wasted no time in making notes. Over the years I found that, just as is the case with dreaming, it is important to document the awareness we bring back from the meditative state as soon as the experience is over.

I started by writing down the two phrases that had played in my mind before the shower:

'The pain your body is feeling now is not a sign of weakness, it is a sign of your spiritual fortitude.' And 'We made it difficult for you.'

Interestingly, the Master made it clear that the pain was in the body. I was feeling that I had totally failed the spiritual Path by losing a relationship that I thought would be an integral part of the Path. What he said, though, located the pain on the body, and somehow, released me from the notion that I had failed spiritually. Just knowing that the pain was physical, and not spiritual made a huge difference to me at the time.

Then there was this issue of the pain being a sign of spiritual fortitude, not weakness. That part of the lesson I had trouble with. The whole notion of associating pain to spirituality both made sense to me and bothered me immensely.

Three ideas were clear to me at the time regarding pain and spiritual fortitude:

1. I could medicate the pain away with drugs and carnal sex. Not engaging in either magnified the pain, but also made it possible to trace it to its very root, so I could finally heal.

2. I got into this situation because of my loyalty to an agreement with a person, the commitment to the notion of radical forgiveness, and the devotion to love, framed as the need to find and be with my soulmate. The easy thing for me to have done was to have walked away from Liaran when the lies started, which was from the very beginning. Instead, I was committed both to my agreement with her not to leave, and to the notion that to love is to forgive, no matter what.

3. Most importantly, the breakdown I was experiencing was an important part of the Path, not an impediment to it. Breaking down mental constructs and conceptions of reality that keep us tied rigidly to this type of physicality is an integral part of the Path. Finally, I was understanding that God's plan is indeed perfect; there had been no failure.

But it was that second phrase that sealed the deal to me. 'We made it difficult for you,' to me, meant that I had not been off the Path, I had not failed the Masters, or my Initiations. Instead, the Masters had been with me throughout this process, which was clearly a part of my chosen and accepted Path. Rather than being abandoned by the Masters, they had been there all along; perhaps making lessons more difficult for me, but only because they thought me worthy of higher lessons.

Suddenly I remembered thinking that John was distracted when he asked me about injustices while talking about Joseph. I had told John what I considered to be three uncalled for injustices Liaran perpetrated against me, as was the case with Joseph.

Now it all made sense to me: the breakdown was an important part of the Path. Because of what the Masters saw as my fortitude, it took a lot of 'insults' to bring about the break down. But like Joseph in jail, I was on the Path, albeit not at its end.

After writing the last note on my journal I put on my suit and tie in preparation for the banquet.

I said hello to a few old acquaintances, then stood by the banquet hall door as if waiting for someone; I felt terrible anxiety.

Frank Baler Finds T.H.

The session with Arturo and the Assembly of Masters had awakened something within me that I could not let go of.

The way I understood the Masters, there was no failure on either of our parts. Furthermore, there was no weakness in me for feeling what I felt, and I was not garbage. In fact, I felt the Masters saying that the plan was perfect as it was.

The reason I was suffering, I concluded, was because God's plan, which is always perfect, was not complete yet. This was like talking to Joseph when he was still incarcerated. Had we not known that he would become second in command of Egypt, had the story ended with Joseph in jail, it would all seem like a huge failure. But Joseph in jail is not the end of the story, Joseph in jail is the crisis that awakens the spiritual giant in Joseph capable of reading Pharaoh's dream and interpreting it. The real end of the story is that joseph saves the Israeli people from famine.

The last entry on my journal that night read:

'This is not the end of story'

Then I went to sleep.

Frank Baler Finds T.H.

STRANGE ENCOUNTERS

———○———

While doing laundry one morning, I remembered a new friend I had made at the conference. Allen and I had several deep talks while at the conference. His wife, Mary, is a superb therapist and speaker. Allen is a thoughtful and generous man; he invited me to spend a few days with them, at their lovely home in New Mexico. He suggested that a few days in the desert would do me some good. We made plans for a September visit. Little did I know at the time what life had in store for me.

I picked up a car at the Santa Fe airport and drove about 2 hours to their home. I drove slowly, looking around, crying, and reminiscing about Liaran. Their home is in a development with about 2000 other houses, but the area is so large that you feel a profound sense of expansion. As soon

Frank Baler Finds T.H.

as I got off the car on their driveway, I was in love with the place. The silence! Oh, I loved the silence.

There are no words to describe how incredibly nice and generous this couple was with me. Allen and I went for long walks in the semi-desert, while having awesome deep talks. Mary prepared lovely meals and produced the comfortable feeling of a home, that I believe only a woman can produce. I got to visit Mary's office; she was incredibly generous to offer me the opportunity to sit on her chair while the three of us talked for a while.

This last bit of honor may not make sense to a non-therapist, and a therapist would not need an explanation. I guess you could compare sitting on a renowned therapist's chair to driving a racing car in which someone became a champion.

"If I ever write a biography," I told Mary and Allen, "I will mention that I had the honor of sitting on Mary's chair one morning." We all laughed like college students and went to eat at a nice place in downtown.

During the following three days, my friends took me to a number of awesome places, and several sites that are sacred to the natives of New Mexico. I was aware at the time that this was no ordinary trip. The sites we were visiting, the things I was seeing and feeling, plus the indescribable

Frank Baler Finds T.H.

generosity my friends had extended to me, was touching a deep fiber within my being. Among the awesome places we visited were art galleries and a chapel, Loretto chapel no less!

I was quite familiar with several accounts of what happened at Loretto Chapel, but being there, touching the walls, smelling the air, was a singular gift I felt immensely grateful for.

I feel a profound sense of reverence for all sacred sites because I believe that the feeling we all experience, when it comes to the sacred is the same, no matter our particular beliefs about how that feeling is elicited. The German philosopher and theologian Rudolf Otto spoke at length about this feeling, which he called the *numinous*. I loved Otto's book *The Idea of the Holy* and wrote a few papers on it when I was a philosophy major in college.

"It is amazing," I told Allen, "how one book can change a student's life, imparting ideas that remain with him for a lifetime!"

During the days I was visiting New Mexico, I began to sleep deeply, although at most 5 hours each night. Waking up before 5 in the morning was the new norm for me, and I was beginning to enjoy the crispy air of early mornings.

Frank Baler Finds T.H.

One afternoon we visited a large volcano crater. We drove into the crater, where a small park ranger station actually had restrooms and a helpful ranger who was happy to explain the magnificence of what we were experiencing.

That night I fell asleep a bit earlier than what was usual for me at the time. After about 2 hours of deep sleep I woke up and felt an incredible urge to go for a walk outside, under the night sky at the edge of the desert. It was just after 1am when I walked out of the bedroom. I did not know where I was going, but I walked as if I did.

I started down the same path Allen had taken me on a few days earlier. I found the large brown house with the solar panels on the ground, saw the water tower to my right, and eventually reached the railroad. Allen had mentioned that it is illegal to enter the railroad easement, even though there were no fences or signs that I could see. I wanted to stare at those rails head on, until they met in the distance, under only half moon light, however.

After I walked for several minutes between the rails, I took a left turn into some low bushes and found another trail. That trail led me to a hill, which I climbed. From the top of the hill I could see Santa Fe, New Mexico, in the distance.

I was absorbed by the thought that sounds and sights could seem so different there. Because it was so quiet, for instance, you could hear sounds that came from further away, but being a city dweller, be deceived by the notion that the source was close by. Sights were very deceiving; structures which seemed to be 'right there' could actually be fifty miles away, or more. It occurred to me how dangerous a place like this can be to a person who gets lost and ends up walking until they become dehydrated and possibly die.

I still thought a lot about the alternative to living at that point in my life, but when I reached into my pocked and realized that I had forgotten my phone, I panicked. I really had no idea where I was, or how to get back to the house. I had no idea how long I had been walking or what time it was. I had no water with me. From where I was, I could not see any of the structures I saw from Allen's house. Judging from how my feet felt, I knew I had been walking for quite some time, but because I had been distracted on my way up here, I was not sure I could retrace my steps. When I left the house, I thought of relying on the phone's GPS to guide me back, but I left the phone charging, I now remembered.

Worst case scenario, I thought, daybreak could not be far away. I would find some trail, and somebody would be around. I could just rest right there, I thought, until I realized just how cold I really was.

Frank Baler Finds T.H.

What happened next amazes me, as I recall the events and now put them into words. I went through every emotion I experienced during the past ten months. I felt intense anger for putting myself in that precarious situation, and for certainly importuning my friends when they woke up and did not find me there. I felt blessed for being under the most magnificent sky I had ever seen, for being healthy, despite the severe abuse to my body over many months, and for my four daughters. Then I deeply regretted every mistake I ever made, millions of images raced through my mind, so many mistakes, so many people I hurt as a result of my selfishness and ignorance. I realized I was totally alone, not just up there on that hill, but in this world; worse yet, I had no idea how to connect with another human being, and I really did not think I would ever heal. I felt doomed to total isolation forever. Finally, I had no idea what to do, despite having been an avid outdoorsman for most of my life. For now, I felt lost and doomed to certain annihilation.

As if asking God to finally take me home, I laid down on the ground looking at the heavens. I outstretched my arms, open palms, and finally faced my true situation: I had failed.

'That is not true,' I found myself saying, or thinking, I am not sure which. 'It is not that you have failed, Frank, it is that you are a failure, and those are not the same thing.'

Frank Baler Finds T.H.

Someone gave me a Mystical book when I was eleven years old. I read the book, but hid it from my parents, for I knew that what the book said was different from what we learned in church. Since I saw that book, though, my life has been about the Mystical Path. I had given up on everything else in search of more Light, and now I laid there, on a cold hilltop in the middle of the night, God only knows where, preferring annihilation even to death itself, for I had failed, and I was a failure.

I had not found any Light, I had hurt every person in my life, I had built nothing, I had done nothing worth doing, I never made any money, I simply was utterly incapable of making a woman happy in a relationship with me.

It was obvious to me at the time what had gone wrong: I equated the love with a woman to the spiritual process. I felt that the union between a man and a woman was reminiscent of the bonding between a human and God; I felt that by being a better lover, in all senses of the word, to a woman, I would reach God. In short, I felt that I needed to love a woman to feel close to God. That profound need, combined with a completely dysfunctional childhood, produced a conflicted man who was simply not capable of a normal life. That conflict made me see women both as the path to God, and, at the same time, an impediment to my union with God.

Frank Baler Finds T.H.

So much sacrifice by so many dedicated teachers, I thought; so many miracles in my life… all for nothing. I would certainly die here, my body would be consumed by beasts of the desert, and I had never lived. I was always preparing for the day when life would start. That day, post-enlightenment, post illumination, post union with my true soulmate, when I could become the man God wanted me to be, I could make a woman happy, a family functional, and I could share the Light with those who cared to receive it. That was a life, a life I would not get to live.

I was fried, gone, done. I was burned beyond repair; I finally accepted that I had lost my mind, my life; I had lost it all, it was finally time to let go of life itself.

"What about those 40000 sessions, 300 exorcisms, 43 babies from mothers who could not otherwise conceive, 3000 students, 57 professional licenses… What about the teenagers who never killed themselves, and the marriages that are now happy, the families that are functional and happy? What about those?"

I snapped to my feet in total fear. There was a definite man there, the voice was way too real to be a hallucination. I instinctively checked my pulse, concerned about exposure and hypoxia. My lips were not cracked, I was not dehydrated to the point of such realistic hallucination, I concluded. The voice was not in my mind, there was a definite human being there on that hilltop, who knew details of my work.

Of course, I thought, Allen knows of my work; he realized I left the house and came to get me. How awesome, I concluded within milliseconds.

The only problem with my conclusion was that Allen could not have known what I had been thinking while laying there. Unless, I thought still inside of the first few fractions of a second, unbeknownst to me, I had been speaking aloud instead of just thinking. Yes, that was it, I determined, Allen heard me speaking. I thought I was all alone on the hill, but Allen had let me vent my frustrations to the sky above before intervening.

"What I mean," the voice continued before I could be totally sure of its source or identity, "is that the people you have served would not say that you failed, or that you are a failure. The God you say you seek certainly does not see you as a failure. And the Masters have already told you that you did not fail the Path."

There was a definite man standing a few meters away from me, I could now see; he was wearing a white shirt and had a beard. I recalled Dr. Radin in medical school saying that the odds of having an auditory and visual hallucination simultaneously is extremely low, even for psychotic patients. I had never had a psychotic breakdown, took no medications, drugs or alcohol. I was sleep starved, I conceded to myself, and perhaps a bit hypoxic. After all, I reasoned, I lived at sea level, and where I was the air was thinner than what I was used to. Then I remembered Rene Descartes famous line: *Cogito Ergo Sum*, 'I think therefore I am.' I was thinking fast, something some psychotic patients reported experiencing, but I was thinking coherently. I was not hallucinating, I finally concluded.

"Sorry, your name is?" I figured we would have a proper introduction.

"Frank, I am happy for you," he said." "You finally know that you don't know anything. Now we can get to work."

His use of my name did not startle me; he quoted some work statistics I have published, so he would certainly know my name, and probably a whole lot more.

"What do you mean?" I finally asked.

"Intellectuals and academics like you who seek God intellectually often feel that they lose their minds prior to major breakthroughs. We have to wait for them to conclude that they do not know anything to then help them make progress. Intellectuals are arrogant creatures, however; they think they know it all. When they are ready to learn, life breaks them down first for them to give up on the notion that they know anything at all; only then they can learn something useful."

"Are you saying that what happened was part of some intentional plan? Are you saying that the plan was designed to guide me toward the Light, not to finish me off?" I asked without specifying what I meant, since he seemed to know so much about me.

"Yes, and yes." Then he let me know that he knew a whole lot about my life with the following explanation: "The demise of the relationship you fret so much about is absolutely inconsequential in your life. You did not fail her, and you are capable of pleasing a woman. Liaran does not define your identity… her opinions of you were expressed at a time of extreme anger and frustration for her." Then he said: "She is fine, and your children are fine; it is time for you to wake up."

The mysterious man who seemed to know details of my personal life, gave me time to absorb what he was saying, and actually seemed to welcome questions. So, I continued: "If the breakdown was an intentional part of the mystical process, why does it still hurt so much?"

Frank Baler Finds T.H.

"Because you are still holding on to antiquated ideas. Life will not waste this unique opportunity; as long as the breakdown started, it must be completed before we can build a new man. Truth is Frank," he completed the thought, "if the pain stopped now, you would go back to your old ways. You are not ready to stop hurting yet my friend!" He said smiling, almost sadistically.

For some reason, I remembered at the time, my dentist explaining how it was important to completely remove decay from a dental cavity before filling it. I acknowledged that I harbored much mental decay internally that needed to be purged from my system, and that this breakdown gave me the opportunity to clean house in many unanticipated ways.

"Tell you what Frank," he said. "You just said right there that your life was over; seems to me," he continued, "that you have nothing to lose. How about we get to work and see how far we get?"

I wanted to believe that the pain had a purpose; I wanted to believe that I could come back to life. I wanted to believe that there was some process whereby I could heal once and for all. I wanted to believe that I deserved to be happy and to live a normal life. I wanted to believe that I would make a woman happy. But I did not. I felt doomed. I felt dead. I felt isolated, angry, regretful, hopeless and helpless.

Frank Baler Finds T.H.

"When you say get to work…"

"Never mind that" he interrupted me. "Just sit down." He pretty much ordered me. Then he continued before I had fully settled on the ground:

"Tell me what happened to you Frank, tell me everything." then he added, "I have time… please tell me how you came to feel so sad."

'Sad?' I thought. All this time I have tried to describe what I felt to others, to therapists and friends. I had never used the word 'sad'. Then I remembered how much emphasis we placed in therapy on identifying and naming the feeling correctly; how we always told clients that naming the feeling correctly is the first step toward healing. I never connected with the idea of sadness.

"Well, as far as I can tell, it all started soon after my fourth daughter was born at home. I was happily married then. I asked a teacher for more responsibility on the Path."

"Frank," he interrupted again, "did you ask the Grand Master from Europe for the High Initiation? Did you finally request what you earned years earlier? Did you finally speak up and claim what is yours? Is that what you mean by 'more responsibility on the Path'?"

"I did ask the European Grand Master for the High Initiation," I said realizing that this man knew something, "but I never thought of it as something that was mine, I always thought of it as a privilege that I would be lucky to be granted." He listened, so I continued.

"The Grand Master I requested the Initiation from warned me that my life would change if I persisted with the goal of receiving this Initiation. I was young, bold and immature. I felt strong and invincible, so I did persist."

"Meaning today, knowing what you know, you would not have persisted?" He asked.

"Oh, quite the opposite, knowing what I know today I would have done what I did much sooner and more intentionally."

"Okay," he said. "Go on, please."

"Within about one month of asking for the Initiation, my then wife broke up with me. Soon thereafter I met another woman who seemed to be my true soulmate. About one month into that relationship, she left the house with her baby, following a photoshoot that did not go according to her wishes. Three months later we had a car accident so serious that people who saw what was left of the car said that we had all died in the accident. The night of the accident I mentioned to her that the accident was an omen, meaning that we should get our relationship right. She agreed that the accident was an omen, but to her, it meant that we should separate. Two

Frank Baler Finds T.H.

months after that, she asked me to leave the house the day of her daughter's birthday because we disagreed on how to keep the drinks cool at the party. When the party was over at the park, I packed her car and she left me there. She made it clear that our relationship was over. I felt horrible because she was pregnant at the time, but it was obvious that she no longer wanted to be with me.

"Did she have the baby?" He asked.

"She had a miscarriage. We got back together, but the relationship was really horrible after that. Later there was another pregnancy from someone else; she aborted that baby, despite me asking her and her mother for her not to. By then she was already working on another relationship. By thanksgiving she stopped talking to me, I went to sleep at the office, and her new boyfriend moved in 3 days later."

"What about your life? Did you move on?"

"Oh no. There were two relationships in close succession, both failed the same way. I made the same mistakes with both of them, and never spoke with either woman again. After the second failed relationship, and the troubles that followed, I kind of broke down."

"Tell me more about this soulmate of yours." The stranger urged me on.

Frank Baler Finds T.H.

"Her name is Liaran. She moved into town and signed up at the gym where I worked out at the time. She was good looking and had awesome legs. I think what made me fall in love with her, however, was that she was pregnant at the time. She and her boyfriend had a falling out in California, and she decided to move to Florida to have the baby close to her family. Liaran and I were an instant hit together." I paused reflexively, remembering how hot Liaran really was.

"So, yes, about two weeks after my second wife left me, I moved in with Liaran."

"Okay, Liaran was hot, had awesome legs, just as you like them, and, being pregnant, she probably needed you, didn't she?" He continued before I had a chance to answer. "You seem to be describing the ideal scenario."

"Yes, I felt in heaven. In fact, that is how I described my feelings to Liaran: heavenly. I loved everything about my life and about being with her, except her."

"Wow, I see." He said. "How come?"

"Before I ever went to her home the first time, I asked her about her relationship with her parents. Specifically, I asked if they lived together. Liaran told me categorically that they did not live together. When I went there for the first time, however, they did. Liaran blatantly lied to me."

Frank Baler Finds T.H.

"Oh dear, I am sorry, that must have hurt." He said mocking me.

"No, that was not bad. Bad was what happened afterwards. First, she lied about the lie, something she did more and more each day until the end of our relationship. That was not bad either. The really bad part is that what she did was unacceptable to me. I told her that what she did was a deal breaker to me; I offended her for her immoral lies and lies about the lie. Then we ended up in bed, making passionate love for hours. I kissed her belly with all my love and spoke to the baby. I loved her, except that I could not stand her for what I thought was her complete lack of character. 'No wonder your boyfriend dumped you pregnant' I would tell her; 'you can't stop lying…'"

"Oh, I can see the danger in that," the strange man said.

"The danger was that what happened that night became a vicious cycle, meaning it was worse each day. She would do something totally unacceptable to me, she would lie about whatever it was that day, I would catch it, offend her by calling her a liar and selfish, and end up making passionate love to her. That happened each and every day of our time together. Sometimes more than once in one day."

"What would she do that was so unacceptable to you?"

Frank Baler Finds T.H.

"Yeah, thank you for that question." I said. "I thought a lot about that. I felt that I was crazy for a long time, because, looking at it from the outside, she seemed like the perfect woman. A little lie is nothing, right? No one is perfect, I am not perfect, so why was I so activated all the time while with Liaran? The answer to that question cost me months in therapy…"

"'Activated' … you have been doing your homework son…" he said.

"Yeah, my attachment system was activated all the time, in full alert, or full panic. I loved her, wanted to be with her, but constantly felt the danger of losing her. That activation caused a profound regression in me, to the point that I did behave like a child, eventually no longer being the man she needed or wanted.

"Don't tell me about the man she needed." He interrupted sternly. "You are stuck on the man you think she thought she needed. Liaran is a capricious child herself, expert at snaring the men she wants, but she is not ready for what she needs."

He was differentiating between what Liaran wanted and what she needed. I had no idea how he could possibly know either of those two, but I was focused on a train of thought, so I continued talking.

Frank Baler Finds T.H.

"My attachment system was activated because each lie was the break of an explicit promise. The greater promise was that she would love me 'forever' and grow with me. So, each lie about a little promise chipped away at the big promise. Had I known this at the time I could have addressed it more maturely."

"I get the lie, and the break of a promise Frank. What is awesome is that you just told me that your sadness comes from not having been then who you are now. We are going to fix this by helping you be excited about who you are going to be soon." Then he added some therapeutic jargon… "a bit of future pacing[6] in the mix will bring your awareness to the present." Then he revealed something that I still cannot forget: "That is the secret to joy."

"Wait, what is the secret to joy? and why is joy relevant to the Path? I thought the work was what mattered on the Path" I asked because he was losing me with these complex explanations. Then I continued "I feel that I lost

---

[6] Future pacing amounts to describing to a client a possible desirable outcome. The description forms images in his mind that impress the subconscious. Once an image is established in the subconscious mind it tends to be realized, manifested, or fulfilled.

something… did you just explain to me where the sadness comes from?"

"Yes, that is the Frank I know; my dear intellectual with lots of clarifying questions…" He said patiently. Then he proceeded to indulge me and explain ideas to me at a pace that I could absorb.

"Yes, I just revealed to you what you never got in hundreds of hours of therapy: What you feel is true sadness. Your sadness does come from not having been in the past who you are in the present. I told you how we fix that: we help you become excited about who you are going to be, in the future. That fixes the sadness; placing your awareness in the future creates a huge amount of energy and drive, but no joy. As the sadness lifts, and the drive returns, we bring your awareness to the present to create joy."

"What about the Work on the Path? Why do you keep on talking about joy?" I did not follow this at all.

"Oh, there is no Path, or Work on the Path without joy. If there is no true joy, your soul is not there, and the work becomes the product of your mind. In the long run, that only leads to the breakdown of the mind." Then I thought he was being sarcastic when he said: "Should I mention a prominent example of such breakdown?"

Frank Baler Finds T.H.

"Okay, I think I know who you have in mind, but it is not a prominent example. It is true that I never felt joy, and I never cared, because I thought work mattered, not joy." He laughed with joy, as if his student was getting something.

"Would you kindly tell me what is the secret to joy, and why joy matters?" I asked with a hint of sarcasm this time.

"Of course!" He answered. "The secret to joy is to live in the present. There is only joy while your awareness is focused on the present, not in the past or in the future, but in the present. Your soul can only express itself through you while your mind is focused on the present. Past and future are inexistent concepts, fabrications of the mind only, but the soul lives in a world of eternal present moments. When the mind is focused on the past or future, it is out of syntony with the soul."

"No soul, no joy!" I said with a huge 'aha moment' intonation.

"Exactly," he said. "Just as sexual pleasure is nature's way of ensuring reproduction of the species, joy is the soul's way of ensuring focus on the present. Joy stands at the very center of depression and anxiety. Think of the past too much and you end up depressed. Worry about the future and you end up anxious. Live the present and you have joy. Or," he seemed to be on a roll, "become joyous and you will find yourself focused on the present. Live in the present and your soul will find expression through you, hence the joy."

"Not peace?" I jumped in.

"There is peace in joy, and joy in peace. But if you navigate your life by seeking peace you will end up frustrated because you will not have lived. Seek true joy instead." Then he continued: "You like the bible, all those guys that were fed to the lions in the Old Testament, what does the bible say about them?"

"I see," I said. "They had joy."

"The feeling you seek within yourself Frank is like the destination address you enter into the GPS. You have been navigating your life by the notion that you should have peace. You have had some peace, but with a whole lot of pain as well. Your pain, nothing else, should be an indication that something has to change. Navigate life by joy, not peace.

I was stunned. Could I have gotten life more wrong if I tried? I thought. What he was saying was making sense, but at this point, it seemed too late for me. Then he continued:

"And it is never too late to awaken joy in a man's life… the soul is there… the joy is in there, screaming to get out… a little nudge and you can't help it but to live an awesome life."

Frank Baler Finds T.H.

"Yeah right!" I said faking a sarcastic laugh. "If you only knew it…"

"That is okay," he said. "We go back and forth, past and future, until you find the present, until you find joy. Tell me, what else happened?"

"Well, Liaran had a miscarriage and obviously didn't want to be with me after that, but she never said so, she never broke up with me. Instead, she started blaming me for everything, suddenly everything was wrong with me, I couldn't do anything right. It was constant bashing, nonstop screaming. If I stayed, she kicked me out; if I left, she accused me of abandoning her. There was no way to please her in any regard, except sexually. We made passionate love each night; we exchanged promises and words, so I thought she really loved me, as I loved her, but was upset because of the hormones of pregnancy."

"Hormones of pregnancy? I thought she had a miscarriage."

"Well, she had a miscarriage, and soon after threw me out of the house. I was gone for about 2 months. When I saw her next, she was pregnant again, and announced to me her decision to have an abortion. I begged her and her mother not to, but she said it was her decision. I just loved her so much, that I told her not to worry about the pregnancy, we

Frank Baler Finds T.H.

would raise the baby together, regardless of who the father was. But she insisted on the abortion claiming that 'there was something wrong with the baby'. She proceeded to kill the baby, despite my insistence to the contrary. After the abortion, we got back together."

"Do you know who the father was?"

"Yes, her second husband with whom she had one baby already. This man actually paid for the abortion, gave her $500 in cash for the procedure at MWC." Then I added: "biggest coward I know of, he paid to have his baby killed so his then wife would not be upset about the infidelity."

"What happened then?"

"The lies only got worse and more blatant. Eventually she accused me of violence and worked really had to put me in jail. When we investigated the case in my legal defense, we discovered that she had secretly been accumulating police reports to build up a case against me. She would come home screaming at me, I never knew why she was so upset, so I would go out to prevent an escalation. As soon as I would leave, she would call the police and tell them I hit her and left. There was never any evidence of violence because I never hit her in any way, but she had 12 police reports by the time our relationship was over. She used all that to build a huge case against me."

Frank Baler Finds T.H.

"Were you upset about that?"

"I knew I had not, and I would never hit her. I knew the accusations were false and there could not be any evidence of wrongdoing, because there were no deeds. But one thing got me upset, and the other made me, I guess, sad, as you explained."

"Go!" He said.

"It made me sad that she spent so much time, effort and money to have me incarcerated, particularly when I offered her many times to leave her if she was not happy with me. I was sad because I felt her efforts finally confirmed what I felt all along, which is that she really did hate me."

"Wait, you felt that she hated you?" He asked.

"Yes, and she would say so from time to time, but the love making was so passionate, plus my view on hatred is that of a spiritual illness that has nothing to do with its object. I did not think that an illness on her part warranted my departure, so I did what I could to help her heal, but immaturely, since my attachment system was activated."

"Dude, we have a lot of work ahead of us. Let me guess," he said pretending to be in deep thought, "did you feel that your mother hated you as a child?"

"Can we please save that for next session?" I asked alluding to the therapeutic notion of a session after the current. "You asked me two things, I want to cover them both."

"What got you upset?" He asked without missing a beat.

"That's complicated. It took me months in therapy to even be able to talk about that because I was so ashamed of it. But here it is: Liaran beat me up several times, really beat me up."

"Oh, she accused you of what she did? Frank, if that happens over a cookie crumb on the floor, we call it 'projection'. If it happens on a greater scale, you know it is a PD." He said, I assumed referring to a personality disorder. "So far, based on what you have said, I am guessing NPD, BPD, and ASPD. The DSM[7] talks about 10 PDs, but you know they often co-occur," he said.

Then he said, after some introspection:

"You mentioned the abortion after throwing you out of the house. The kid was not yours, right?"

"Only if my sperm lasted one month inside of her..." I said dejected.

"How do you know the kid was not yours?" It felt as though he was cross checking what I had just told him.

---

[7] The Diagnostic and Statistical Manual of Mental Disorders

Frank Baler Finds T.H.

"She actually told me, including about the $500 payment for the procedure, which she got on August 28."

"Okay Frank, the conclusion is obvious, she wanted you out because she already had someone else. That is common," he continued, "in the old days, generals would send soldiers to their death in the front lines of battles to keep their wives. She wanted to eliminate you from the world to decrease her guilt for cheating the second time."

"Most likely third," I added.

"Yes, I would not be surprised," he concluded.

"We had to investigate her whole life in preparation for the criminal trial which never happened. We found out that she was married three times before, and did the same thing to each previous husband, leaving them each nearly dead. Furthermore, she was indeed in another relationship by then with her now current husband. The reason why she manipulated her previous husband into impregnating her, while involved with two other men, was because the previous husband was a cop. She needed his help to create false accusations and formal charges against me. The man who paid to have his own baby killed betrayed his own badge and helped her commit a crime, which they got away with."

Frank Baler Finds T.H.

"Okay," he interrupted me. "What happened to you as a result of all this? I have a picture of who she is now, I was able to tune into her already, and I am sorry to tell you, it is worse than you think. She is not just a liar and cheater Frank, there is more there, and that is why you were plucked from there; you were saved from her."

"What the heck is that supposed to mean?" I asked frantically.

"Frank quit pretending! You know exactly she was sent to eliminate you."

"What the devil does that mean?" I was almost shouting now.

"Frank, it was not her fault. A spirit was sent to her, she incorporated it. You know her mother was possessed, and her father is a deep alcoholic. The family has a long history of using black magic; the maternal grandfather was 'deranged', you found out later. The spirit felt natural to Liaran. It was not so much Liaran, it was the spirit that was sent through her to take your life away, and you know that."

When I heard those words, I began to cry violently. I bent over and placed my forehead on the ground. I cried deeply, while the mysterious man just watched kindly, holding space for me.

"Yes, I knew about the possession. But several things happened. One, I felt guilty for not protecting her better. I felt it was my fault that she was attacked, because of my work with exorcisms. Two, I blamed her for being so spiritually weak that she could not deflect the attack. Third, I wanted her to come to me with the problem..." He interrupted me again.

"Frank, the family has a long history of dabbling into black magic," he repeated. "When she began to dislike you, she actively sought help from the entity to empower her to leave you because she was also attached to you. She was not a passive victim. When she met this other man, another victim, she gave the entity full control of her actions to have you eliminated. The idea that you are a criminal did two things for her: it created a focal point for her to project her guilt for cheating, and elicited pity from the next weakling she snared."

"Are you saying..."

"Yes, dammit," he actually raised his voice, "what is so difficult about accepting that she wanted you dead? DEAD" he emphasized, "not in jail."

He let me digest the enormity of what he was saying for as long as I needed to. When I breathed deeply and raised my head, looking at him, he continued:

Frank Baler Finds T.H.

"Please don't tell me that you are not aware of explicit attempts to eliminate your life."

"Well, the beatings she gave me were not life-threatening… when she pushed me down the stairs as I ran away from one beating, I guess I could have tripped and fallen, but I would not have died. The first time she poisoned me with her mother's medications in my food, she was trying to help me sleep. Yes, I went to several doctors, and almost had a few car accidents because I would fall asleep while driving, but she really meant well; she wanted to help me sleep better. Sure, she forgot to tell me about the medication in my food, but that was just because we were both very busy at the time. The second time she overdosed me on metoclopramide I ended up at the hospital for a couple of days, but I was the one who drunk the stuff she put in my water." Then I paused.

"Come on, go!" He said.

"Fine, she almost ran me over with her car three different times, but I can't say that she veered her car onto me to hit me, maybe she was avoiding a cat on the other side of the road that I could not see. I don't know man, I can't see what you mean about she wanting me dead… I think you are exaggerating a little."

Frank Baler Finds T.H.

"Yes, perhaps she was avoiding a cat on the other side of the street the three times she veered onto you. But did she hit the brakes?"

"No! Surely she got nervous and hit the gas accidently."

"I am sure there are videos of these events. Right?"

"Well, yes."

"Does the video show her looking at a cat on the road?"

"No, actually she looks at me, veers onto me and hits the gas. Two officers saw the event and ordered her to pull over. She fled the scene of the incident, but I am sure she probably was just in a hurry to get to a bathroom, or something."

The man did not seem to lose hope with me. He seemed compassionate, but it seemed like he was trying a different angle now:

"You have been on the Path most of your life. What have you really not seen? Who can really fool you at this point with the occult? Plus, you are probably one of the most experienced therapists around; 40000 sessions? 300 exorcisms? Come on! Now tell me, Doctor, evaluate patient Frank the year before he left Liaran and give me your diagnosis."

Then he added again, somewhat sarcastically:

"Please Doctor, go on…"

"The patient suffered from a delusion and had a major personal weakness. The delusion was the romantic notion of love for ever more, the soulmate for life hypothesis, and the sacrificial model of love, as in 'to love is to sacrifice' as Jesus sacrificed his life because he loved us. The weakness was his attachment style. Two attachment styles have been identified: secure and insecure. The insecure can be anxious, avoidant or disorganized. The patient fits into the disorganized category, not the anxious, and that was a major personal weakness."

"Brilliant analysis Doctor. Would you now factor in the mystical quest, please?" He asked.

"Yes, the patient in question has been a mystic in each incarnation known, therefore we must understand events in his life in terms of a mystical purpose."

"And what purpose did a full cluster B[8], narcissistic woman who love-bombed him to death, pun intended, serve him?"

---

[8] He was using therapeutic jargon. A 'full cluster B' would be a person who qualifies for the diagnosis of all cluster B personality disorders on the Diagnostic and Statistical Manual of Mental Disorders. This would be a person colloquially identified as "crazy".

Frank Baler Finds T.H.

"First, it was a test that he chose. He knew the experience might have killed him. As a warrior after all, he wanted to test himself in battle. If he did not die, he figured, his mind would be totally broken, which would make way for the Light in his heart. It was a costly, but effective pathway to Illumination."

"I see it," he said. "What you are saying is no different, in principle, to chemotherapy or insulin oncotherapy."

"What?" I asked.

"Frank, chemotherapy kills everything in the body, the hope is that it kills more cancer cells than healthy ones. In insulinic oncotherapy they do the same thing, they inject massive doses of insulin to the point of inducing coma, hoping that tumor cells are starved before the brain dies. You said the same thing: break the man down completely, hoping that the heart emerges open."

"I never thought of it that way," I said.

"Yes, you did, doc. What you mean is that you never gave yourself credit for being who you are. You never owned the totality of who you are. Don't worry, soon you will…"

He looked at the sky for a moment, then he continued:

"You have explained your personal life to me in detail, and you are about to relate the personal to the mystical. The day is about to break, however, so go home and meet me tomorrow night."

"Where?" I asked as he walked away.

"Just go for a walk again, I will find you." He said before I could ask for help finding my way home.

Returning to Allen and Mary's house, I felt like a teenager who took dad's car without authorization and was now coming home quietly not to be detected. As I jumped in the shower, it occurred to me how awesome the walk back home had been, particularly considering that I felt guided by a remarkable intuition.

After breakfast, we made plans for another great day out. We went grocery shopping, we stopped at the hardware store to purchase a drill bit, we put gas in the car… I felt like a local resident doing normal things with my friends, who felt like family by now. Of course, as soon as I would disengage my mind from focusing on something specific, I would hurt immensely. Often tears would come down my face, but I no longer cared about that.

That night I was in a hurry to retire to my room in my friend's house. I still don't know why I thought my escapade had to be a secret. Looking back, I could have told Allen 'I am going for a walk', but I wanted it to be a secret.

Frank Baler Finds T.H.

Again, at about 1am I walked out of the bedroom. This time I checked several times that the phone was in my pocket and turned on. I checked that the pin had indeed been dropped at the house's location. I was much safer now, I thought, as the GPS will guide me home if I got lost. So, I relaxed and simply walked freely, without a destination in mind. Inside, I was expecting this man to come up and continue our 'session' together. At the time, however, it did not occur to me just how unlikely the whole thing was.

Who was that man? How did he know so much about me? What did he mean by 'finding me' when I came for a walk tonight? At the time, none of those questions mattered to me. I simply walked around the semi desert in and out of trails, with absolutely no concern on my mind, just a heavy heart filled with guilt, shame and regret about a past I was now determined to fix.

I found myself on a trail that seemed to go down, not uphill. Suddenly, it got really dark, so I pulled out the phone, turned the flashlight on and placed the phone just below my navel, held by my belt, which I tightened one notch to keep the phone in place. I had used that same strategy climbing out of Angel's trail on the Grand Canyon a couple of years before. That little light on the phone, on a dark trail, made it seem like daylight.

Frank Baler Finds T.H.

The narrow trail I was walking on became a little steeper; I was definitely going downhill. I figured I might reach a creek or perhaps a dry riverbed somewhere, so I kept walking. I came to what looked like a ledge, a large rock hanging on the side of a mountain. When I got close to the edge, there seemed to be no bottom to that precipice. I felt that uncomfortable tingling sensation in my peritoneum and walked back slowly, not to slip down. I noted the self-preservation spirit at work within me, and thanked God for its return.

As I turned the flashlight to my right, now in my hand, I saw that the trail continued in that direction. The problem was that, as far as I could see with the phone's flashlight, it was a narrow trail on the face of the mountain. To my right, if I walked on the trail, was a vertical wall, the side of the mountain. To my left would be an abyss whose bottom the phone's light could not reach.

I would not want any of my daughters to do what I did next, for I now think that it was irresponsible of me to do so; I followed the trail.

The trail curved to my right, then became a very steep short downhill. It then curved to the left, and I seemed to no longer be next to a precipice. Then there was a flat clearing. Then total darkness.

Frank Baler Finds T.H.

The phone simply died. My eyes had been adjusted to the light from the phone, so for a while I could not see absolutely anything. I knew that in a few moments, vision would return, but under the circumstances, it felt like it was taking forever. I rubbed my eyes, removed my glasses, placed my hands in front of my face, nothing worked. I was not able to see anything.

The year before, driving in Costa Rica at night, I had a similar moment. Perhaps I am low on vitamin A, I noted to myself as I sat on the ground waiting for night vision to return. Indeed, by the time my buttocks were on the ground I could see the side of a mountain in front of me.

"Don't you charge your phone?" The voice coming from behind me asked. It was him again; his voice unmistakable. "I was just wondering about that. I checked that the phone had been plugged in before dinner, I made sure I had it on me when I left the house and made sure that the pin was dropped. Even with the GPS running the battery should not have died so soon."

"Maybe the mountain spirits sucked the power out of your phone…" He said laughing freely and joyously. I did not think the joke was funny at all.

"Frank, let me try to appease you. You are not crazy for feeling broken. You don't miss Liaran either. You miss two

Frank Baler Finds T.H.

things: you miss who you were when you met her, and you miss how you felt having her in your life at the time." Then he continued.

"You are not the only one suffering narcissistic abuse injury; there are millions of people on the same boat. Sad thing is" – he said – "nobody knows how to help them, as you already found out."

"Is that a thing?" I asked. "NAI?"

"Absolutely! Listen," he said, "the narcissist love bombs you to death, or, more appropriately, until you become addicted to the love bombing. Then they devalue and discard you. The discard would be bad enough, but they also destroy their victims. Can you recognize those stages in Liaran's behavior?"

"Your model seems to fit the data" I said in a low monotonic voice.

"The important thing" he continued, "is that missing that feeling, the love-bombing, does not mean that you are broken, the feeling feels good. There is only one problem…"

"What's that?"

"Well, what did you call her when she was love-bombing you, in the beginning?"

"Fake, she was a fake. She had no interest in my life, in my pursuits, in my dreams. She never asked a single question, she never cared to get to know me. She never cared to build something together. She lied all the time and lied about her lies. So, yes, I thought her extreme love was fake, and I told her that several times."

"See the cognitive dissonance there? Your better judgement knew that something was not right, but it felt so good, so you stayed, hoping for a change, true?"

"True. And I never asked for much. I asked for better communication and plans together. She mocked me, saying that she could not produce the feeling of bonding with me, since I clearly had a problem accepting love."

"Once you gave in to her version of love, which seemed like madness to you, since you had separate lives, what happened?"

"She clearly devalued me publicly and eventually discarded me in the most brutal of ways, as she had done with her previous husbands."

"Any campaigns to discredit you?"

"Oh please… can you just tell me how to become normal?"

"Tell me Frank, it was not just discarding you in private, right? She constantly involved other people, spread lies about you, discredited you, and made sure to turn as many people against you as possible. Is that true?"

Frank Baler Finds T.H.

"She did all that in a vicious way, including to the Police and other authorities, yes."

"Classical narcissist, Frank. The injury you suffered may not be in the DSM yet, but it will be in the next edition. Narcissistic abuse injury is real, and it is serious. Most people who suffer NAI end up dead, one way or the other." He paused, then continued:

"What happened after the discard?"

"She got pregnant elsewhere. She announced an abortion. I pleaded with her not to have the abortion, remodeled her house a second time as a gift, and begged her to rebuild the relationship."

"Did you make it up yet again?"

"We did." I said.

"Why do you think she got back with you at that point?"

"I have several videos of her hitting herself, and of her hitting her head on the wall. She wanted those videos deleted, but I refused to delete them. She took me back in order to have access to me and to my things, so she could delete the videos. She came to my office one afternoon and scoured my computers. She found the videos and deleted them. She accessed my phone remotely and deleted the videos there as well. She stole 2 SD cards from my laptop at home. Only a drive with backups of all the videos showing her deranged behavior survived. She does not know I backed up the videos."

"That is true," he said. "She was driven to delete those videos and having access to your things made that easier. Incidentally, he continued, kudos to you for backing up the videos… they will be useful soon. But, that is not the only reason she went back to you."

"Really? Why else then?"

"Frank, the other reason was that she actually loved you. You surprised her. She never intended to build a life with you beyond her original pregnancy, but you actually loved her, made many changes, worked diligently on yourself, the relationship, and your lives together. Your response to her discard took her by surprise; it awakened a feeling within her that she is extremely scared of."

"What was that?" I asked.

"I told you, she felt love. Frank, you said so yourself, she never loved before, not her parents or even her child. Certainly, none of the previous men in her life. Remember how you said she would always delegate her child to her mother and not bond with her? She is extremely scared of love. You did something so innocent and genuine that she actually felt love."

"So why not become vulnerable and live the love with me?"

"Fate my friend. That is what we are going to talk about tonight: fate. By the time she felt love with you her fear of that opportunity was at an all-time high. She was literally scared. This is why her lies were worse than ever; remember that? The other problem was that by that time she already had a commitment with someone else. She lied to you and to him. She felt the threat of real love with you, and the opportunity to control him. So, she chose him."

"Why not break up with me then?"

"Oh, that would require honesty and valor. She was afraid of the love, she already had a man she could control and manipulate. Plus, her true and only relationship is with her parents. You know that. Her parents, as a unit, are her wife. She likes that life, bossing her parents; she is an only child after all. Plus she feels safer with a man she can control, rather than love."

"Okay, but you said she wanted me killed. What happened?"

"That was accidental. She wanted you completely out of the picture, and because of the love in your heart, you kept forgiving and coming back with more love, hoping that she would correspond your love. When you refused to simply disappear, and I don't blame you, for she never broke up or asked you to leave, she asked for help from her mother. Her mother works a form of African earth religion that is amoral. They provide their saints with vital energy in exchange for favors.

"That was when your mystical and personal lives intersected. She just wanted you to 'look the other way' and disappear from her world. The entity that was sent took the opportunity to execute a plan you needed to face: your own death."

"Wow, she was a different person at that time..." I said. "Oh yes, she was fully possessed and changed. She took on a toll, and this chapter of her life is not over. She contracted another heavy karma, as you would call it."

"Another?"

"Come on... three cancer surgeries by the time she was 27 years of age? This woman is loaded, and there is no sign of change in sight. But that is not your problem, and we will no longer talk about her."

"So, the death thing was real, but it was accidental?"

"Well, it was accidental in so far as her not pulling a gun and firing it; it was accidental in that she wanted you 'gone'; but it was not accidental in that she actively called the dark forces to herself. Frank, she called those forces into your

Frank Baler Finds T.H.

lives, while telling you that she loved you, and that she wanted a life with you, if only you would be perfect. Not all cases of NAI involve the use of black magic, of course, but they all involve a severe contradiction that splits the other person in two; hence the injury. Once split, and profoundly injured, the narcissist tells you he or she is a victim of yours. This 'turning of the table around' is absolutely universally known when it comes to narcs like this woman. Because of who you are, in this case, the only way to produce that split, was to use heavy black magic along with the sweetest love you have ever known.

"You were split, you were severely injured, and to a large extent you 'lost your mind'. Fortunately, your love and service to others made it possible for you to avert death. But that energy, once put in motion, and she put it into motion, must now go somewhere. Unfortunately, just like undelivered mail is returned to the sender, this type of energy always finds its way back to the sender."

"What?" I almost shouted.

"Frank... I said that the subject for tonight was the intersection of your mystical and personal lives. I only reviewed what we talked about last night for you to have a sense of completion and closure. Also, we want you to know that you are not crazy, and we want you to know that,

Frank Baler Finds T.H.

although Liaran did you a huge favor, as you will see tonight, she is not what you call the love of your life. That love does exist for you in the form of a woman in this lifetime, but we have some work to do before you are ready for her."

"Please man, can't you just give me her number?" He laughed joyously and abundantly, then he said: "I have something better for you."

He looked deeply into my eyes, as he approached me. Suddenly he struck my forehead with the open palm of his right hand and shouted:

"Sleep!"

I remember laying down on the ground and dreaming I was flying like an eagle. Then I opened my eyes.

"I must have Esdailed[9]," I said referring to a deep hypnotic state, "because I have no awareness of any verbal suggestion."

"There were no verbal suggestions. I just worked on your heart, a little."

"A little? I need a lot!"

---

[9] This refers to a deep hypnotic state in which the subject loses awareness of the surroundings. The state was named after the Scottish surgeon James Esldaile (1808-1859).

Frank Baler Finds T.H.

"As is the case with the mind, the heart cannot be opened too fast because that would leave the person so vulnerable in the physical world that they would initially be non-functional. In the past, people have died from having their hearts opened too fast because they would stop eating, they would lose interest in a world that felt hostile and unreal to them."

"Is my heart open?" I asked always wanting to be a good student.

"You are doing better than last year, much better in fact. But we have a lot of work ahead." Then he became introspective and asked:

"Frank why do you think we are having these conversations?"

"That I know professor," I said trying to sound funny. "I am being prepared for a higher mission."

"Yes son, yes." He said deflated. "Thing of it is, the only mission that exists is to find yourself. You actually think you are on this earth to help others integrate; your only mission, the only mission that exists, is to integrate yourself."

"Well, according to the Tradition…"

"Wow, wow, wow," he said interrupting me sternly. "Ease does it, boy. Confucius said: easy, boy."

Frank Baler Finds T.H.

I remembered him saying the night before that I was now ready to begin the work because I finally knew that I knew nothing. So, I got quiet. Then he said, wasting no time at all:

"Tell me about the other side of the coin. You lived two lives; you told me about your human, now tell me about the mystical during the same period."

It occurred to me that this strange man covered what happened on our previous encounter then moved on to the subject for this encounter. I did the same thing in my sessions with clients at the office. I would always comment on the previous session before starting the current. I felt that, by doing that, clients would better situate each session within the overall therapeutic journey.

"Well," I started hesitantly because I really wanted to continue talking about Liaran. "I told you about requesting the High Initiation, and a freaky car accident that could have killed us all. Two years after the accident Liaran and I were separated during a trip to Costa Rica. That night I was sleeping at a beachside hotel. It was about one o'clock in the morning when I felt that the beach was calling me. There were no electrical lights or air conditioning sounds. The windows were open. I heard the waves and the wind. I got up and went to the beach. There was nobody there. The moon was not visible. It was as if the beach was emotional, the ocean at times was very quiet, and at times very agitated. 'Footprints', the poem in which a man is walking on the beach alongside God, was on my mind. I walked back and forth from about one in the morning until the sun came up at about six o'clock in the morning, walking back and forth, up and down the beach, many times.

"I was very agitated. I could not stop crying as I clearly remembered details of many instances as a priest or a person of civil authority in different lives judging people for what I thought was inappropriate behavior. I was ashamed of that past. I did not know what to do. I could feel the same pain that all those people felt. At one point, I questioned whether I would make it off the beach alive because the pain was so intense that I worried about a heart problem. I was hurting.

"Eventually I decided that it did not matter if I died that night on the beach in Costa Rica. The important thing would be to never hurt anyone ever again, that would be my priority. Little did I know that night that the pain I felt then was just the beginning of an experience that would go on for at least another couple of years.

"I made serious changes in my life after the Costa Rica trip. Liaran and I reconciled, but from my point of view, she never made any changes herself, leading us to that fateful thanksgiving night when we finally separated permanently."

Frank Baler Finds T.H.

I hoped to hook him into talking about Liaran some more, but he did not flinch. I made a mental note that I must look at my need to keep on talking about her as a true addiction. Then I continued:

"I did not sleep at all for about three months once I left Liaran. I would doze off for a moment, then immediately jump up startled. I have come to think that a great deal of the problem I am facing stems from a prolonged period of sleep starvation."

"Yes, lack of sleep exacerbated the problem." He concurred.

"About one month into that ordeal, I had an experience that changed me drastically. It took a while to piece together what happened that night. At times, I thought of what happened as an out of body experience, and at times I described it as a near death experience. There are no recorded signs of clinical death though, so I guess the NDE label is not appropriate."

"Frank, can you please tell me what happened? Save the academic definitions for your books…" He said.

"What books?" I asked startled!

"Oh, you will write and publish many books my dear doctor. Your books will be a source of inspiration and healing to many people."

Frank Baler Finds T.H.

"I see what you are doing: future pacing and getting me excited about who I am going to be! You told me we would do this last night."

"You have been paying attention, son. But I am not programming you to write books. The books are in you already. At the appropriate time you will birth them. I am just telling you what will happen."

"Are you a prophet?" I asked intrigued.

"Frank, please focus. Please tell me what happened that night." He said with an air of frustration, I thought.

"Sure. I definitely experienced life outside the physical context. Bathing in 'nothingness', while at the same time feeling an all-loving presence clearly changed me in ways that I still cannot describe."

"You use the word 'bathing', suggesting a context, or medium, within which you were. That hardly suggests the idea of 'nothingness'." He pointed out.

"Agreed. I first experienced nothingness. Then I noticed that I did not feel alone, that is when I became aware of some sort of all-loving presence. That is when I felt enveloped or bathed by that awareness. Looking back, things developed apparently in response to my awareness. For instance, when I noticed that I was 'nowhere' yet did not feel alone, I experienced the 'presence'. Then one side seemed brighter than the other. As I gravitated toward the lighter side, my four daughters 'appeared' on the other side, which now felt like my left."

"Oh, were your daughters afflicted somehow?"

"No! Complete peace and total absence of any emotion or judgement. There is nothing in this world I can compare to that sentiment. I guess there were no…" I got lost in the remembrance of that moment outside of this realm.

"No what Frank?" He finally asked to get me back into the conversation.

"I guess I drifted back into that 'space' for a moment. Man, there was no desire?" I was not sure if I was saying it or asking it.

"Ahh… now we are getting somewhere son. You experienced what we call 'zero-desire'; indeed, a concept foreign to the human condition. Here, we always want something. We live immersed in a sea of desires. In many ways, true meditation is about the zero-desire state."

"But don't people meditate to achieve something? Is that not the expression of a desire?" I asked curiously.

"People are addicted to their desires, and they will do anything to try to achieve what they want, including pretending they meditate. It never works because the more they pretend to meditate to try to achieve what they think they want, the more they affirm what they lack. Meditation is the experience of fulfillment, not the affirmation of a lack. Most people never catch on to that obvious contradiction. Now please continue telling me what happened," he said.

"Well, I have described and talked about how different my relationship with my daughters feels here versus there, during the experience. Here, I always feel that I want to give them more but feel incapable of it somehow. There I felt a profound sense of completeness, as if we are all complete, and no transfer of benefit is needed in any direction."

"Hummm... that is interesting," he said. "If there was no transfer of benefit in any direction, as you describe, how do you account for the positive effect the experience had on you? I ask," he clarified "because I read a book called 'The Philosophy of Therapy'[10] by one of your colleagues, in which the author talks about the therapeutic effect and the transfer of a benefit." Then he added: "Some incredible work you therapists do..."

The question took me by surprise because it was so simple, yet I had no clue how to answer it. There was an obvious effect to the experience, I had changed as a person

---

[10] The Philosophy of Therapy, by Flavio Ballerini, Ph.D.

as a result of that experience. But if nothing was added into me, or removed from me, how did the change actually come about?

Suddenly I started to imagine myself as a boy on a beach in Brazil. Sometimes we would play soccer on the beach for hours during summer vacations. When we got home, we would be amazed at how 'burnt' we were. Then I got it.

"When exposed to the sun, we would not say that the sun itself came into the skin, although 'vibrations' from the sun, or what we call 'radiation', does promote a chemical reaction on the skin that changes its color. Exposure to the sun changes skin color. Similarly, exposure to absolute acceptance was what changed me during the experience. The bit about my daughters was an opportunity for me to practice with them what I experienced there."

"Remarkable. So, you are complete and whole. You do not need to be fixed because you are not broken. Therefore, the experience of divinity on the earth is not about becoming divine, or humanly perfect, it is about accepting your true essence, accepting your divinity. You can do that by exposing yourself to 'radiations' from divinity; that will change you enough, just as radiations from the sun changes the color of your skin"

Frank Baler Finds T.H.

"Yes, I guess…" I said not sure I totally understood what he was saying. Then I continued. "But at some point, I wanted to come back and offer a contribution to others."

"And what happened at that point?" He asked slowly.

I could not answer that question, because my next awareness was of being in bed, in a different room. This was difficult, I thought.

"I do not know. I guess I have not recovered that part of the experience from my unconscious mind yet."

"Tell me the sequence you are aware of" he said.

"I told you: I wanted to come back and help others. Then I recall being in bed, awake, having slept, rested. No dreams; just rested."

"You see?" He asked "The moment you thought of yourself as special, as coming back to help others, of being the savior again, the experience was over because you were no longer in syntony with your natural state of divinity called what?" I guess he was asking me a question, so I tried to be a good student: "Zero-desire?" I said hesitantly.

"Exactly!" He said somewhat triumphantly.

"I was thinking about my daughters, and how much more I want to give them though. Isn't love about giving?" I asked myself when he interrupted again:

Frank Baler Finds T.H.

"Frank, your daughters are just fine, and you are a good father. We are talking about the mystic side of the coin; focus, and please be more concise in your descriptions because we have a lot to talk about!" The man said sharply.

"Fine, I said. You already know about the hypnosis session at the conference in May where I was able to get in touch with the Assembly of Masters. That experience was fundamentally important for me because I realized that I had not failed the Path and the Masters had not abandoned me." Then I continued, again lost in thoughts and endless elaborations…

"Another impressive experience at the conference happened the morning before the hypnosis session with Arturo. I had been at the same hotel with Liaran the year before to present a paper on the use of hypnosis to improve menopausal symptoms. As usual, Liaran used that opportunity to create all kinds of fights with me; I had no idea what the fights were about. We walked around the pool area arguing. I would walk away, she would follow me, scream some more, bash me some more. I would walk away again; I never understood what she was upset about.

"This time, when I went to the same hotel, it occurred to me to retrace the same steps I had taken the year before and erase those memories of Liaran with me, at that hotel. I was

Frank Baler Finds T.H.

wearing a suit and tie, since I was presenting a bit later that day. I walked around the pool and the outer lobby of the hotel, stopping at each station where we had an argument the year before. At each station I would stop, look around, mentally get back to the state I felt the year before, forgive, and discharge the feelings from within my person.

"While I walked around the pool area, for probably about a good 45 minutes, unbeknownst to me, a man watched me from a balcony on the 7th floor of the building.

"Later that evening he recognized me at the conference and told me that he was intrigued by a man walking around the pool wearing a full suit and tie, stopping periodically, looking around, and walking some more. He told me that he thought I was the hotel manager, inspecting different aspects of the operation.

"When he told me that story, I realized that no matter how much we hurt, how lost we feel, how alone or abandoned we feel; no matter what we try to do on the ground, there is always someone watching us from above. The man watching me from above turned out to be my new friend Allen; he taught me a valuable lesson that day."

"Frank, I appreciate your poetic flair, and the candor with which you relate these experiences to me. Daylight is about to break; you need to go to sleep now."

Frank Baler Finds T.H.

"Yes, but what about..." He interrupted me, again!

"Go to sleep now; we will talk soon." He said as he disappeared in the darkness.

Perhaps daylight had already broken, or perhaps my night vision was getting sharper already, I don't remember which; but I had no trouble finding the trails and my way home that night.

When I finally made it to my bedroom that late night, almost morning, I plugged the charging cable into the phone again, and had no response. Tracing the charging cable, I found that the other end had come out of the charging block on the wall. The phone had been plugged in, but it had not charged.

The next day I had a few moments to write on my journal after the three of us had breakfast. I reflected on the experiences in the desert the previous two nights and understood how years of crust were being removed from my being to expose my true nature in preparation for a glorious future. The similarity to the story of Moses was uncanny.

The last entry on my journal that day read:

As unlikely as this story is turning out to be, I must admit I met Moses.

Frank Baler Finds T.H.

Little did I know as I put my journal away, that another encounter, perhaps even stranger than the man in the desert, awaited me in New Mexico.

During my last full day with Allen and Mary, I met a barber by the name of Maharay who claimed her dead grandmother communicated with her, and sent me messages. Maharay would turn out to be a pivotal person in the months that followed.

THOU SHALL LIVE

The retreat took place at a small, out of the way, mid-level hotel in the West Coast of Florida. We were required to stay at the hotel for the duration of the event, presumably to increase immersion into the healing process. There were conferences, group exercises, and individual sessions with a therapist. Outside of official activities, we were not allowed to talk, again, presumably to increase immersion in the process and to encourage deep introspection. The rules made it clear that a participant who broke them would be dismissed without a refund of the fee.

The entire first day there was only one session with the main therapist putting the event on. The session was essentially a lengthy interview covering every aspect of my life, since birth. While other participants were being interviewed, we had a movie room playing inspiring movies

Frank Baler Finds T.H.

all day, and another room where games and fun exercises were happening. We were allowed to talk that day.

At 7PM we all had dinner together; there was a lot of pain and nervous energy in the air. At 8PM we had our first session, a conference with the head therapist, Thomas.

When Thomas and I had been talking privately I thought he was too lethargic and passive to conduct this kind of retreat. Thomas was from Oregon, in the northwest of the United States, an unusually beautiful part of the world. Slightly taller than I, possibly 6'1", thinner, and definitely more muscular than I, Thomas seemed very healthy. His hair and short beard were orange blond, and he looked no older than about 35; too young to know much, I thought. Thomas eyes, however, told a different story: they pierced me with a deep look that revealed some type of special knowledge that I could not quite place. Perhaps, I thought intermittently, it was not knowledge; perhaps it was just the particular shade of deep blue that made his eyes seem impressive. Thomas spoke in a calm and deep voice that was reassuring, although he often hesitated at the beginning of a sentence creating more anxiety for me.

Frank Baler Finds T.H.

Now Thomas was standing in front of the room; he filled the room and seemed in complete command of the entire process. The first question he asked of us was:

"If you are hurting so bad that you no longer care to live, please stand up."

We had just discussed the importance of confidentiality and safety in the group; furthermore, I figured, if I had a chance to heal, I would have to be brutally honest with myself, and, by extension, with the group.

I knew that I was not frankly suicidal because I had locked the balcony of the fifth-floor apartment where I lived, and I stopped going to the roof of the building to meditate in the mornings. I remembered pulling back from the edge of the precipice in the desert in New Mexico, so I felt that my survival instincts were operational.

There is a difference however, between wanting to die, and not wanting to live. The therapist asked for those who no longer cared to live to stand up.

I stood up, thinking I would be the only one, but no one remained on their chair. I was not alone. All eleven other people there were on the same boat as I. Somehow, I felt hope.

The next morning, we had to be up by 5:00. The meditation on the beach started at 5:30 sharp. The deal we

Frank Baler Finds T.H.

signed on was that all events were mandatory, and that tardiness would not be tolerated. When we got to the beach it was dark still. We each received a card with a simple line written on it. I suppose all cards were similar or equal because, at least on my card, there was no name written:

Walk around looking down into the sand. Recall everything that happened to you before you got here.

I knew I was broken, just like the advertising e-mail said. About one year had passed since I left Liaran knowing fully well that I was dying a slow death with her, and that I would probably die without her. I still had trouble with just about every aspect of my life, including the all-important desire to live. Yet, I knew one thing: this exercise they asked of us was not good. These people clearly had made a mistake. If a person who does not want to live walks around looking down, for sure they will feel worse. I knew then that the people putting on the event did not know what they were doing.

A plan showed up on my mind: I would do as they asked me to do to prove them wrong. I started walking, looking down. Soon, my shoulders rotated inwards, my back slumped, the breathing became shallow. Thoughts became

Frank Baler Finds T.H.

dangerously gloomy, and anxiety set in. I paid attention to how terrible I felt, and reached a full panic, right there on the beach.

As the panic mounted, I felt worse, eventually noticing that I was talking to myself. I kept noticing how I had been right, and they were all wrong. The inner speech continued:

'I know more about healing than they do; I would never ask a broken person to look down and think of what happened to them; of course I feel terrible; in fact, no, no, no, I feel worse than terrible, I am literally dying.' It went on and on, all in my head.

At 6:00AM they sounded a horn and asked us to gather around. A boom box played loud music. Thomas, the head therapist, asked us to 'shake it all off':

"Dance, scream, jump, bite, do whatever it takes to shake all that stuff off your system… just focus on the music!" Thomas said.

I am not the dancing type, but it occurred to me to stretch and to do a few karate moves I had practiced years earlier. I am not the screaming type either, but a few mantras came to my mind. Buried by the loud music coming from the boom box and the screams of others, I pronounced the mantras generously.

Frank Baler Finds T.H.

Next Thomas asked us to stand side by side, forming a line, all facing the ocean. He told us simply to focus on a deep, slow breathing until we felt relaxed again. My heart rate had not gone up too high because I had not been jumping that much, so I just enjoyed the silence and the slow breathing.

Then he asked us to close our eyes, listen to his voice and do as he said.

Thomas started to talk about the sun as if it were something alive, aware of our existence, almost as a God, I guess. He explained to us that the ancient Egyptians represented the God Ra by a figure that often included the sun with hands reaching down onto us.

That depiction of the sun, Thomas said, is symbolically accurate because the sun is indeed the source of all life on earth, and as such it is the closest thing we can understand as a God.

Those words touched me deeply because I had never considered that the human mind, simply cannot comprehend the totality of what life really is. The mind, it occurred to me, as in the intellect, is like a person trying to appreciate a large museum through a keyhole. The mind simply cannot grasp a complete picture of reality; therefore symbols, myths, legends, parables, analogies and metaphors have evolved over millennia for people to reach a little higher into their subjective minds and grasp a slightly larger slice of reality. Some people, however, defended the idea that the myths are to be taken as real, and the history of religious wars started. Another word for 'religious war', I thought, is a 'belief war'.

Suddenly I imagined a large crowd, millions of people walking aimlessly. My eyes were still closed, and Thomas was still talking in a calm, paused voice. I could see, in my mind's eye, the war going on inside of all the people walking around the earth, they each were, themselves, the grounds where a huge belief war was taking place. Every now and then, I imagined, massive bombs went off, and the person exploded in anger and rage toward the outside. Other times, the bomb went off in that belief war, imploding them into depression and sometimes suicide.

Thomas then asked us to look out and up, but still with our eyelids closed.

"Look out and up, keep your eye lids closed. Do as I say. Stretch out your arms forming a cross. Hold that position, relax, but hold the position. Breath nice, easy, slow and deeply. I will count from 3 down to 1. When I reach 1, take a deep breath as you open your eyes…"

When I opened my eyes, the entire sun was just above the horizon on the water. As I took a deep breath in, it felt to me that I pulled the sun into my being. I felt as though the rays of light entered my whole being and saluted me, or that I saluted the sun, or both. We saluted one another and merged, it felt.

I started crying, but these were very different tears from the ones I had been crying for the last year. These were tears of profound joy. I felt fortunate to be alive, to be there, and to experience the sun as a live entity.

As I cried and looked out onto the horizon, my mind brought me back to that image of the crowds walking around aimlessly. This time, however, it seemed that the mental image zoomed in onto one person on the aimless crowd. I looked deeply into that man's mind and heart. His heart was filled with joy, but his mind was loaded with conflicting beliefs and pain. I mentally sent him a beam of forgiveness, appreciation, gratitude, and above all, compassion.

That one man on the crowd, no different from the millions of others, was on the earth. The truth of his true identity veiled from his mind while he navigated life based on what he was told and learned from the outside in. That man had been broken, not as punishment for being bad, but as a reward for being a dedicated Seeker of the Higher Truth. Breaking his mind was the most efficient way of letting the Light in.

Frank Baler Finds T.H.

I felt so much compassion for the man that I started seeing moments in his life. I could see moments of joy and triumph, as well as moments of terrible pain and sorrow. Then something amazing happed.

I had always been seen as a weak man, in that I accepted the unacceptable from others, particularly from the women in my life. I had always disliked myself for the weakness I had been told I had. Everyone always told me, if I mentioned some of the things that had happened in my life, that I should send this or that person to hell, turn my head, and never look at them again. That suggestion never felt right to me because I always saw the other person as someone who was hurting and who needed to complete a process with, or through me. Somehow, I understood what had been portrayed as a weakness as my biggest strength, my biggest gift to those around me. I loved that one man on that crowd, but I could no longer find him there.

I collapsed on my knees and cried so much while the warm sun caressed me. I was happy, the tears were joyous. I was now safe, I thought, because those around me were now safe.

Moments after that, we were all in a small room having breakfast. After some time eating in silence, Thomas asked each of us to stand up and share with the group what we had experienced earlier that morning.

When it was my turn to talk, I mentioned my doubts, or my certainty that their methods were mistaken, and how I had decided to prove them wrong by doing what was asked of me. Then I continued:

"I noticed that by looking down and thinking of what had happened to me I felt initially sad, then desperate and hopeless to the point of panic. Later, when I looked up, opened my arms and welcomed the sun in, breathed slowly and deeply, I felt great. Only two things changed, both in my control: my body and the focus of my attention. Looking down and focusing on what happened to me, seems to cause depression, whereas looking up and out and focusing on what is ahead seems to produce joy. Furthermore, realizing that the power to change how I feel is actually within me was wonderful." As expected, and agreed upon, there were no comments or reactions.

After breakfast we spent the entire day in lectures, all briefly interrupted by sharing our thoughts and feelings about what was being discussed. At one point I shared the following thought with the group:

"It wasn't that I didn't want to live; it was that I no longer knew how to live. I didn't know how to engage with life.

Frank Baler Finds T.H.

Again, I said, it is not that I wanted to die, it was that I felt I already died."

When I sat down after sharing that thought, I noticed that I had spoken in past tense. Something had indeed changed within me.

My turn to have a private session with Natalie, Thomas' assistant therapist came the next day, soon after breakfast. Natalie tapped on my shoulder very lightly and motioned me to follow her into another room.

Natalie told me that she had observed a change in my demeanor. She actually said that my aura was brighter, and that was good, she said. She told me that our time together was an opportunity for me to discuss any deeper issues that I had not shared with the group. Any doubts, concerns or issues whatsoever were fair game in this confidential session. She repeated and emphasized that I should not hold back, even if I felt embarrassed about a topic, I should bring it up now.

"What still troubles you Frank, tell me, we have time." She said as she leaned back on her chair.

I started to apologize for thinking that the organizers did not know what they were doing the day before on the beach, but she interrupted me:

Frank Baler Finds T.H.

"Frank, thank you, but perhaps we can get into something a bit deeper in here…"

"That's just it, I said, I am trying to get into it. I got this way for following my heart… sometimes I do not know what to think… I got it all wrong…" Suddenly I made no sense, not even to myself.

Natalie was patient, empathetic, and a remarkably effective therapist. She suggested a brief guided meditation to help me gather my thoughts and focus on what was important for us to discuss during that opportunity that the universe had given us. She said:

"Don't think of me as a therapist and of you as a client, or a conference participant. Don't think of me as put together and of you as broken. Don't think of me as knowing and as of you as not knowing. Think of us both as two souls that the universe brought together to share some Light with one another. I want to see your Light," she concluded.

She was so loving, wise and, dare I say, beautiful, that I started to cry again. Natalie just held space for me and looked at me with love, compassion, and respect. She did not see a looser or a broken man. Natalie saw Light, and I sensed that from her. Soon I said:

"Natalie, I spent my life on the mystical Path, practicing it and teaching it. I lived by Jesus words 'sell it all and follow me' my whole life. All my decisions were based on the mystical Path; often I seemed irrational to others, but I always comported myself according to my interpretation of what was mystically needed at that time."

"Was that a problem for you?" She asked.

"No, I was happy to live that way, but I know that I inflicted pain on those around me. I never made any money, I was never able to have a good relationship with anyone, let alone a woman, and offended every person I ever spoke with."

"Why was the money thing relevant?"

"Well," I said, "because I was never able to support a woman and a family properly. I just never cared about any of that… I cared about the Path, or what I thought was the Path."

Wisely, she let me continue.

"I thought I was not complete or capable mystically of carrying out my function without a woman. I thought I needed the female complement; I thought the two of us together would be one unit that, together, could spread Light around the world. That was my thought, all of my life. So, I prayed and asked God for the right woman for me."

"That's beautiful Frank. What happened?"

Frank Baler Finds T.H.

"I met a woman named Liaran whom I immediately thought was God's answer to my prayer. She was perfect and awesome, except that our relationship was absolutely, unbearably horrible. Liaran was very violent, and she lied all the time. I would engage her on her constant lies, leading us to hell."

"Conjugal relations can be very difficult Frank…"

"No, no, you have no idea. She used to beat me up severely, draw blood, cut me, kick me, then call the police and claim that I had hit her. I never hit her, of course, but she built up a whole life for herself based on the notion that she was a victim of my physical abuse."

"Frank, I read on your chart that you are a therapist and a philosopher. The chart says that you were a biomedical engineer and attended medical school. I suppose you know that you are describing a true sociopath, right?"

"What I am trying to get at is not Liaran's diagnosis." I continued firmly. "I am trying to come to grips with my response to that craziness." Natalie inhaled as if to speak, but I pressed on. "My breakdown was not for lack of Liaran, my breakdown was because I felt deceived by everything I knew, practiced, and taught."

"Oh, I see now. And how did you respond to the craziness?" Natalie asked.

Frank Baler Finds T.H.

"That's the thing," I said. "first of all, I approached the relationship from the perspective that we were ordained by God to remain together for the rest of our lives. Even months after our final separation I still thought that we had a misunderstanding that would soon be repaired, and that we would be happy together, forever." Then I explained how Liaran reinforced that belief by constant promises during nightly love-making sessions.

"Frank, if you felt ordained to remain together and if the relationship was horrible, you must have suffered quite a bit…"

"Liaran was very effective at blaming me for everything, including all the beatings she delivered. Each beating I received, according to Liaran, was my fault. I accepted my responsibility in each of our troubles, and always looked for the correction I could make that would improve our relationship. I trusted she would do the same thing, but she already thought of herself as perfect; she would actually say that she had nothing to correct because she had done nothing wrong."

"Well, again, classical narcissistic sociopath, doctor…"

"Again, I am still trying to get somewhere with all this. I really don't know how to say this…"

Frank Baler Finds T.H.

Natalie sensed my struggle and suggested I take several deep breaths and focus on the one idea I needed to get out of my system. "Just tell me, tell me like it is Frank… there are no wrongs in here," she said kindly.

"I prayed constantly. I asked God to show me who she truly was. I wanted to know her heart and soul. I thought she was crazy, I thought she was selfish, absolutely dishonest and totally fake. But that was my human perception of her human manifestation. I wanted God to show me her true heart and soul."

"Oh wow, the conflict runs deep…"

"I used mystical techniques to seek out, experience and merge with her soul. You know… the classical 'magical mirror' meditations. There was so much Light I could barely stand it. Her soul was so bright, she is pure Light, truth and love. I was absolutely in awe of her Light to the point of thinking of her, and telling her, that she was a goddess."

"But the relationship was horrible," Natalie said, showing me that she was getting my conflict.

"Yes, yes, it was. Not only that. The lies became legal calumnies. She purchased stolen merchandize on the street, she cheated and lied all the time. Eventually she had one, then another affair. She got pregnant and had an abortion. The more Light I experienced during those 'mirror meditations', the more deranged she became as a human being. Toward the end, she went totally crazy. By then she was a total goddess to me. I was devastated, but I would pray, get in touch with her soul, and experience total Light, love and truth. So, I knew I was garbage, I threw myself out. How could I have seen such an illuminated soul as an immoral person?"

Natalie looked at me with compassion because she saw that my struggle was sincere. Her slight smile indicated that she knew something I didn't. I soon discovered what it was.

Natalie was also a hypnotherapist. She asked me to close my eyes and take a deep breath. Soon I was in a deep hypnotic state, the state I spent so much time in each day with clients. The only suggestion I remember hearing was that if there was anything else I wanted to get out of my chest, I should. Now.

In my mind I saw that man in the desert. The white shoes, black pants, white shirt and beard. Even in my mind his voice was unmistakable. This time I noticed that his necklace contained a green stone, an emerald I thought, where his heart would be. I could clearly see and hear him telling me:

"Tell her about the betrayal."

When I opened my eyes, I said:

Frank Baler Finds T.H.

"One night we were separated because, as was often the case she had done something absurd. There was no way to talk to her, so I would leave to prevent an escalating fight. She called and asked me to come over, presumably for sex, because that is how she would always get me back without having to talk about what caused the separation in the first place.

"That night, instead of going to bed, I sat on the living room of our place, closed my eyes, and meditated deeply, for the first time, while in her physical presence. When I felt 'connected', I asked for the true pain between us to be revealed.

"Suddenly I was in absolute pain myself. For a moment I felt that I became her and felt what I thought she felt deep inside. It was endless, excruciating pain. There was such deep betrayal that the pain was unbearable.

"I eventually opened my eyes, panting, and asked her whether she ever felt betrayed. She mentioned her first husband. I knew that story really well, because she would never stop talking about both of her two previous husbands. I knew both stories in detail. She betrayed them both, according to her, not the other way around. But that night she said casually and dismissively: 'Yeah, Lesser betrayed me, I guess.'

Frank Baler Finds T.H.

"I hugged her and caressed her. Inside though, I thought she was being disingenuous. I knew that Lesser had not betrayed her. It was much deeper than that, the betrayal ran deeper and was more painful than a simple extramarital affair. I was determined to help her heal her pain, so we went to bed and made beautiful love.

"You connected with her and felt her pain for being deeply betrayed, in her past?" Natalie asked.

"Yes, I have been practicing those techniques for years."

"So," Natalie, pressed on, "you felt compassion toward her?"

"Yes, deep compassion, and love. Our troubles were not her fault Natalie, she was pure Light and love... her soul is pure truth. Furthermore, she had been deeply hurt by a past betrayal. If only I could create a better situation for her, she would feel free to tell me the truth," I concluded.

"So, you rekindled the relationship after that night?"

"Yes, more determined than ever before to be better for her. I would constantly ask her what would please her..."

"How did that work out?" Natalie asked a bit concerned, I felt.

"Well, I was never able to fix myself enough. I was needy because I wanted to feel the conjugal bond with her... she told me that I had a problem for not feeling the bond; and

Frank Baler Finds T.H.

she was right. Then she constantly screamed at me and bashed me. She called me 'garbage', she told me I deserve nothing, she literally spat on my face, told me she hated me, and that she despised me. The beatings continued, and so did the police accusations."

"I see, then what?" Natalie shifted on her chair.

"Well, Liaran was right. I was not a good enough man; in fact, I was not a man at all. She told me I was not a man, I was a coward, and just pure garbage. The lovemaking became even more intense and passionate, but so did the screaming during the day. It was all my fault for not being a good man."

"Frank, Natalie said, maybe there was something else going on there…"

"That's the thing Natalie, that is the whole thing," I said. "There was something else. Liaran has a soul that is pure Light and love and has been badly betrayed. I was not able to love her enough; that is why I deserved the beatings." I looked down for a while, then I said:

"In the end, her plan to destroy me became evident. I spent tons of money in investigations because they wanted to put me in jail for a crime she accused me of, that I had not committed, of course. So, we knew there was a long and elaborate plan to destroy me. I felt like garbage for a while

Frank Baler Finds T.H.

because I was not able to make a 'perfect' woman happy... But also, I always thought that there was more there, something else going on, and I just couldn't access it. That is when I came to think that I had failed the Path."

Natalie made a few notes on her pad and concluded the session. She explained that the purpose of our meeting was not to carry out a full therapeutic intervention, all the way to final resolution, but simply to have the opportunity to express whatever else we had not expressed in the group setting. She felt, she told me, that I had expressed adequately and sufficiently for now.

On the last day of the retreat each person told each participant one great thing they thought about them, including Thomas. We each heard twelve great things about ourselves. It was a very emotional moment for all of us. It was the first time during the retreat that we addressed one another, and it was to say something great about one another.

Soon the retreat was over. We had a massive party. There was great food, music, dancing and three comedians that made us laugh until our bellies literally hurt. It was awesome!

I eventually retreated to my room to write on my journal. The desire to live was definitely back, and somehow, it had

Frank Baler Finds T.H.

come from within my being. I wrote about having met Samson and went to sleep.

Frank Baler Finds T.H.

DISLODGING GRUDGE

---o---

Back in the mid 90's my friend Paul, a descendant of the Lakota nation, and a High Initiate in their sacred traditions, offered me a ceremony that would, essentially, make me one of them. Paul reasoned that, being born in Brazil, and having native blood in my father's lineage, the Initiation would be mutually beneficial. The nation needed adepts, and I would be empowered by a 'spirit' I would receive later.

Paul gave me all the instructions I needed for the ritual, including how to prepare physically and spiritually the weeks before the ritual. I had to be at the place at 5AM, and back then I dreaded waking up early.

The first step in the ritual was to start a fire using only traditional tools and methods. By the time I left at 2PM,

Frank Baler Finds T.H.

clearly getting the message that the Gods did not want me in the ritual, there was still no fire. Paul told me later that as soon as I left, they started a fire and had a beautiful ritual well into the night.

For the twenty five years that followed Paul's offer and gracious invitation, I dismissed any conversations that had anything to do with native rituals, because I understood that my spiritual Path did not intersect with theirs. That was my mindset as I happened into the clearing where the lodge was.

The actual lodge was already set up, the fire was lit and the people were already sitting in a circle with the Shaman, shirtless, in deep meditation. There were 22 participants there, plus the Shaman, and an assistant managing the fire.

After some time in silence, the Shaman opened his deep, dark eyes, clearly visible in the glow of the large fire carefully tended to; he asked if there were questions about what was going to happen next.

Two or three people asked some procedural questions, which were met with quick answers. Then the Shaman began to talk while smoking something out of a pipe that he kept lighting up again and again.

"Find a spot inside that small tent on the ground, the sweat lodge. At the center of the tent there is a shallow hole. Hot rocks will be placed in the hole and I will splash water on the rocks. That will create steam, a lot of steam. The tent is all closed shut, and dark inside.

"From time to time I will open the door and request more hot rocks. At that point, if you believe you are done, if you believe you got what you needed, you may exit the tent.

"There is no point in staying beyond what you need. You will know when you are done, and you should exit at that point.

"I may or may not speak inside. You may or may not see things. You are free to do what you wish. Lay down if you want to, remove clothes, scream, just do not touch others or speak to them directly. Each of you will have your own experience, respect others and do not disturb anyone.

Then he asked:

"Are you ready?" He went around the circle, looking at each participant and waiting for the affirmative answer from each.

The Shaman explained how to enter the lodge, physically and reverentially.

I lost count of how many times he opened the door and requested more hot rocks. At some point he asked the people still inside to exit, wash off, and drink plenty of water. We were encouraged to urinate on the plants if necessary.

Frank Baler Finds T.H.

It was the middle of the day, judging from the bright Florida sunshine, when I exited the dark tent for a break. I could not believe what I saw: I was covered in so much dirt and sand! I even found sand inside of my ears! Had I been rolling around on the ground inside of the lodge, and not aware of it? I thought I had been sitting on the ground, staring in the direction of the rocks I could not see, while listening to the Shaman tell stories about animals and spirits. My body, however, told a different story.

A ¾" white PVC pipe emerged from the ground, ran for about 1 meter, then a 90-degree elbow brought it out of the ground. A ball valve was strapped to a wooden pole and another elbow about 2 meters high made the pipe horizontal again for about 30 centimeters. The open end of the pipe was the 'shower' we used to wash off the sand and dirt.

I drunk a large bottle of water, urinated behind a large tree, and moved my belongings, the car key, one shirt, one towel and my eyeglasses, to a spot I thought was safer under a tree. Theft was not the concern; the spot was safer, I thought, from being stepped on by dizzy participants who could inadvertently smash my eyeglasses when coming out of the tent next time. A few of us, five I think, sat on the ground awaiting instructions.

Frank Baler Finds T.H.

Soon I was sweating profusely again inside of the dark tent. The Shaman told another legend and opened the door again. One participant exited. More hot rocks were ceremoniously brought in and the sweating continued.

Then the Shaman asked us each to say something we were grateful for. There was complete darkness inside of the tent, yet we seemed to sense when it was our turn to talk.

"I am grateful that my life was protected while I suffered and didn't care for it." I said.

There were no comments, or feedback from anyone, as instructed. Not even the Shaman, who also spoke as one of us, commented.

More hot rocks, another person exits the tent, more stories, and the Shaman asks us to say one thing we regretted.

"I regret leaving my home," I said, and began crying.

When we were asked to take another break, it was dusk already. I did not care to even calculate how long we had been in there. I drunk a lot of water from a jug they had for us, but this time did not urinate. I noted the lack of urine and wondered whether I could have lost bladder control inside of the tent, or whether I was getting dehydrated.

This time one woman and I sat in front of the tent while the Shaman talked some more. We got in, more hot rocks, and she left the tent. All I remember then was that I felt tired and sleepy, at least that is how I identified the feeling at the time. Looking back, I was probably passing out.

I figured I would rest on the ground for a while until the door opened again, then I would leave. Once again, I thought, this thing is not for me. Nothing happened, other than a whole lot of sweating and time wasted. Then I heard a voice in my mind telling me:

'There is really no hope for you.'

About then, the Shaman started playing with a couple of small drums; soon he was chanting, and later emitting wild sounds I associated with animals. Then he said something weird:

"Show me your darkness!"

I remained motionless, hoping that this was a part of his ritual, but he insisted in a commanding voice, clearly directed to me:

"You, laying down, hiding your pain, show me your darkness!"

If you told me the story of what happened next, I would not have believed you. I do not blame you for not believing me, but what you are about to find out happened as I describe it to you.

Frank Baler Finds T.H.

I got on my knees, faced the hot stones and screamed louder than I thought a human is capable of:

"I loved the devil! I loved her and she hated me. I was building a life; she was destroying it. I was planning a future with her; she was planning one with someone else." My forehead instinctively touched the ground, then I came up and screamed:

"I hate what she did, I hate what happened, I hate who she became."

"Oh son," he continued, "show me your darkness."

"I hate her for becoming Jezebel." I finally said. "She could have chosen otherwise, we could have separated peacefully, she could have come to me if tempted by Jezebel, but no, she had to give in and become the slut she became." I would not stop now. "She cheated on the way in, she cheated on the way out. She cheated during the relationship. She is the fu***** devil itself, pretending to be pure and clean, while actually enjoying destroying each man in her life. She plays victim, but she is a fu***** thief and a goddam slut, a fricken Jezebel who meticulously planned my destruction for two and a half years while making passionate love to me and promising me love forever."

I said all kinds of other things. I screamed and screamed. I said it all. Apparently, I was not the composed man, depressed and sad for losing something precious. Apparently, within me, there was quite a bit of anger. Eric, a friend, had been right; I held on to a lot of grudge.

The words I said, and continued saying for a long time inside of that hot tent, are not as important as what happened at some point. I started feeling sick. I had not eaten all day, but I figured the water they gave us was contaminated, for I felt sick.

Eventually I vomited. I vomited and vomited stuff that could not possibly have been in my stomach. I could not see what came out, but it smelled fetid and putrid. It was when I became aware of the smell, that I noticed I had lost bladder and bowel control as well. I defecated all over myself, since I now laid on the ground again. So much stuff came out of my body that I had no idea where it could have been.

I 'showered' outside the tent and put on the dry clothes I had brought. I went to the Shaman who stood there, looking at me peacefully. I wanted to say 'thank you', but I could not speak. I approached him and started tearing softly. He hugged me and matched my breathing. We breathed together for a while, hugging, until the crying stopped. I calmed down and said, "thanks man".

The Shaman looked at me and said:

Frank Baler Finds T.H.

"Each moment is all you have. Focus on the moment, the present. Move from moment to moment as a puma leaps from rock to rock." Then he turned around and left.

I filled my water bottle again, drunk quite a bit, and started walking to the car slowly. There were three cars out there, one being a crew cab pick-up truck; it was already dark out, but it looked grey to me. The light inside the cabin was on, so I could see Rosie, the friend I had come with, talking to two other people. As I approached the truck I saw that a fourth person was asleep in the back seat.

"Oh good, you are done," Rosie said climbing down from the truck.

"Sorry it took us a while," I said. "How long have you been here?" I asked.

"No worries, we've been talking for about two hours," she said.

"Did you all have a good experience?" I asked.

One man said it was too hot for him, then explained how he had to leave because of a heart condition. The woman, possibly his wife, said that she felt much lighter. Rosie said that the whole thing was really 'cool', which I thought was an interesting choice of adjective, considering how hot it was inside of the tent. The last person never came out of the truck.

Frank Baler Finds T.H.

All of us were obviously tired. So, we looked at one another, hugged gently, wished one another well, and left.

I could not sleep at all after my proper, hot, soap shower at the hotel. I was hungry.

I didn't want to leave Rosie hungry in her room, without a car, in case she was awake, but also, I didn't want to wake her up either if she was asleep. I figured the least likely to wake her up in case she was asleep would be a one word text message. I typed 'awake?', and it was never read. She was asleep, I figured.

I drove twenty minutes into town. The GPS took me right to a large store that remained open 24 hours. I picked up a number of things for me and for Rosie, so we would have choices, depending on our mood in the morning. I ate a Caesar salad, bread and cheese, chocolate, and drunk a bottle of a sports drink with electrolytes. I grabbed a whole case of sports drinks and stopped at a park I had seen on the way to the store.

At first, I sat in the car reflecting on everything that had happened during the day. I had said some pretty harsh and horrible things in that tent. Suddenly, I found myself feeling guilty for having said what I said in the hot tent. Then I had to urinate; I figured there had to be a public restroom in the park.

Frank Baler Finds T.H.

By the time I saw some trees, I could no longer hold the urine, so the trees received extra hydration that evening. As I joyfully voided my bladder, in the peripheral field of vision to my left, I saw what appeared to be a lake.

There were large rocks around the edge of the lake. I was about to sit on one of them when a voice startled me to the point of almost falling down.

"I know you feel guilty for saying all that, but did you say it all?"

This time I could clearly see, in addition to the white shirt, he wore black pants and white shoes. He wore a long beard. His voice was unmistakable.

"I thought you were from New Mexico, what are you doing in Florida?" I asked.

"Cute," he said. "Did you say it all? Don't change the subject on me!"

"No Sir." I said. "I wouldn't."

"Then complete the entire process, say it all; now. GO!"

By now I knew better than to argue with this man. No wonder I could not sleep, I figured. I had lots of questions for him, but decided to wait and ask them later.

"Fine. Liaran held back. She was extremely selfish. While I spent two years working on making corrections to my personality and figuring out ways to make our lives better, she spent the same time working on herself alone, and on ways to move on with her life with someone else."

"Go on," he said.

"The extreme selfishness Liaran displayed could only be perpetrated by being totally dishonest. Not only did she lie about everything, and I mean everything, she lied about the true source of her unhappiness. She had me running around and working 7 days a week trying to please her, while she made plans to live with someone else. She never told me that she never intended to stay with me, quite the opposite, she asked me to make sure we could get together younger in our next lifetime together. Liaran later wrote that she frequently questioned whether she was in the right relationship. To me she always said that she had no questions, that we were meant to be together forever. She also wrote extensively about her lying as a way of meeting her needs for certainty."

"You are not done, I sense," he said.

"Okay. She was a fake. She would be screaming at me, she would be miserable, complaining about everything, she would be crying like a silly baby, then she would stop and take several pictures of herself smiling. She would post those pictures on social media and create the impression that her life was heavenly. She was a fake."

Frank Baler Finds T.H.

"Okay, Liaran was a fake, a liar and selfish. Now let me ask you: were you happy while with her?"

"No, no way. My life went backwards with Liaran. I was not able to sleep well with her, she stole from me, she poisoned me at least twice that I was able to confirm, once I ended up in the hospital, I gained weight, I stopped developing myself. Liaran screamed at me if she saw me reading a book; she said I should be working instead. Liaran constantly said I was a bad man and a bad person. Liaran's nickname as a child was 'Cyclone', and that is what she was in my life and in the lives of her two previous husbands, based on what she said herself. With Liaran I came to develop depression, anxiety and severe panic. In short, I was miserable with Liaran."

"I see," he said. Then he went quiet for a while. Finally, he asked: "Why did you stay with her? If it was so bad, what were you doing there?"

"That is what I hate about myself," I started saying. "I had what I now call a 'sacrificial model of love', meaning that to love was to sacrifice; the more I sacrificed for you the more I wanted you know how much I loved you, crazy! I was crazy. Then I had a profound sense of obligation toward her. I met her pregnant and felt responsible for the kids, all of our kids, and for my promises to her. That was idiotic of me!

Frank Baler Finds T.H.

"Then there was the soulmate crap, that I despise now; I thought she was a gift from God and that we were meant to stay together forever. I thought she was my soulmate and that I would be with her until the very end of our lives."

"You thought she was a gift from God?"

"Yes dammit, I prayed and asked God for a good woman with whom we could build a beautiful life together. The only thing I asked God for was that she had a good heart. Liaran turned out to have no heart at all. God betrayed me; God punished me…"

Another huge catharsis followed. This time I thought I got to the bottom of my grudges. I resented God for what felt to me like a betrayal. The story of Moses was on my mind as I screamed on the edge of that lake under the night sky. God had asked Moses to talk to Pharaoh about the Israeli people, but God simultaneously hardened Pharaoh's heart. Here I felt the same way. I asked God for a godly woman with a good heart with whom I could grow, and God gave me a communist with no heart at all. Simultaneously, God took my better judgement away, hypnotized me so I could not see what was happening until I was completely destroyed. God hated me, betrayed me, and punished me. For what, I asked, what was my big sin that warranted total destruction by a woman I loved sincerely?"

Frank Baler Finds T.H.

"You loved Liaran sincerely and never questioned that you would be together until the end of your natural life. Is that what happened?"

"Yes, absolutely," I responded.

"Frank, are you familiar with the Tarot?" He asked.

"Yes, I am," I said. "And I know where you are going with this. Yes, I felt so much love for her, but she was so unhappy and miserable all the time that I would consult the Tarot to determine what changes I needed to make personally to make her happy."

"And what would you determine?"

"Oh man, I would always see the most brilliant Light ever. I would see a soul filled with pure joy and Light, and absolute love. I would perceive a total commitment to honesty, healing and above all, forgiveness. That is how I knew it was all my fault, and that I was totally messed up. When it came to my person, the 'answer' was always the same: forgiveness. I would forgive non-stop, everything... right down to the infidelity, pregnancy, abortion, physical violence, and the constant reports to the police."

"What else did you do to determine how to fix the relationship?"

"Well, the conventional exercises to join with her soul in my deepest meditations. I would enter a higher dimension and seek her soul; I would experience pure love and joy. Then I would come home and make passionate love to her because I knew she was a divine goddess. I must have been a mess, so I would apologize and beg her for forgiveness, for she was so elevated and brilliant spiritually."

"So, you constantly consulted the tarot and contacted her soul mystically to determine how to improve the relationship. You experienced the highest caliber of Light you could possibly imagine, so you concluded that you were junk in comparison to her. When it came to her crimes – yes, they were crimes – you always forgave her. Am I correct?"

"That sums it up, yes." I said. "And you tell me, how can such pure Light, how can such an advanced soul betray me so mercilessly? How could she be so cruel and calculating, to me and to her two previous husbands? How could such an enlightened soul take pride in the destruction of three men, as a measure of how good she is? That is only possible if God hates me"

"Hold on, did you also say that in comparison to the way you saw her soul mystically, you felt like spiritual junk?"

"The Light that emanates from her soul has no equal. Yes, in comparison to her Light, I am nothing."

"Did she ever call you 'junk', or 'garbage'?"

Frank Baler Finds T.H.

"Yes, she used a word in Spanish, presumably to hurt deeper; she called me 'bazura' all the time. Why would you ask me that?"

"Wow, never mind that. She called you the same thing that you felt next to her... amazing." Then he said in a commanding voice: "Close your eyes!"

He touched the center of my forehead when I closed my eyes and ordered me to 'sleep'. I recognized the hypnotic technique, and quickly relaxed my whole body, and mind. He guided me through an induction and deepening. Then, just as I do at the office, he did a few test-regressions, asking me to visit birthday parties and relate events verbally. I remember thinking 'allow yourself to immerse in the regression'.

He asked me to imagine Liaran, her parents, and even God. Then he asked me to add to that group anyone else who had wronged me. My parents soon joined the party in my imagination. I knew I was deeply hypnotized because his voice was distant, and I lost awareness of the physical surroundings.

In the hypnotic state, the mind is able to accept suggestions that the intellect would not even comprehend. There was a part of me that was excited to see what was going to happen next. I still remember what the next suggestion was:

"Take a good look at the group in front of you. This is the group that has hurt you, violated you, wronged you. Look at them all and look at each of them as you search your own awareness. Is someone else missing from that group?"

I motioned my head in the negative. The group was complete, it seemed. He continued:

"Group them..."

Three groups formed in my awareness: 1. My mother and Liaran, 2. My father and God, 3. Her two parents. Even as I write these words, I am amazed, despite being a hypnotist for 23 years, at how the subconscious mind interprets and executes suggestions. All he said was 'group them', and three groups emerged in my imagination.

"Talk to each group," he said.

I went to Liaran parents, in my imagination and said:

"You never approved of my union with your daughter, but you gave us your blessing when I asked for it. Then you spent two years doing your best to separate us. You are dishonest, you work under the radar, behind the scenes. You remind me of a thief, a thief who under the cover of darkness, at night, hidden from view, undermines other people's happiness. You have no life of your own, and you use your only daughter to derive a sense of significance. You pretend you care for her happiness, but you truly all hate one another. You sow hatred and darkness wherever you go, but you pretend to be nice people. You are not authentic."

"Good," he said. "What part of you have you just spoken to?" The question made perfect sense to my subconscious mind.

"The devil. The part of me that does not allow me to be happy. I call it 'the misery', or the miserable."

"Look at them again," he said, "and do something about it."

"I want to thank you both," I said. "You tried to destroy me and your daughter's two other husbands; you damaged your daughter immensely. Yet I thank you because you brought the misery out of me. You served me by being a screen upon which I could project all of my misery, and now that I see it, I know it is out of me, for had it been in me still, I could not see it. Thank you for your service."

"Pretty nice. Next!"

Liaran and my mother were now in front of me. I looked at them and noticed how identical they were, in every aspect. Then I said:

Frank Baler Finds T.H.

"I want to thank you for being so damaged, both of you. My need to fix both of you defined my life. For a while I thought I had failed, I thought my life was over because I had been incapable of fixing you. Then I understood that in not being repaired by me you showed me that no one is in need of repair, and more importantly, I no longer have to live with the burden of having to fix those I love. I love both of you as you are. And from now on I decree myself capable to enjoy loving a woman as she is, without having to fix her. Thank you for this beautiful gift."

"That's good," He said in a quieter voice. "Go on boy!"

My father and God stood humbly in front of me, as if awaiting my sentence. I hugged them each, then said:

"I love you. My whole life I wanted to make you proud, to have you notice me, notice how good I was. I wanted you to notice my enormous capacity for suffering and sacrifice in the name of love. I wanted to be like Jesus, who loved humanity so much that he gave it his life. The more I loved, the more I suffered, the more I sacrificed. I was miserable my whole life in an attempt to earn extra points from you. I just wanted you to be proud of me. I love you because you never gave me what I thought I wanted. Had you gratified me for suffering and being miserable, I would have learned that you wanted my misery. Nothing really worked in my

Frank Baler Finds T.H.

life, so I learned to accept love and peace; I learned to accept that you love me for who I am, not for how much I suffer. Thank you."

"Go to sleep man, enough fun for one day." That was all I remember him saying as I stood up and found my way to the car.

When I got home, I was rested, in good spirits, and looked forward to beginning to organize my new life. I wrote on my journal about the sweat lodge and the encounter with the mysterious man who now obviously was in Florida. That night, the last entry on my journal read:

"The goliath is grudge. I am ready to be king now. Thanks David."

THE END OF MAGIC

When I was in Daytona Beach, in May of 2019 for a conference, I made many friends.

For the first time in my life, I spoke freely and openly about my personal problems, and the deep trouble I was in at the time. I told everyone I met, and old friends alike, that I was not well. In fact, at the time I was fighting hard to come back to life.

There is always magic in life, I thought at the time; in fact, that was my sign-off line on e-mails sent from the office to clients and prospects. The magic at that time was that Lisa, my girlfriend at the time, would listen to me for hours and always give me really insightful feedback, even when I was wrong, which was most of the time, but she never judged or criticized me. This woman was so loving and giving, that to this day I think of her as a real angel. She, and several other friends, really saved my life.

One beautiful evening at the conference, a group of ten or twelve senior therapists were sitting around a table by the pool. The hotel was beautiful, the conference was going great, and the ocean was right there to my left. The night was clear, the moon was out, the conversation was fantastic. The jokes were funny; most of them had to do with the oddities of being a therapist.

I had agreed to call Lisa at ten o'clock, but the evening was going so well that I texted and asked if we could catch up the next day. The decision to postpone our phone date was very serious to me. Although I was having a great time among fellow therapists, even laughing at the jokes, I was suffering from immense anxiety and constant panic. The panic would only decrease when Lisa and I spoke or spent time together. She and I talked abundantly about the medicinal and addictive effect that she had on me, but both decided to continue enjoying the relationship.

After my angel not only agreed to postpone our phone date, but actually encouraged me to have a great time, the anxiety shot way up. I turned to the woman next to me, also a senior therapist, and simply told her: "I am having a massive panic attack."

Frank Baler Finds T.H.

Mathilde did not blink. She said firmly:

"Look into my eyes, now! Tell me everything. Come on, talk!"

Suddenly I realized the absurdity of this situation. I did not know Mathilde before, I knew of her as a great therapist through other conferences and publications, but she and I had never spoken before. My mouth started trembling, tears gushed out, and I simply could not pronounce a single word. Then she did it.

Mathilde punched the center of my chest, right on my heart. She punched hard. The other therapists around the table carried on with the jokes, as if that is a normal occurrence in social life.

"Talk dammit, talk now!" She said loudly.

At that point our noses were almost touching. She was right on my face. She repeated, now in a soft voice:

"Take a deep breath and tell me the whole story, we got time..." She said this as she leaned back on her chair, made herself comfortable and, never taking her eyes off of mine, let me know softly: "We can talk, I am a good listener."

I asked her whether she would enjoy a walk on the beach. Mathilde enthusiastically told me that she would love to go for a walk on the beach. Ever since I was a child, I loved the

Frank Baler Finds T.H.

beach at night. For some reason, I love looking into the dark ocean at night.

Our toes were in the sand, the water was warm, the breeze caressed our faces. The evening was magical. I did not know it at the time, but Mathilde had attended my lecture the day before, and had heard about my crisis.

"Frank, that was a powerful talk you delivered."

"Oh, were you there?"

"How could I miss it? I have read your papers… I enjoy the depth you bring to the field."

"Oh, the only depth I know of is about death…"

"Tell me about that Frank. What really happened?"

Maybe it was because the moon guided me, or maybe it was because Mathilde's therapeutic skills were superb; whatever the reason, I started talking. I gave her a broad overview of the conflict within me, the pain. I held nothing back in terms of feelings, but I did not talk endlessly about details of events. I gave her a proper summary of the 'case' as I understood it then, which was before the trip to New Mexico, the TSL retreat and the sweat lodge in Florida.

Mathilde followed my lead and continued seamlessly:

"Interesting case doctor Frank, how should I proceed with the intervention?"

Frank Baler Finds T.H.

Only she could get away with that comment without coming across as mocking me, I thought. She was cute, I had to admit, and a dam good therapist.

"Well," I said, "part of the guilt he is feeling is good to a certain extent because it is driving him to heal parts of himself that really needed healing. He has no aggression or resentments toward her, the concern there, I continued being professorial, is that he may be in denial. His suffering is really coming from feeling attached to someone he does not want to be near."

"Thank you, professor," she joked, then continued "be at my room tomorrow morning at 9."

Mathilde explained to me that when a man and a woman are sexually intimate several types of bonds form between them.

"The first type of bond is purely chemical. The bodies exchange many chemicals, which function as a drug we become addicted to. Sex is meant to bond," she said, "and the first level of bonding is purely chemical."

"In addition to the exchange of chemicals, each body itself produces a plethora of chemicals during sexual encounters. Neurotransmitters such as dopamine, oxytocin and serotonin play a huge part in the sexual equation," Mathilde kept explaining. "The proportion and amounts of those chemicals within your own body also create a bond with your sexual partner; almost like an addiction," she said as an afterthought.

A distant streetlight across the boardwalk beyond the beach illuminated half of Mathilde's face. She kept explaining to me the consequences of having sex with someone, to the point I wondered if she wanted to have sex with me. The more she explained the unseen effects of sex, the cuter I thought she was, and the more I convinced myself she was flirting with me.

I stopped walking for a moment and faced her directly… we never broke eye contact. I looked at her lips and begun to move for a kiss, right there on the beach, at night, under the moon light. As my face approached hers, she said softly:

"Then there is a mental aspect to sex… the fantasies and stories we tell ourselves, about ourselves and about our partners, regarding sex. There is a spoken and an unspoken narrative going on in our minds before, during, and after the sexual encounter." She continued relentlessly. "We also bond with that narrative… or the narrative creates the illusion of a bond with our partner."

Suddenly I stopped. I heard something that disturbed me a little. "Illusion?" I asked concerned. "Do you think it is an illusion?"

Frank Baler Finds T.H.

"Frank, you are a hunk, and you know it, but you and I did not come together for sex or romance, and you know that too."

I gently turned my body and smoothly proceeded with the walk, pretending that I never thought of kissing her. She was right, of course; there was something much more profound happening between us... we should not waste this opportunity by turning it into a short romance.

"Yes, I believe you are correct," I said trying to sound academic, then I continued "the narrative I entertained was that of a soulmate for a mission together, no matter what..."

"All of these bonding elements make sense from an evolutionary point of view, right? After all, sex does have a lot to do with the propagation of the species."

I perked up again "yes, and we are commanded to populate the earth, right?" I said with a smirk on my face indicative of total desperation. Fortunately, Mathilde either ignored my comment, or pretended to ignore it. Instead, she continued her explanation:

"Then there is an invisible cord, almost like an umbilical cord that binds a mother to her children for life. A man actually becomes bound to a woman he loves through this invisible cord.

"Do you remember wonder woman?" Mathilde asked me.

Frank Baler Finds T.H.

"Yes, I was just thinking of the lace she used on the crooks, they had to say the truth once in her snare."

"Frank, you told me you loved this woman for real. Did you ever lie to her? About anything?"

"No, quite the opposite, I was always seeking to tell her more and more. My 'need' to tell her everything was so intense that I really lost myself. I was no longer able to make decisions on my own…"

"See what I mean? She put a lace around you. Sorry, but she is a witch, and a fearful witch. She did not set you free to love her, she snared you with her lace, she bonded you into oblivion. She wanted to eliminate you, consume you. Sorry man, she may have loved you, I don't know, but her desire to destroy you was certainly bigger than her love."

My head was spinning. Mathilde was wise; what she was saying sounded and felt true to me, particularly because, before the relationship was broken, I was already experiencing massive panic attacks. I knew what was coming, and I knew that what was happening was not good, but I knew that I was powerless to avoid it. Strange, I thought.

"A wise, loving woman knows about her power to snare a man, but she cuts him lose and gives him freedom. Curiously, the man then becomes powerful in the world but gentle with her. A true man will never leave a true woman. He will never hurt her either." Then she continued.

"Verbal offences are common from women to men, they call this 'nagging', and 'being a bitch'. Men accept that as part of the deal. When a man verbally offends a woman, however, this is a huge sign that something is majorly wrong. Unless a man is a true sociopath Frank, he would never verbally offend a woman unless he felt that his power and or freedom are being taken away from him. In other words, he offends when he feels castrated and bound because of the snare I told you about." Mathilde would not stop…

"A man's nature is to be free and to seek pleasure. A man stays with a woman who nags because, on the whole, the balance is positive. But if his power or freedom is compromised, his first instinct is to leave her. He would only stay if he was held back, and he can only be held back by the snare. A woman who snares a man in is as evil as a man who really hits her. Sorry, but to me she is a jealous witch, and I don't like jealous witches," Mathilde said.

Wow, I thought, this is no different from a strong man knowing that he would have the physical power to hurt her, but not daring to use that power that way. A woman has a different kind of destructive power – oh my gosh, I thought, as if suddenly illuminated: the same things happened to

Frank Baler Finds T.H.

Joseph and Samson. A man who is destructive, destroys a woman overtly, he harms her physically and the evidence is clear for all to see. A woman destroys a man covertly, by removing his freedom or power, or both. No one sees what she did... yet he is neutralized.

Suddenly I understood the occult meaning in the Samson story of going to sleep prior to having his hair cut off. The story says that Samson 'got drunk' and 'fell asleep' before being betrayed by Dalila. Samson allowed himself to be neutralized before he could be taken down by 'the guards', the agents used by psychopaths to destroy others. Eventually I said:

"That explains why I felt increasingly weak at work as the relationship progressed. That also explains why I kept needing her more and more."

Mathilde smiled and listened, as does a wise therapist who knows that she has made her point for this session.

"What's the prescription, doctor?" She kept joking, while being serious. She was lovely, and remarkably effective.

"We need to cut that cord at once. That will take some real magic..." I continued, half joking.

"As I said, 9AM sharp, room number 953."

Frank Baler Finds T.H.

How odd, I thought, we are meeting at 9AM and I just turned 53 years of age. Somehow, in my mind, that coincidence translated into 'be there, it will be good for you'.

The cord-cutting ritual was nothing short of high magic. Over two hours of battle, similar to an exorcism. Mathilde later told me that I had been holding on to my ex-partner.

"There is real love there," she said, "but it was mostly about your commitment to the idea of the relationship, sacrifice, and the soul-mate for life."

Mathilde and I became friends. Before we said goodbye the last day of the post-conference workshops, she said:

"I just sent you a text with a link. I want you to click on it and apply. Frank, I know you are going through a rough patch right now, but I read your papers, you need to be there." Then she said: "remember who you *really* are," and left.

The page that opened up when I clicked on the link within her text message referred to a conclave on high magic. The event would take place in November, in northern California. The page said that in prior conclaves, which happen only once every four years, over 900 people apply, but only 33 are chosen to attend, in addition to the 7 organizers of the event. Below that short preamble there was a button that simply said "Apply".

I clicked on the button and saw the enormity of the application. I decided to look into it at a later time.

When I sat down two nights later to consider this high magic event, I knew that I would probably not attend. First of all, the application consisted of 16 pages of questions. They asked details of Initiations, rituals, and degrees of magic I had performed. They asked for personal references, and for other magicians who knew of my occult work. They wanted it all, no details barred. One question, 'Why you want to attend the Conclave?' required the answer to be submitted telepathically, according to a certain set of parameters they would explain after you submitted the questionnaire, and a 33-page paper simply titled 'On Magic and Miracles'. No other instructions were given.

No wonder over 900 people apply and only 33 go, I thought. The academic in me, though, thought that it would be a good exercise to answer the questions and write the paper, even if I never heard from them again. Coincidently, in the previous two months, I had been reading books on magic by Dion Fortune and Eliphas Levi.

At that time, however, I read mostly to reduce anxiety; I could not remember what I read, since I was not sleeping.

Frank Baler Finds T.H.

Somehow, however, the 33-page paper and the answers to questions emerged. Three days after I hit 'send', almost to the minute, an email comes in simply telling me to visualize a certain situation and deliver the answer to the final question telepathically.

It was a June South Florida morning. I was sitting in criminal court, awaiting my fate for a crime I had never committed. The wait was long, and there was nothing I could do. Phones and books were not allowed in the court room. There was literally nothing I could do, other than witness the fate of other people accused of crimes until my name was called.

Somehow, I thought that this would be a perfect moment to 'upload' the answer to the question the organizers of the event wanted. I took a deep breath and closed my eyes. The sound of the judge's voice became distant.

Then someone shook my shoulder.

"You Frank?"

"Yes madam," I said to the officer who woke me up.

"You are free to go; your case has been dismissed. There is no evidence against you."

"Thank you, madam," I said not quite coherent yet.

I walked out of the courtroom emotionless. Of course, I had not been physically violent against that woman, ever. I

Frank Baler Finds T.H.

had called her a liar, and that is wrong of course, but accusing a man of a crime he did not commit just about validates the verbal offense.

'My first priority now, I thought, is to retrieve the will to live, the will to inhabit a world in which I do not feel needed or wanted. A world in which I find no pleasure, and a great deal of pain'.

'Strange words,' I wrote on my journal in the parking lot of the Courthouse before driving away.

Then I wrote a few notes about the pathway John and his wife Priscilla had laid out for me. I confirmed on my notes how the experience with the Assembly of Masters had been transformational for me, but acknowledged to myself, and to my journal, that the will to live had not returned[11].

---

[11] Looking back now, I see how firmly establishing a priority in writing on that Courthouse parking lot set events into motion. I attended two important events in October of that year: the TSL workshop, after which the will to live was restored, and the Sweat Lodge ritual, after which the deep grudge was released.

Frank Baler Finds T.H.

The e-mail I received in late July shocked me. First, because I had forgotten all about the conference on magic; in fact, I did not think they had received my answer telepathically, since I was so weak mentally back in June. Second, because their request for clarification on one question indicated that they might have been considering my attendance to the event, but dismissed me on the basis of my answer.

One question, among many others in 16 pages, was:

'Has the HCM ever investigated an experiment you directed or participated in?'

My original answer was 'yes'. Now they requested clarification on that investigation.

The HCM is the High Council on Magic, a group of 12 elder Magicians who monitor the experiments and activities of young magicians, to make sure we do not violate cosmic law. At the end of the day, the HCM protects us from our own ignorance and arrogance. That is why, when a man died as a result of one of our experiments, I did not wait to be called in, I went to the HCM and explained everything we did, in detail.

There is no dialogue or debate in the HCM. You present your feelings and the facts in 12 minutes. The elders confer among themselves, usually in silence, and one of them

Frank Baler Finds T.H.

delivers their findings. No appeals or further clarifications are allowed. A student of magic is not obligated to abide by the HCM findings, but not doing so results in immediate expulsion from the SOM, the School Of Magic.

Previous students who have been expelled are typically known as "black magicians", perhaps because they were at one time "black-listed", I suppose.

The man who died had committed a crime, he boldly told three of us one late night while having coffee at an outdoor cafeteria in Miami. The three of us, eager students of magic, looked at one another but said nothing. I assumed the man would have confessed to his crime to the police voluntarily sometime during the following three days, but instead he was killed on the fourth day at a traffic accident.

I requested an audience with the HCM the day after I learned of his death. My buddies did not feel implicated in the death, so they did not go. Later, both of those students left the SOM. One had brain cancer but survived a complex operation. He went back to civilian life. The other almost died on the sidewalk one day. A rescue truck driving by stopped and took him to the hospital. He was hospitalized for 60 days; doctors had no idea what was wrong with him. Suddenly he was well again and returned to civilian life.

Frank Baler Finds T.H.

The HCM told me that my actions were not directly related to the man's death, although his karma was precipitated by our encouragement that he turns himself in to authorities, and his subsequent conscious decision not to. I was told I was a loyal student and allowed to continue my studies on magic. One Elder praised my presentation.

Within three months of my appearance before the HCM, my first wife broke up with me. I recovered the marriage, had another child with her, but still ended up divorced in three years. Not only that, 12 years after the first divorce, I married another woman, and the events were repeated down to minute details.

Being examined by the HCM, no matter how we frame their function, is not something to be proud of, I thought. After I sent the clarifications, therefore, I was pretty certain I would never hear from the organizers of the conclave on high magic event ever again.

That is why the following e-mail really shocked me. The subject line read:

EVENT DETAILS

Inside there was one phrase, a name, a link and a picture.

We appreciate the fortitude and authenticity with which you submitted the results of your experiment that took place in 1996 to the HCM. - Matheus

Frank Baler Finds T.H.

Please join us in Northern California, among giants. Click here:

The picture was of giant sequoia trees.

I could not believe my eyes, so I kept reading the e-mail over and over. I checked the address they sent the e-mail to and from; maybe there was a mistake, I thought, but there was not. They invited me to attend a very special event; all the details were inside.

We had to be at a small high school, north of Shasta at 9PM. The group was small, but there was electricity in the air. We all felt that something special was about to happen. Doors to the auditorium opened at 9:30. At 9:45 the Master of Ceremonies made a few announcements, briefly welcomed everyone, then delivered the rules for the night:

No visual aids

No recording of any type, not even written notes

No interruptions

No questions

No applause

No delay getting on or off the stage

There will be 9 speakers randomly selected

First speaker will be on at 10, sharp.

15 minutes per speaker, then the buzzer sounds

Frank Baler Finds T.H.

As he got off the stage, he said, we will have a banquet afterwards!

I wondered who the speakers were, but no announcement was made. I assumed the speakers had already been selected, so I relaxed on my chair. I calculated we would be getting out by about 1AM to eat, I assumed at the school cafeteria.

The first five speakers were absolutely fantastic. One was able to cure physical diseases by absorbing them into his body, then discharging them to the ground. The second speaker was able to interact with subtle energies to the point of levitating small objects. The third speaker could cause a person to faint and drop to the ground, as if a toy had been turned off. The fourth speaker was an alchemist. He was known as a philanthropist, but he was able to generate vast amounts of wealth without an obvious business. The fifth speaker described herself as a fireball. Whenever anything needed to be dissolved, she would emit a fireball in the causal plane and dissolve it.

As the sixth speaker was being announced, someone taped on my shoulder and asked me to follow him. I do not recall what that magician spoke about.

Frank Baler Finds T.H.

The seventh speaker wore black pants, a white shirt, a strange necklace and something that resembled a makeshift sword on his left side. He said something like this:

"The physician is rewarded for saving the patient by killing the germ. Equally, the surgeon is also rewarded for saving lives, by killing the tumor. When a baby is born, there is no more fetus. Life and death, ladies and gentlemen, are two faces of the same coin, just as white and black magic are.

Remember this, my esteemed colleagues: The next time you look at a decaying corpse, tell yourself: this corpse is teeming with life, even if I cannot see it. And the next time a baby is born, tell yourself, there is one cute dying thing, for only death is certain to all who are born.

I spent my life defending the idea that I practiced white magic. I abhorred black magic. I do good things, I save lives, I help people. Black magicians do bad things, they get in people's ways, they block the Light. I always told myself that I was good and that I opposed the bad; I fought the bad, I eliminated evil.

How come then, how come my dear friends, if I was a white magician, how come I was so miserable? How come my personal life did not work at all?

Frank Baler Finds T.H.

The answer was to be found in none other than the great, the triple great Hermes.

Life, good, and white magic are but one pole of spectra. Whenever we invoke one pole of any spectrum, we automatically must deal with the opposite pole. I felt doomed after doing white magic, not because I am secretly a black magician pretending to be good, not because I hid my dark shadow under a fake cloak of white goodness, but because I called misery upon myself for thinking of myself as good.

Good and bad are opposite poles on the same axis. I can only think of myself as good by judging others as bad. When a magician judges another as bad, he is doing black magic, for his thoughts actually hurt others. Conversely, thinking of others as good, makes me bad by comparison; still, one son of God is being harmed.

I can now tell you that I am not good. In fact, the worst thought I ever had was that I was good. After 30 years of magic, I once called my closest adepts and confessed to them what were my five biggest mistakes on the Path. Number one on the list was thinking that I was good.

By not thinking of myself as a white magician anymore, I no longer have to do black magic by creating enemies that were not there before. By not creating enemies, I am now

Frank Baler Finds T.H.

free to live life; life is pleased my me simply living it because its purpose is now fulfilled.

In his evolution, eventually the white magician must bring magic to an end because magic is a binary idea, as in white and black magic. The binary notion of magic must be logically rooted in a binary view of the cosmos. Go with the cosmic grain and you are a white magician, go against the cosmic grain and you are a black magician.

Both the white and the black magicians will eventually call an end to magic on their evolutionary paths, because neither can do one without also being the other.

Furthermore, if the cosmos is an expression of unity, it cannot at the same time be dual; there cannot be a cosmic direction against which the moral value of magic is evaluated. The true magician is the magician who no longer needs magic, for he discovered that the only duality in existence is the illusion of his perceptions.

Think of your three higher chakras for a moment. They are associated with physical glands in the dense body, the thyroid, the pineal and pituitary glands. The thyroid gland has 2 lobes, the pineal has 1 and the pituitary has 2 lobes as well. The thyroid gland, associated with the chakra responsible for expression, can be impressed by the pineal or by the thymus, meaning that a person can speak his mind or his heart out; his physical voice reflects that difference.

The objective mind is associated with the cerebral cortex, which has 2 hemispheres. Our perceptions come into a dual mind through a dual gland, the pituitary and through two sets of sensory organs. Our common perception is one of duality, but cosmic perception which comes in through the singular pineal gland is itself singular.

So long as we perceive the natural world with our natural eyes, we will see a world of duality, a world of good and evil, a dark world that needs the light of the white magician.

If good and bad are opposites on an axis, what is at the center? The heart is at the center. True love is at the center, between good and bad, just as the present is between past and future. When a magician perceives the world through his heart, he no longer needs magic.

By seeing the wildest and most ferocious beast as an expression of life and divinity, no defenses are needed. No white magic against dark forces are called for.

That, my friends, is how you put hungry lions to sleep."

I did not catch the following speaker either because I was backstage drinking water, pacing back and forth. The top of my stomach was hurting; I had felt that pain before when too much energy circulated in my dense body. The organizers of the conference offered me cold water and suggested I walk back there until I felt better. Soon I was back on my seat.

Once the last speaker, the ninth, finished her talk, the MC came on stage and simply said:

"There is a banquet right outside."

There were no concluding remarks, no praise, no adulation to or from anyone. There were no announcements about future events, or purchases one could make. Nothing for sale, and no requests for donations. There was an understanding in the air that everyone there was awesome in some way that puts them well beyond the need for attention, recognition, or praise.

Another surprise awaited me outside of the auditorium. I had assumed we would eat something at the school's cafeteria, but the banquet would take place at the large foyer to the auditorium instead.

There were a few odd things about the so announced 'banquet'.

Instead of a huge party with music and dancing, there was one long table with all kinds of foods on it. Orthogonal to the long food table, there were three long tables with place sets on them. There were 7 servers behind the food table, and a convex mirror on the ceiling.

Frank Baler Finds T.H.

The image of the tables on the mirror on the ceiling was definitely that of a letter 'E' with 7 dots along the vertical.

On the other side, opposite to the food, there was another table with drinks and deserts of all types. Three servers stood behind that table.

Something else about this banquet felt odd to me: there were way more people there than the 33 plus 7 who had been inside the conclave. I did not know who these extra people were. I eventually assumed they were either students of magic, or spouses and children of attendees.

I hung out by the beverage table for a moment because I was very thirsty. My mouth was dry, and I was not quite hungry yet. A few people come up to me and said 'hi'. For the most part, however, I was enjoying the opportunity to observe the scene from afar. Eventually one young woman to my forward right caught my attention.

What was Maharay doing here? She is a barber I met in New Mexico when I was visiting Allen and Mary. Maharay claims to hear her dead grandmother talking to her. What an odd coincidence that she would be here, I thought as I fixated my gaze on her. She seemed to be alone, more attractive than I remembered her, and definitely waiting for something to happen or someone to approach her.

Frank Baler Finds T.H.

Just when several people were moving in my direction – perhaps going to the bathroom, I thought, I carefully made my way through them and approached Maharay.

"Hi there, remember me?" I asked. She looked at me as if at a ghost and said:

"*Abuelita* asked me to come here and tell you something."

"Oh no," I said. Then I thought: the dead grandmother thing again…

When I woke up at the motel room late the next day, I reached for the journal and took some notes. I wrote about the weird circumstances that got me admitted to this strange event, and about some of the lectures I remembered. For months after that event I recalled the following phrase, which I wrote all over my journal:

'That is how you put hungry lions to sleep.'

I noted on my journal how the thought that one person is evil is only possible when we think of the other person as being godly. In this case, 'evil' and 'godly' are opposites that cannot exist without one another. Just as the seventh speaker in the conclave explained that black and white magic had to be transcended, so does the idea of evil and godly people.

Frank Baler Finds T.H.

It made sense to me that the polarity between evil and godly, or between black and white magic is analogous to the polarity between a hungry lion and a just man. As long as the polarity exists, the hungry lion tends to eat the just man. Taming a hungry lion, putting it to sleep, is analogous to eliminating the polarity between it and the just man.

There cannot be a polarized universe, I wrote. There cannot be duality in a 'uni' verse. Our perception of reality is polarized; our task is overcome the perception of polarization to find reality, truth, unity in all things. That is what the strange speaker meant by 'the end of magic' and what the Biblical writers meant by putting hungry lions to sleep. 'Thanks Daniel', I wrote and closed the journal.

Frank Baler Finds T.H.

A WARRIOR IS BORN

The airplane door was closed, and the plane began taxing. 'Too late now, whether I am a devoted mystic or a lunatic, I will land in Recife, Brazil, in about 8 hours,' I told myself. 'You better be awake and alert because you will only have 90 minutes to go through customs and catch a flight to Campo Grande, Mato Grosso,' I continued with the instructions to myself. Then I dozed off.

I had been exhausted. I still slept very little. I had to care for my two daughters with Hana half the time, run the office, teach classes, take care of clients, try to keep up with my adult daughters, and otherwise manage my life. I had presented at an international conference on therapy, fought a

Frank Baler Finds T.H.

massive criminal case, and had been on five major trips this year, each of which proved to be instrumental on the Path.

Now I was on a major international trip that frankly made no sense to me. What was worse to me was that I was on this trip on account of a message Maharay, a barber from New Mexico, received from her dead grandmother, especially for me. Nothing could be weirder; so weird in fact, that I kept taking copious notes on everything that was happening, as if to remind myself that it was all real.

The trip was uneventful, except for the fact that the airline offered me an upgrade to first class on the flight to Campo Grande for only $45.00. I hesitated, of course, but eventually accepted the offer when the pretty Brazilian attendant smiled at me. I could not read her name because her name badge was turned toward her, but it did not matter because I could not take my eyes off of this woman's lips. Her lips were so perfect; the shape, size and 'consistency' were simply mesmerizing. I was wondering what it would be like to marry her when she handed me the boarding pass saying "*tenha boa viagem doutor*". I was having a good trip, I thought, as I walked toward the gate.

From Campo Grande I took a bus to Corumbá. I was famished and sleepy, but decided to take a taxicab to the port,

Frank Baler Finds T.H.

as instructed by Maharay's grandmother. Funny, I thought, now that I am here, her grandma does not feel 'dead' to me.

The so-called port seems more like a busy market on the Paraguay river. All types of boats are moored there, people all over the place, and lots of donkeys carrying cargo to and from the various boats.

By then I was fully immersed in what I thought was a great adventure, James Bond style. I no longer wondered whether I had lost my mind for being here, I enjoyed the game it felt I was playing, and I respected the process I thought I was undergoing.

My instructions were memorized, I was told not to write anything down. I was to find a restaurant facing the river. There would be seven steps from the pier to the eating floor. Facing the front door of the restaurant, if I looked toward my right, I would see a church, if I looked toward my left, I would see city hall. Don Jimenez would be waiting for me at 3 in the afternoon. Finally, Maharay said, "be aware of false prophets!"

The port curved around the river's bend. I first located both the main church and city hall. In my mind I triangulated a spot on the river's bend that would give me an equal angle view to both structures. There were mostly gear stores and small fish markets in that region of the port. As I was about to walk away, I noticed that one fishery had a small stairway behind the fish stands leading to an elevated area where I could see the backs of chairs.

I carefully counted the steps, hoping to be wrong because I felt uneasy and anxious about walking into that place; it just gave me creeps. I realized that maybe I had been impressed by a particularly fierce-looking black fish, a good 3 feet long, propped up on ice cubes on one of the stands. Putting my trepidations aside, I climbed the seven steps counting again to make sure this was the right place.

A man sitting alone wearing a white linen suit smiled warmly as I approached him and said "I am Frank". The man started describing to me where we would go and how much it would cost me. I accepted that there would be a cost to take the voyage, so I grabbed my wallet out of my pocket to make the payment, but I hesitated, and he perceived it. The man then asked me a question that caught me by surprise: he asked me whether I preferred her to be Indian or Brazilian.

Once I actually understood what the question meant, I felt as though I had failed some sort of test. I thought that my sexual nature had lowered my vibrations, and that my aura was probably pulsating red or pink. True, I had not been sexually intimate with anyone in a while, and the frustration was probably so obvious that tour operators were now offering me prostitutes to sweeten a deal. Maybe I should spend the afternoon with a prostitute, I thought, overcome this sexual frustration, maybe that was a part of the process I had gone there to live.

Just then one thought occurred to me: I did not feel sexually frustrated at all; I wanted more Light and healing, there would be plenty of love-making with the right woman later... then I remembered Maharay's last words, excused myself and left.

As I walked out of the restaurant through the fish market, I noticed the black fish was no longer there. I quickly re-established my bearings by finding the church and city hall and turned around to count the steps to the eating floor again, hoping to find what I obviously missed before.

I walked toward the river, crossing the pier. From the water's edge I looked at the façade of all the buildings on the port. Then I noticed a narrow door right between what I now noticed were two fish markets, not one. A plain, wooden door; closed but unlocked I discovered when I tried it.

As I went up the steps behind the door I felt the tingling sensation of excitement of a new adventure that was about to unfold. I counted six steps to the top though; maybe I missed something. As I went down the steps I noticed that the last step was perfectly flush with floor downstairs,

Frank Baler Finds T.H.

making it almost impossible to see it on the way up. It occurred to me that the first step on any mystical journey begins where one is at in life, never one step beyond where one truly is. I figured I was at the right place and climbed the steps again to find Don Jimenez and Marali waiting for me with a glass of iced tea.

Marali smiled and told me plainly:

"That is right, most people who come here walk away thinking that they should start their journey one step beyond where they really are; they fail before they begin because they are not authentic. The mystical Path," she continued, "meets you where you are at in life; it never asks something of you that you are not, or that you cannot give." Now I was sure I was at the right place.

I walked out of the restaurant with a hammock, precise instructions, and my head spinning. I was to show up to peer 43 at ten minutes before nine that night. I was to report to the captain of a barge named Xororó and tell him I would get off at Porto Coqueiro. I was to follow all instructions from the captain, but not to listen to anyone else. Easy enough, I thought, wondering what the hammock was for.

Marali's words would not leave my mind. I felt like I had failed on the mystical Path year after year. I was unhappily divorced, not successful in any aspect of my life, despite

Frank Baler Finds T.H.

seeking more Light my entire life. Was I not authentic before? I had just lived the most difficult and painful three years of my life, culminating with 10 months of intense crying, lack of sleep, and utter desperation. Suddenly, I seem to find the 'right door' and someone on the Path tells me that most people do not find that door because they are not authentic enough. Was all that pain and suffering the catharsis I had needed to become more authentic? I realized I no longer had anything to lose or anyone to impress; was this what they meant by 'authenticity'?

Hunger spoke louder than my philosophical inquiry. I found food and a hostel to lay down and take a one-hour nap. I wanted to be alert for the trip to Porto Coqueiro.

At about 8:30 that evening I was close to the Xororó. The boat was a flat barge with a small roof toward the back supported by many metal columns. Behind the barge there was a small tug boat covered in soot. I waited for the appointed time and walked right up to the Xororó, asking in a loud voice:

"Permission to come aboard, captain." A tall, lanky black man came forward and identified himself as the captain of the Xororó.

Captain Pedro showed me to a metal column and pointed to a hook. He told me I could hand my hammock there. He

Frank Baler Finds T.H.

mentioned that at 5 in the morning there would be plain coffee and dried meat at the bow of the tugboat. We would be at Porto Coqueiro around 7 in the morning, God willing and weather permitting. He wished me a good night and walked away.

At 9 o'clock the engine started. Oh no, I thought. A one-cylinder diesel! I could hear individual explosions within the low-revolution sooty engine. For almost 12 hours that engine thumped deep into my bones, as I wrapped the edges of my hammock around me to ward off the mosquitos. When I went to get coffee and dried meat at daybreak, captain Pedro told me that the wind was fierce all night, making us about two hours late.

I watched two men roll a 55-gallon drum of diesel from the barge to the tugboat and counted 12 more drums. I asked the captain how long their journey would be.

"We should be back in 10 to 15 days, God willing and weather permitting," he said as he shouted orders to his deck hands. I learned that the Xororó was a cattle barge. The captain would take her to the highest point on the river empty, then coast down the river picking up cattle from various farms for the slaughter market. About 1000 animals would be sacrificed at the end of this journey.

Frank Baler Finds T.H.

The bow of the barge was the furthest point from the sooty diesel engine; the distance, plus the head wind we faced made the bow of the barge the quietest point on the boat. That is where I sat with my backpack to watch nature and wait for the adventures at Porto Coqueiro.

The thumping of the one-cylinder diesel slowed down. Weird I thought, since there is no port anywhere to be seen. I wondered if we had a problem when the barge approached the river's margin. All the way from the tugboat, Captain Pedro shouted "Porto Coqueiro". There was one plain coconut tree at the margin of the river, but where was the port?

Several men shouted at me telling me to jump off the barge quickly because they were late. I jumped into water above my knees, unhappy about having my boots and socks soaked.

The James Bond, the mystic and the chicken in me began to argue. Later the man showed up. Bond thought this was a great adventure, something fun was bound to happen. The mystic felt intrigued, observing how the Cosmic was using all events to bring me closer to the Light. The chicken checked my phone and, not only found no signal, but the

Frank Baler Finds T.H.

battery was about to die. My only clock, my last reference to civilization, was about to disappear.

Then something almost funny happened. Being all alone in the middle of nowhere excited me. I began to think about the women that man had offered me and wondered what it would be like to love the Indian one right there, under those bushes. I sat down in a half shade, had a sip of water, being conservative just in case I had a long walk back to civilization, and closed my eyes. I could feel her scent and the excitement of caressing her strong thighs with my lips.

"Doutor!" a man said, bringing me out of my fantasy.

When I opened my eyes, I found a man apparently in his 60's atop a black horse, pulling a brown horse.

"We must leave quickly" he said "so we get there under day light."

"Where are we going?" I asked.

"To the main house" he said while strapping my backpack to his horse. "And don't worry about the river, these horses can swim with a man on their backs."

I understood we were pressed for time, which meant it was a 6 to 8-hour horseback ride which would take us through a river deep enough that the horses would have to swim. I decided not to ask about the *piranhas*. I had not been on a horse since I was a kid, and probably only in some sort

Frank Baler Finds T.H.

of amusement venue. The Bond in me was ready to go. The mystic knew it would be okay. I did not allow the chicken to opine. The man was making secret plans to go talk to that same man about the Indian woman he mentioned when back in town. I was already in love with an Indian woman I never even met.

Camacho handed me a belt with about 20 bullets and a 38-caliber revolver.

"What is this for?" I asked.

"You know how to use it, don't you?" He answered. I pulled the revolver out of the holster, opened the barrel, confirmed that six unfired bullets were loaded, spun it around, and locked it again.

"This will be fine." I said strapping the belt to my waist. As I mounted my horse feeling like John Wayne, I was reminded of a recent trip to the shooting range when I put all twelve 9-mm bullets into the center circle. I felt like a champion as my horse actually moved under my command.

We were both mostly quiet throughout the journey. We stopped at strategic points on the journey, dismounted our horses, drunk water and ate some dried fruits and meat. The horses grazed. Camacho seemed to be a man of few words. He always answered my questions, but economically, and never started a conversation.

Frank Baler Finds T.H.

We arrived at the main house eventually. I thought I would have to be airlifted to the nearest intensive care unit. For one thing I could barely walk. My back hurt like crazy, my arms, hands, face and neck had so many mosquito bites that I worried about shock. I felt that my back and head were sunburnt, despite wearing a heavy shirt and hat. I guess I was hungry and thirsty but felt too weak to eat.

The so-called main house is nothing more than a tiny two-bedroom cement house with ceramic tile roof and no ceiling.

Carlos was waiting for me. Camacho placed my backpack on a chair on the porch of the main house and disappeared with the two horses. Carlos showed me to one room with a spartan single bed, and a bathroom with one toilet and a pipe out of the wall for a shower – no shower head. There was no air conditioning or heater. The water was not hot.

I took a shower, removed mud from all over, apparently picked up while crossing the river, put on dry clothes and washed the wet ones in the 'shower'. Carlos offered me some rice, beans and dried meat. After I ate, he suggested I rest for one hour, since the ceremony that night may run late, he said.

I did not ask any questions. I simply removed my slippers and laid down on my bed. Once I got past the discomfort on my back and hands, it downed on me that I had not slept

Frank Baler Finds T.H.

much in almost two days of travel. I imagined kissing the airline attendant in Recife good night and fell deep asleep.

I remember dreaming that I was at a Japanese garden where a gong was sounding. I loved the sound of that gong and just wanted to keep on hearing it, but the man next to me on the park kept roughing me up. It turned out that the man moving me was Carlos, trying to wake me up.

"Didn't you hear the gong?" Carlos asked. I did not answer, opting instead to get ready as quickly as possible.

I had no idea what time it was. I felt a little disoriented, a very uncomfortable feeling for me. I have always associated that feeling with drunkenness, so I rarely consume any alcohol. I felt dehydrated and totally jet lagged to the point of being a bit dizzy. But it was time to go, and that was why I was there.

Carlos had brown pants on, with the hems rolled up to his knees. An untucked white dress shirt on and no shoes. The night was warm, but thinking of the mosquitos, I wore my grey sweatpants, a navy-blue long sleeve shirt and black socks, no shoes.

Carlos told me that we were going to the *caramanchão*, a gazebo, right behind the house. I had not noticed any other structures in the vicinity of the main house, but then again, I had been disoriented and distracted long before we got there on horseback.

The gazebo was enclosed. There was an entrance, but I could not see any other openings because it was totally dark inside. Carlos nudged me to a position that I estimated to be roughly at the center of the structure, told me to sit on the dirt floor and meditate. I remember thinking to myself: 'Sure, as if even the slightest relaxation was possible under the circumstances.'

Sitting on the hard, compacted dirt actually felt good for a change. I eventually closed my eyes to introspect a bit more, even though the utter darkness was already having that effect on me. I did not know if there were other people in the gazebo, but I could hear at least one person on the outside.

Perhaps I dozed off, because the sound of a gong startled me. I opened my eyes without moving and saw a man coming into the gazebo with a small lit torch. He went around the periphery of the structure and lit five torches which I thought were dangerously close to what seemed like a cloth curtain enclosing us.

When the last torch was lit, soft music started playing. The scene was so out of this world that I actually wondered if I should escape it. Opposite to the entrance, which was

Frank Baler Finds T.H.

now closed, were three men. In the middle, on an elevated wooden platform, was a chair. Standing in front of the chair was a man in full Indian garb, majestically watching it all but hardly moving. On either of his two sides was a man standing in a lesser Indian garb. They each held a spear taller than them on the hand furthest from the center.

To the left of the entrance there was a three-man band. One played the *berimbau*, a typical Afro-Brazilian instrument, another played drums and the third played a large bamboo flute. The music was soft and relaxing. Opposite to the band, to the right of the entrance were three people sitting down. I was not able to discern if they were men or women at this point. That was it. I was the only person sitting on the ground.

At some point the music seemed to wind down, but it never stopped completely. First the man to the left of the center figure, opposite to the entrance, spoke:

"Get up and walk in circles." Then the man to the right spoke:

"We will let you know when to stop."

I did as I was told. Having received dozens of Initiations in several countries and mystical orders, I was able to relate to what was happening in terms of the symbolism I was familiar with. That familiarity kept me relaxed to a certain

Frank Baler Finds T.H.

extent, but it would soon change drastically, in the most unexpected of ways.

The main man at the center of the three-man formation stood up almost upset and spoke in a stern voice:

"You told me he was ready! He has too much tension in his body. Tell him to come back when he is ready."

I could not believe my eyes and ears. The three men at the elevated wooden platform walked out of the gazebo! I stood there frozen in space and time. A part of me remembered a therapeutic technique I studied once, whereby the hypnotherapist would tell the client that she was not ready to be hypnotized and walk out, preferably slamming the door for show, only to walk back in shouting instructions that would just about force the client into the hypnotic state. I thought I should practice that technique with a real client, since I had paid to learn it, so I did. To this date I regret the pain I put that lady through.

'This is my karma,' that part of me said. 'This is my karma. I hurt the client now I will not receive the Initiation.'

That voice turned into a feeling, the feeling turned into reality, and soon I was sobbing. What? Yes, I was sobbing! My entire life is about the mystical Path, I had given up on everything in order to pursue and find more Light, and now I had failed out of the Path because I hurt one client; no, I

Frank Baler Finds T.H.

thought, I hurt everyone all the time, that is why I do not deserve this Initiation.

The music intensified a bit, reminding me that it had never stopped. The realization jolted me out of my self-pity trance, and I noticed that the other three people were still sitting to the right of the entrance, opposite to the musicians.

One person, a man by the sound of his voice, told me to dance to the music in order to shake the tension off my body. I thought that was silly, so I barely moved, even though the music was changing and becoming more fun. At some point another person, whom I could now identify as a woman, came up to me and told me that she would blind-fold me so I could get into the music more and shake the tension off my body.

Three tight blind folds later, with not even a sliver of light coming in, the first man told me to dance and shake the tension off my body. I had no idea what these people were saying. I had been thinking of doing some stretches because I sit down most of the day with clients and often felt tension in my body, but nothing that has to be shaken off as they were saying. These people were definitely weird, I thought, 'Why can't they just give me the Initiation and let me go being the same jerk I have always been, except now Illuminated?' I thought.

Frank Baler Finds T.H.

Blindfolded the music seemed more colorful. It often seemed to be coming from several places at the same time. Maybe the men were moving around me, or maybe I was moving more than I thought. I remembered meeting a shaking instructor years ago. That lady seemed very relaxed to me, but at the time I remember wondering if her brain actually included a left hemisphere, such was her apparent disconnection with objective reality.

This is crazy, I thought, as the music intensified both in tempo and volume. The drums were also more noticeable to me, and I found myself tuning into them and hitting the ground in synchrony.

Just when I was getting into the music and moving more, noticing beads of sweat forming on my forehead, a man grabbed me and told me:

"Fight me!" I still smile at my immediate answer:

"No, I don't want to hurt you." I said as if I *could*...

We were now grabbing each other's shoulders, foreheads touching, sumo style. He was taller and definitely more muscular than I. By the sound of his voice, he seemed a good 20 years younger than I. He was relentless, repeating in a commanding voice:

"Fight me!"

Frank Baler Finds T.H.

"I don't want you to get hurt. I will never fight; I will never hurt anyone again!" I screamed surprised at the words just spoken.

"One of us will be hurt if you don't fight," he said, grabbing me so quickly that I did not have time to react until I was flat on my back on the dirt.

This is not a typical symbolic Initiation I thought. Then the severity and absurdity of my situation hit me: I was in the middle of a jungle, somewhere in Brazil, possibly in Bolivia, there was no way to communicate with civilization. No one knew I was there or when to expect me back home. There were no emergency contacts, here or back home. No cell phone signal and no 911 service. I am blindfolded inside of a gazebo with people I really do not know at all. Even if I could scream, no one would hear me. A man clearly stronger and more skilled than I just threw me on the ground.

This was not what I expected, and I was not about to risk an injury or even death for no good cause. Besides, I had serious doubts about the mystical legitimacy of this ceremony. True, I felt no pain, but this man just threw me on the ground! Three possibilities ran through my mind:

Frank Baler Finds T.H.

1. These were legitimate mystics testing me to make sure I had no violence left in me before giving me the Initiation I came here for

2. These were legitimate mystics seeking to extract any remaining violence from within me through a catharsis induced by the fear of bodily harm

3. These were real savages about to either harm or kill me

I needed a quick plan to sort this out. In all legitimate mystical Initiations, if a candidate expresses the desire to leave or interrupt the process, the process is mandatorily over. That person will never be permitted to receive that Initiation again in the current incarnation, but the process stops immediately.

There was no anger within me at all, so I was not concerned with differentiating between possibilities 1 and 2. I was concerned about the possibility that these were savages and that my life was in danger. While opting out of the supposed initiation would give me the answer I needed, if these were real savages, attempting to opt out would not free me from them. On the other hand, attempting to opt out of a legitimate ceremony would ban me from it for the rest of my life. Opting out, therefore, was not a good option for me, I thought; the risks were high and the potential benefit negligible.

I was at a real loss for my next move. While I fervently desired the Initiation, being thrown on the ground did not feel mystically legitimate to me somehow. By then I was standing and found my hands reaching for the blindfold, very slowly. Before I could unlace the blindfold though, the man grabbed me again and shouted a command:

"Fight me!"

My concerns were allayed; these were legitimate, compassionate mystics trying to protect me from my own fears. They prevented me from interrupting the initiation; furthermore, if they meant to harm me, by now they would have already.

I still did not get the point of simulating a fight, but I started thinking of the several judo and karate moves I had learned over the years. Each time I thought that fighting this stranger for no apparent reason was ridiculous, I would relax my grip and intensity. He, on the other hand, would respond by intensifying his grip on, and aggression toward, me.

I began to consider several martial arts maneuvers, but they were energetically costly, and I did not know how long this would go on; furthermore, this man was heavier, taller,

Frank Baler Finds T.H.

clearly more skilled than I, there had been at least five other people in the gazebo, and I was blindfolded.

Eventually, my right leg began to hit the back of his left foot in an attempt to knock him down. I was just experimenting with this move when I noticed that each time my right foot hit him, his left foot was firmly planted on the ground, it would not budge.

Then, somehow, time seemed to slow down. I was able to perceive his movements and mine. Eventually I was able to shift weight off my right foot when he shifted weight off his left. The fight turned into a dance!

Then, in a move faster than I thought my body was capable of, I swept his left leg off the ground as I pushed him forward. He fell flat on his back and I jumped on top of him, still blindfolded. My hands immediately found his neck, and I began to squeeze.

Just then it occurred to me how absurd this situation really was. 'What was I doing?'

I stood up with my hands outstretched and open. I knew where the man was, even though I was still blindfolded. I reflexively bowed down to him, karate-style, then brought the palms of my hands together in a sign of gratitude. I actually felt he did me a favor, letting me pretend to 'win'.

Frank Baler Finds T.H.

The mind works in mysterious ways. At moments like these, the mind can either speed up and think millions of thoughts in seconds, or it can slow down so much that a single focus can be held for what seems like an eternity. I had been feeling like a complete looser for a few years now, professionally, personally and even spiritually.

The folks who put on this Initiation knew a lot about me. I remember the pages and pages of questions they sent me when I requested the Initiation, and then I had to write an essay. I bared my soul on those pages merely days before arriving, after Majaray told me about this opportunity when we met in northern California.

Maybe they actually read the papers and thought that they had to give me a taste of manly victory to jolt me out of my personal misery before the real initiation could begin. So, I held my hands together in front of my heart, blindfolded and slightly bent over, with my head low, thanking my opponent and teacher.

I could not have been more wrong. The man I fought, his voice was unmistakable, approached me and spoke into my ear in a solemn voice:

"You are a warrior! Fight the real enemy! Fight until you win, never stop fighting, but fight the real enemy!"

Frank Baler Finds T.H.

Those words cut so deep into my soul that I started feeling weak to the point of wondering I could keep on standing. Two other people embraced me and gently helped me to the ground. I laid down on the dirt floor drenched in sweat, still blindfolded. The music was soft and pleasing, mostly the flute now.

Two hands gently touched my chest. The touch was like no other touch I had ever experienced. It was remarkably light, yet it penetrated my entire body. The most impressive thing to me about that tough is that it brought a phrase to my mind, followed by the deepest, most gut-felt tears I had ever cried.

'Our struggle is not against flesh and blood, but against the rulers of darkness. Put on the armor of God, so that, in the end, you can stand firm.'

That is not the full accurate quote from the book of Ephesians, chapter 6, of course, but those were the words that came to my mind at the time. Here I was, not even sure of where I was, laying on the ground with two people trying to comfort me, realizing that this could very well be the 'end', and all I had done my entire existence was struggle against flesh and blood, while *protecting* the true ruler of darkness.

The tears came from such a deep place within me that my body began to contort itself in ways I did not know it could. I screamed sounds I did not know I could produce, while scenes of my lives flashed within my mind. Finally, I screamed with such intensity and force that I thought my entire body had turned inside out:

"I am sorry!" I shouted.

The hands firmly touched my forehead. Then I opened my eyes. Nothing in between; no sleep, no dreams, nothing.

The day was bright and warm. I was alone in the gazebo. There were no walls or curtains, no torches, no music, no one around. The blindfold was gone. I felt remarkably fresh and rested, particularly considering that I had obviously spent the night on the ground.

'Wow,' I thought. 'That was wild and unexpected.' I focused on the taste in my mouth, and carefully inspected both arms. Had they drugged me? I asked myself, realizing how silly my own question was. They turned me off by touching my forehead, I concluded. 'Now, that is good hypnosis right there,' I giggled to myself.

Frank Baler Finds T.H.

Fragments of sentences kept replaying in my mind. I knew from past experience that I would have to sit down calmly and rebuild the events in my mind, something my experience with hypnotic regressions had helped me with in the past. Then I had to make notes and read them. Once I read my own notes, I would have assimilated the experience. That, however, would have to wait because I was famished, and I had to urinate urgently!

The main house was within view, but I thought it would be fun to wet the local plants with warm urine, something I did justifying to myself that the organic compounds in urine are good for plants.

Then I walked to the main house reciting to myself:

'You are a warrior, make sure you win, fight the real enemy, don't fight against flesh and blood, the real enemies are the rulers of darkness…'

I repeated those words, as if to commit them to memory, while I walked to the main house. As I stepped into the house, I felt tense though. I knew exactly where the tension was coming from, and worse yet, it felt to me as if everyone else knew it too. Shame was back, and it had nothing to do with urinating on the plants.

Telma and Jurandi were smiling; they both hugged me warmly while saying 'congratulations'. Their sincerity was

Frank Baler Finds T.H.

through the roof, these were genuine people, truly happy for me. They offered me black coffee, dried meat and yucca flour. There were also bananas and fresh water on a side table.

I went to the bathroom to wash up a bit, but really, I just needed to think for a moment before I ate. The Initiation had been exceedingly powerful, but it exposed something that I could not ignore. I decided not to fake joy, or anything else. I was deeply concerned now, but very hungry as well.

As I got back to the kitchen, Jurandi calmly explained that Carlos had to go check out a water pump some two hours away from the main house on horseback. Telma continued, while serving me her delicious breakfast, explaining that I may want to go to the grotto and 'pray' for a while. Jurandi explained that Carlos wanted to leave at 2 am because a fishing vessel will go through Porto Coqueiro sometime tomorrow morning, on its way back to Corumbá.

The dried meat was delicious, the aroma of the black coffee felt heavenly, the company was angelical, and all I could think of was – a fishing vessel, please dear God, let it have a quiet motor.

Jurandi and Telma did not let me do anything around the main house. There seems to be some urgency in the air, and Jurandi literally walked me out. Once outside, I made small

Frank Baler Finds T.H.

talk, inquiring about the water pump Carlos went to check on.

"It is a wind-driven pump. There is a well and an elevated tank. All the fresh water we get here comes from that tank. They installed it some 15 years ago. Twice a year somebody has to go there and fix it." I assumed he meant 'maintain it'.

With no hesitation or time wasted, Jurandi turned me around and pointed to a trail head to my right.

"Follow that trail for about 2 kilometers. Stay on the trail! You will find a small green lake. Do not drink that water! Go around the left side of the lake until you see a rock formation. Go through the left, not the right! Look there until you see an opening. Go in and pray for a while. We will be here when you get back."

"Thank you Jurandi, breakfast was delicious," I said as I walked toward the trail by myself.

The walk was very pleasant. I felt like a kid again, free and spontaneous. I hugged a few trees on the way to the lake, I sung aloud, I jogged at times, I sat down at others to take on the scenery. The air felt crispy, but there was no sensation of cold or heat. Suddenly, I imagined what it would be like to live here, in this forest. Just she and I, together… Tarzan and Jane had a good time, I think, why not…

'Stop!' I told myself.

Frank Baler Finds T.H.

'Fantasizing about sex and romance feels really good precisely because, being my fantasy, it always happens as I wish it. Loving a real woman is different because she is a human being as well; besides, sooner or later, they all cheat and try to destroy you.' The thoughts would not stop.

'You are a mystic,' I reminded myself. 'Women are a distraction, you know that,' I continued.

Then another 'voice' got into the conversation, quite uninvited:

'You can only be a true mystic with a woman. You come from one woman; you must go into another to experience true Light. A woman can give you life; be real, you have no life. Look at you, lost somewhere in a forest, looking for a grotto to pray. Be honest with yourself, you call yourself a mystic, but what you really want is to be with what you call 'the right woman', and don't get me started on what you really mean by 'the right woman'! Are you even the right man?'

"Stop it already," I said agitated, this time in a loud voice.

'Of course I am the right man,' I thought. 'I am a deep thinker... and besides, I am a good man... and besides I...'

Frank Baler Finds T.H.

'Dear Jesus of Nazareth,' I, or someone, continued. 'Have I learned anything? Have I gone mad?' What was that spat about?

The spat did not concern me as much as what I caught myself 'saying' to myself. Had I inadvertently expressed my deepest fear to myself, right here in this forest? I felt like laying down right here and sleeping for one thousand years, at least. As I lowered my head toward the ground, though, I spotted the edge of a green lake.

The trail continued to my left; I could now see. Then the trail gently curved to the right a full half circle. Right there, just about in front of me, about 50 meters below, is a green lake. I stood up refreshed, saying to myself:

"It is downhill from here!"

Walking around the left margin of the lake, I indeed found some rocks, but no entrance to a grotto. I kept walking, looking, but found myself back at the trail. It was more like a pond, not a lake, but still, no grotto. I decided to circle back around, letting my intuition guide my eyes.

'This can't be real,' I thought as I sized up the hole on the ground I could now see. 'You don't have a flashlight or a first aid kit,' a voice screamed at me. 'If there is a snake or a scorpion down there you are done!'

Frank Baler Finds T.H.

This time I decided to take my time and consider the thoughts in my head. Two thoughts competed for my attention.

In one book by Paulo Coelho, he talked about his master ordering him to climb a waterfall. He tried to, but his master had to save him. Paulo told the master that he thought this was a test of his obedience. The master replied that this was a test of his wisdom to know what he cannot do.

Maybe, I reasoned, going into that hole is crazy. Besides, why do I need to go into a grotto to pray? I can pray right here at the edge of the lake!

The other thought on my mind was a memory from the King's chamber at the Great Pyramid of Egypt. After I received an Initiation there, my master asked me to express something about the occasion. I said that the entrance to the chamber impressed me. The only way in was by lowering myself, for a large slab blocked the upper half of the entrance.

"That is right," my Master said. "Only those with a humble mind and heart, those willing to lower themselves, ever find the Higher Truth."

Either my wisdom or my humility was being tested. But in the end, the adventure of going into the hole prevailed.

Frank Baler Finds T.H.

There is something about a deep, dark hole that no man can avoid, I thought as I got on my knees and looked inside.

The entrance was quite low indeed, but there was some light inside the chamber beyond the narrow entrance. I decided to go in feet first, firefighter-style, now feeling more like Indiana Jones.

The grotto was probably about 3 meters in diameter, roughly circular. I could tell because it felt similar to my old office in size. The side opposite to the entrance was darkest, but it was time to pray, so I could go back to another meal. I was getting hungry already.

I sat on the ground and closed my eyes. That felt uncomfortable to me. I admire people who can sit lotus style for hours, motionless. I could not relax sitting on the ground, so I laid down and closed my eyes.

"That is a good point, you have to discover what works for you," he said.

Was I dreaming? Was there someone in this grotto with me? Someone watching me this whole time? I was afraid of opening my eyes and finding out.

"No need to open your eyes," the man said, his voice unmistakable.

"You still have not told me your name," I said.

Frank Baler Finds T.H.

"My name is not important. You are fascinated with your version of order. You want my name so you can classify me in your mind in some way. Besides, you are talking today, not I."

I started to get up, but he insisted for me to stay where I was.

"Just relax and tell me what happened last night."

I stated explaining how there was this gazebo with music inside and some torches, when he interrupted me:

"I mean what happened inside of you…"

My mouth started trembling; I could not pronounce the words that came to mind. Eventually I spoke, though; half crying.

"Well, I never thought of myself as a warrior, but I guess under extreme circumstances I can be pushed into violence."

"Every being is built to survive," he said, then continued after what seemed like a short introspection.

"When survival is threatened, each will attempt to restore safety according to the tools available at the moment. A person can fight an injustice with loving prayers, intelligent arguments or weapons. Regardless, they are fighting against the injustice and protecting their survival. Not all people engage their survival mechanisms under the same situations. True threat assessment is related to the tools we use to increase the likelihood of survival. A violent person feels violated easily and fights back with physical force. The intellectual feels insulted easily and aggresses others with sharp words. The spiritual person preaches forgiveness, forgives the aggressor, then goes home and battles himself with what he should have done instead. The religious often battles the 'devil'.

"So yes," he continued, "you can be pushed into violence as you should, for you were created to protect your survival. You will never take a beating again without at least attempting to neutralize the assailant…"

He paused for a long time after that, but I felt that more was coming. He said a lot, and I had to think about that. As a child I received frequent beatings, and the punishment was increased if I attempted to defend myself by putting up a hand or blocking a hit. Was he referring to my childhood, or was he speaking metaphorically?

"Or the enemy," he finally said.

"So yes," he went on, "the enemy can push you into violence. But when was the last time your physical or intellectual survival was really threatened?" I sensed this was a rhetorical question, because I could not think of any examples of real threat to my survival.

Frank Baler Finds T.H.

"Exactly," he said as if reading my mind. "But you have been violent toward yourself and most other people with your sharp words. Where is the enemy?"

When he said 'where' is the enemy, instead of 'who' it is, I got it. The enemy can push me into violence. I have been pushed into violence, so there has to be an enemy. I have not faced any real enemy in my outer life, so the real enemy must be within. Within me!

"Wait!" I wanted to explain and defend myself, but a deep voice, his, said "*deeper*!" as I often did as a hypnotherapist when a client wanted to explain his shadow away.

I smiled warmly seeing me, in my mind's eye, working with a young man at the old office. It felt to me that I was in the room with them, but neither person was aware of my presence. Neither party was totally aware of how deep and true what they are doing really is. This man had come to see me, not only because he had a problem, but because he could bring me a message. This young man could easily go into the hypnotic state, visit several of his past lives, and also report from his experiences in between lives.

On one occasion, the young man was speaking for a Master, who apparently had been aware of our work together and offered to assist. The Master and I engaged in a profound dialogue about the nature of the mind and the origin of suffering. Eventually, I summarized the conversation into one question to the Master, through the client:

"What is the ultimate problem?" I asked.

"Thinking about the problem is the problem," the Master answered even before I could finish the question.

"Wow," I said to the Master at the old office "If the mind is about thinking, and thinking about the problem is the problem, the mind is the problem."

"Your soul is pure Light, it does not need Illumination, for Light cannot be Illuminated. Your body responds to one natural mandate: survival. Your natural life is governed by the need to reproduce yourself physically. Reproduction is encouraged by the promise of ultimate pleasure, but in a world of illusions of duality, that pleasure comes with the danger of great pain as well.

"From the perspective of the body," the Master continued, still speaking through the 19-year-old client "what you experience as pleasure and pain in relation to a woman is simply nature's way of informing you what combinations of bodies can result in good babies. Being with a woman you really like is not a spiritual reward, just as being hurt by a woman is not spiritual punishment."

I was single when that session happened, and I remember wanting to take the conversation into the relationship direction and how to find the ideal soulmate. The Master, however, was not about to be derailed. There was one message to be delivered:

"The body cannot be faulted for complying with a mandate built into it. Therefore, the body is not the problem. If you say that you are body, mind and soul, and the problem is not in the body or in the soul, where is it, then?

"You either do not have an ultimate problem, or you do," he went on. "You asked me what the ultimate problem is, indicating that you do have one. If you have an ultimate problem, it can only be in your mind."

I opened my eyes and scooted up to the wall of the grotto, leaning lazily on it. My eyes were tearing with emotion as I revisited that session at the office so many years earlier.

"Where is the enemy?" the voice coming from the dark part of the grotto insisted.

"Well, clearly the mind is the enemy."

As I said those words, I had an intense flash back of an afternoon in medical school many years earlier. The lecture was on auto-immune disorders. I got distracted and wrote several notes to myself about the 'craziness' of the body attacking itself. I compared auto-immune disorders to self-destructive behaviors. Much of what we do, sometimes in the name of entertainment, is actually self-destructive.

Frank Baler Finds T.H.

Hearing the last sentence I just uttered, made me think of dementias as the mental equivalent of auto-immune disorders; we think of the mind as the enemy, so we destroy it.

"What did the Master say about the ultimate problem?" The voice in the grotto asked me, as if reading my mind.

"Thinking about the problem is the problem", I replied.

"So, where is the enemy?" I detected a hint of a smile on his voice, as if I was about to get something important.

Suddenly I burst out laughing with joy!

"The enemy is in the mind, but the mind is not the enemy. Erroneous thinking is the enemy!"

As I said those words aloud, I started to cry. It was a strange moment of joy and sadness. I felt the intense joy of sudden Illumination, along with the sadness of regret for getting it all so wrong for so long and hurting so many people along the way.

"Interesting," the voice said. "So, what about the rulers of darkness? Who are those?"

I understood that he was asking me about the Bible verse from Ephesians that had come to my mind the night before. – was he really reading my mind? – I asked myself. "Never mind about that for now," he actually said!

Frank Baler Finds T.H.

I sat up, straightened by back, cleared my throat, and spoke with certainty for the first time in a long time.

"The rulers of darkness are thought forms created by the mind as a result of sustained erroneous thinking. They exist as real entities in the mental realm and can manifest in the physical if fed long enough. They are fed by sustained thinking, since thought is energy. Each erroneous thought, fed by thinking it, becomes an entity that comes back to you later. Sometimes those thoughts manifest in your life as people who act out your erroneous thoughts, as an opportunity for you to see what you have been thinking and make a correction. When that happens, you are not being punished, there is no such thing in the universe, you are being given the loving opportunity to make a correction in your thinking."

The voice in the grotto was quiet, as if knowing that I was not done.

"An example of an erroneous thought is what I caught myself saying earlier today: sooner or later all women cheat and try to destroy you. That is an erroneous thought because it is judgmental and not loving. It is judgmental because it attributes a quality to another person that only reflects my pain. It is erroneous because it cancels the other person out. They have no opportunity to love, to make a correction, to

Frank Baler Finds T.H.

be who they are; they simply become a character in my story." Then I said it, "an erroneous thought is erroneous precisely because it annihilates the other person, since it has nothing to do with her reality, only my pain."

I could clearly see how sustaining thoughts such as 'all women hurt you' would create an entity who would literally possess a willing woman, who would then hurt me. That realization explained much of my absurd life, particularly what happened with the women in my life. I could clearly see how I systematically dehumanized them and turned them into an agent of my pain. Eventually the spell would be broken, they would 'abandon' me, and become 'someone else'. At that point I would justify the mess I created by saying that they had only pretended to love me all along.

Detail after detail of my past romantic relationships flashed across my mind. Actually, I did the same thing with all the people in my life, but only felt real pain through the women I had loved.

At that point the shame I felt earlier that morning as I stepped into the main house was back. The shame was intense, not only because I had exposed the true ruler of darkness, but because I uncovered the mechanism whereby it exerted its darkness. Something really interesting happened then.

Frank Baler Finds T.H.

For a moment, I begged the earth to open up and swallow me into oblivion. Then I saw how that man, Frank, sitting on the ground inside of a grotto, God-knows where on this planet, was risking everything to heal. He had given everything up, he held nothing back, he desired healing and Light more than anything else. Frank himself was just another victim of this ruler of darkness. The shame and desire to be swallowed into oblivion was not different from what the ruler of darkness did to the people around him. Suddenly I felt love and compassion for that son of God sitting on the ground. It was not him; it was that which was within him…

My spiritual mother, a nun named Ana Luisa who considered me her spiritual son, and from whom I felt absolute love, came to mind. I actually think she watches over me from heaven. I remembered one conversation where she told me:

"The devil does not want you to speak it out. You must speak it out, confess your sins my son!"

Amidst intense tears and barely able to pronounce the words, I finally blurted it out.

"Once I convince them that they do not love me, I punish them for not loving me. I make them miserable and drive them mad. I do this through words and thoughts… intense criticism, annoyance and judgements."

My forehead was now on the ground. I sat up again and spoke with the authority of a son of god owning up to his own darkness:

"And then, I secretly plan the destruction."

I had been a part of hundreds of exorcisms as a hypnotherapist, but I had never imagined or experienced something so intense as this. The words spoken cut deep into my soul. I never thought of myself as a warrior. I always thought of myself as a peaceful person, but I have been fighting everyone, all the time, my whole life. Now I am encouraged to think of myself as a warrior, but one who fights the real enemy.

The real enemy is within me; it is in the mind, but it is not the mind. And now the exact plot the ruler of darkness uses to spread pain has been exposed. My mission, as a warrior from now on, I concluded, is to defeat that inner ruler of darkness, my mission is to be victorious, my mission is to stand firm in the end, armed only with the truth of God.

Then the voice in the grotto, this now familiar man whose name I still did not know jumped in again:

Frank Baler Finds T.H.

"No, not 'I'. 'It' secretly 'planned' the destruction." He emphasized the words 'it' and the past tense 'planned', as he spoke with authority.

"It is out of you now," he explained. "You no longer have to fight it, because it is out. There is nothing to defeat. Your mission is to stand guard at the gates of your mind. Guard yourself against any form of resentment, judgement, ill feeling, or frustration. Those are trojan horses used by 'it' to come back in. You now have the power to stop it from coming back in simply by raising the flaming sword of love and truth."

I wanted to ask so much, but before I could say anything, he said:

"Close your eyes!"

I closed my eyes and soon felt a slight pressure in the center of my forehead. It felt to me as though his index finger was toughing my 'third eye', but I kept my physical eyes closed as requested. Then he said it:

"I love you."

I remembered feeling exhausted and surprised by his last words as I opened my eyes. How long had I been laying here? The grotto was dark. It was nighttime. There was no other presence, but I did not feel alone. There was deep joy. I felt as though a ton of bricks had been removed from my back. I felt light as I climbed out of the grotto where my life was transformed.

As my head poked out of the hole I had descended into hours earlier, the intense light of the full moon flooded my awareness. 'How poetic, how majestic' I thought. I was coming out of a hole where my life was restored, and I was met by the light of the moon!

The moon represents to me the female energy. Being greeted by the light of moon, to me, at that moment, felt as though all women in my life had forgiven me, and my relationship with the sacred female, and with physical women, was healed. I ran through a mental image of all the women in my life; mother, sisters, lovers, daughters, wives, all of them, while I basked in the light of the moon. I thanked each of them profusely, and I told each:

"I love you."

The way back to the main house was so fun that I never wanted to arrive. I spoke aloud, I laughed, I cried some more. I remembered camping by myself as a youth at Ocala National Forest, in Florida, and running around the forest naked at night. I felt so much at one with the forest now that I removed my clothes and ran through the trees filled with joy. I talked to God, and to my Teachers on the Path. I screamed at times, I was quiet at others. I ran and I knelt on

Frank Baler Finds T.H.

the ground. I kissed the ground and thanked the elemental forces in the forest for accompanying me on this journey.

Soon, the dim porch light of the main house was in sight. The hum of the diesel generator was audible in the distance. I was famished and dehydrated. Still tucking my shirt in, I walked into the main house where Telma, Jurandi and Carlos welcomed me with dinner served.

No one asked anything about my day. The joy all over my being spoke for itself. The three of them conversed as I listened. For now, I really missed my daughters and could not wait to get back home.

Frank Baler Finds T.H.

SHE IS ASLEEP

---o---

The babies were so pretty when I picked them up in the morning, that I ran to them and got on my knees so I could look deep into their eyes. I hugged them and kissed them with so much joy! We went to the park and all three of us played for a while. Then we ate and went home to watch a movie. I had missed them so much during my last trip to Corumbá, and apparently, they missed me as well.

In a few days life was back to normal. Each night I would write down some notes on my last trip, and the depth of the experiences I had lived. About two weeks had already passed when I finally felt ready to call Maharay and thank her for the experiences she helped create for me.

The following Friday morning, I dropped the babies off and hurried to the office to set up for a productive weekend. First item on my list was to call Maharay; she lived in New

Frank Baler Finds T.H.

Mexico... about 11 am her time... perfect; I knew that she started working at 1 pm.

"I am so glad you called Frank, *Abuelita* really needs you," she said before I could say hello.

"Hello Maharay... sure... nice to talk to you as well, what can I do for *Abuelita*? And thank you for the trip to Brazil." I said, pretending to be cool, but my heart was already racing.

"Actually, *Abuelita* needs you to help Tonho in Manaus... he lost it!"

"What did Tonho lose?" I asked thinking I knew where this was going. "Tonho is one of us, but he lost his grip on life, the desire to live. His wife left him for another man. She tried to have him killed so she would not be judged as adulterous. Tonho found out about the plot and lost it. The doctor calls it depression, but we know better, he lost touch with life, he unplugged from the world. You know how dangerous this is." Maharay went on and on, not giving me time to digest what she was saying.

"*Abuelita* is concerned, Tonho would not kill himself, but he is thinking about accidents... don't worry, I can help with all the details, but *Abuelita* needs you in Manaus tomorrow."

I literally dropped the phone out of my hand. "*Abuelita* needs me where? When?"

Frank Baler Finds T.H.

"I already checked," she said. "There is a flight leaving tonight, you can be in Manaus tomorrow... Frank, *Abuelita* is counting on you to bring Tonho back... please, he is one of us."

She hung up the phone before I could say anything. After the trip to Corumbá, I would not deny *Abuelita* a favor, especially when she needed me. The problem was that I already had sessions scheduled at the office, I had to pick up the babies on Monday morning, and to be honest, I had no money at all. I had no idea how many days I would be gone. A last-minute trip to Manaus... that has to be expensive, I thought. There is no way I can help this time. For sure next time they need me I will be there for them.

They are all nice people and all, but a same day international trip to go talk to a man just because his wife broke up with him seems a little far-fetched to me. Yes, they all went all out for me in Brazil last time, but we are all Brothers and Sisters on the Path, we help one another out. I just can't help this time.

This crazy back-and-forth conversation went on in my mind the entire day; so much for productivity that weekend.

Finally, I got it. Now I knew it. I had finally gone too far. The trip to Corumbá turned out great, but that was because

Frank Baler Finds T.H.

the folks at a local lodge read my papers and took over. This *Abuelita* thing was just crazy; it was getting out of hand.

I picked up the phone to call Maharay and politely tell her that she has gone mad with her dead grandmother thing. Just then a text message came in:

'Send a picture of your passport, and a credit card, both sides. Be at MIA[12] at 8.'

The credit cards I had were all either maxed out, or near the credit limit. Still, I took pictures of two of them and sent back with the following message:

'Try the blue first, if it does not go through, use the red. Passport is at home, send later. How many days?'

'What am I doing?' I asked myself. This woman is clearly high on drugs, and I keep on doing what she says. True, she has never lied to me, everything she has said turned out to be awesome, but nobody goes to Manaus the same day just because this woman dumped this guy. Besides, if he needs therapy, he is welcome to call the office. Why should I go there, on my dime, to do him a favor? I actually thought those thoughts in my mind as I drove home to photograph the passport.

---

[12] Miami International Airport

Frank Baler Finds T.H.

By 4 that afternoon Maharay sent me the trip confirmation with the following message:

'Sorry about the return, best I could do. E-mail follows with details. He is one of us.'

'What???' Three stops on the way back? A six-hour trip becomes 25 hours with layovers? What is this? I went online to prove that Maharay must have been high. The only other alternative I found would have been to wait three more days in Brazil and catch a non-stop flight home. Apparently, the non-stop flight happens once a week; the plane leaves Miami on Friday night and returns the following Saturday morning. That option, however, would cause me to miss picking up the babies a second time. Maharay made the right choice, the loving choice. Maharay favored my weekend with the babies over a possible three-day vacation in Brazil. Maharay was a little strange, but I was definitely beginning to appreciate her a whole lot.

I opened the e-mail she sent me when I arrived at the airport. The e-mail said:

Walter will be at the airport in Manaus, dressed in black. He will drive you to Hotel Tropical. All reservations confirmed (hotel/car/airline). Look for the Head Concierge, no one else, and ask for Tonho. Once you meet Tonho, introduce yourself simply as Frank, a friend of a friend, and

Frank Baler Finds T.H.

take it from there. Remember he is one of us, and you will be home in three days. *Abuelita* is counting on you to bring Tonho back. Enjoy your flight!

The favor asked of me seemed unlikely to happen. I could see the logic of asking me for this particular favor: One of my wives had developed a relationship with someone else while we were married, then tried to destroy me in several ways so she would not have to break up with me and explain her indiscretions to me. I lost the desire to live and almost died. While recovering though, I developed several ways of helping people in that same situation. A book called *Awesome Again*[13], with a method other therapists could use in these cases was instrumentally helpful to me. I had perfected many therapeutic techniques for this type of problem, I conceded to myself. I was confident I could help Tonho, but certainly three days would not be enough.

In the back of my mind, I began to formulate a plan to establish some therapeutic *rapport* with Tonho to then keep working through the computer until he was well. Now, however, I needed to focus on checking-in.

---

[13] Awesome Again, by Flavio Ballerini, Ph.D.

Frank Baler Finds T.H.

It was a long line to the counter, fortunately I only had one backpack with me. Eventually I placed my passport on the counter and showed the attendant my phone with a reservation number. I did not feel like talking much after standing in line so long. The attendant typed and typed into her computer, seemed a little distressed, checked my passport again, then finally said:

"Oh, Doctor Frank, please, I can help you over here," indicating another countertop. "I am sorry you waited in the coach line, Doctor."

Was she asking me to follow her to the first-class counter? This time I was determined not to pay for an upgrade, no matter how good she looked, or how eloquent the sales pitch.

As expected, the attendant described all kinds of perks and amenities, including a lounge with champagne and *hors d'oeuvre* while I awaited to be ushered into my private cocoon on the plane.

Naturally, the key to not be suckered into buying what you cannot afford is to not listen to the sales pitch, so I was not listening to Stella describe how awesome it must be to fly first-class. When she was done talking, I simply asked:

"Could you get me an aisle seat, please, as far forward as possible, *please*?"

Frank Baler Finds T.H.

"Doctor, there is an aisle on both sides of your seat; and 1A is about as far forward as we can sit you," she said winking at me with a beautiful smile.

Strange, I thought. On the wide-body planes that typically fly the international routes, coach seat numbers usually begin in the 30's. That is all I need, I thought, maybe this was a small plane with cramped seats.

"Marienne will walk you to your lounge, Doctor. Have a fantastic journey and thank you for flying with us!"

About then it began to down on me that Maharay had gone mad after all. I had sent her pictures of two of my credit cards, specifically saying that one may not even be approved. Surely, she would know that I am broke, that I cannot even afford the coach fare, much less first class, and even less staying at Hotel Tropical. Had she really done this to me? How was I going to pay for all this? If this *Abuelita* thing is true, I reasoned, she would know that I have not been able to work and that I am in deep debt. Why do this to me?

Marienne looked like a fine lady; she was very respectful, and not flirty at all. I wanted to ask her whether this was a first-class seat but didn't want to sound silly. I decided to rehearse in my mind a tone to the question that made it seem like the answer was obvious, and that I was just kidding.

Frank Baler Finds T.H.

"Did she give me the right boarding pass?" I finally blurted out showing Marienne the paper in my hand.

"Yes Doctor, you are on seat 1A, flight 8712 to Manaus, Brazil, leaving at 10:43PM." Then she said, "I am sure you will be most pleased with our first-class service Doctor."

"Thank you, madam, I am very well pleased indeed. Thank you."

At the lounge I finally ate. I was famished! A distinguished looking gentleman introduced himself to me as the president of a large corporation. He asked what I did, and whether I was going to Manaus on business or leisure.

"I am a hypnotherapist," I said. "I am going to Manaus to visit a friend," I added.

The flight was spectacular. Something interesting happened when the plane took off from Miami that night. All my therapeutic logic stayed on the ground, behind me, it seemed. I began to fantasize about miraculous healings and powerful therapeutic techniques I had read about or studied over the years. I thought long and hard about the lecture on magic I had attended in California. Somehow, I figured, Tonho was suffering not because of what happened to him, but because of how he interpreted the events, the story he told himself about what happened. Under the right hypnotic conditions, I reasoned, I could help him change that story.

Frank Baler Finds T.H.

He would come back to life, and I would make *Abuelita* proud, I thought.

I began to see his comeback to the world in only three days as a real possibility. Then I remembered my Mentor on the mystical Path saying that all healing is actually instantaneous; sometimes it takes years of preparation to get to it; it may take years for the mind to accept the healing and let go of its grip on our experience, but the actual healing is always instantaneous.

By the time Walter grabbed my backpack and showed me out of the airport, I was strangely certain that Tonho would be just fine. The flight was awesome, I thought, because I slept very deeply, and could not remember at what point I fell asleep. I felt alert and ready to do good work.

Once again, I could not be more mistaken.

As a kid living in Brazil, Hotel Tropical was supposed to be the epitome of luxury and sophistication. There was a zoo in the hotel grounds and a wave pool. Every amenity, every luxury, and supremely detailed decoration were supposed to be the hallmarks of the famous hotel. I was in awe as we approached the grand entrance of the hotel. I felt lucky to be there and couldn't help but to remember that what probably

Frank Baler Finds T.H.

got me here was a trip diametrically opposed to this in terms of luxury.

The polar opposites of life, I thought…

Walter handed my backpack to the bell person. Another man, actually wearing white gloves showed me to the front desk. There, Manuel surprised me saying:

"Welcome to the Tropical Doctor Frank, your suite is ready for you. Carina can take you there now, or she can show you around the hotel if you prefer. She will also be happy to take you on a tour later if that is more convenient for you.

"These are the keys to your car, Doctor, it is parked on spot number 7 right that way," he said as he pointed to a sign. "Have a pleasant stay with us Doctor, and please let me know if you need anything. I am the general manager of this hotel, my name is Manuel, and my cellular number is on this card."

He continued, "on behalf of my entire staff, welcome again to our hotel, and thank you for the opportunity to serve you."

I could not say anything after that; to be honest, my eyes were teary, and I felt like crying. I brought the palms of my hands together in front of my chest and bowed down to

Frank Baler Finds T.H.

Manuel with a great deal of respect and admiration. He was simply perfect.

Carina showed me to a large room with a King bed. The walls were covered in dark wood. The large window opened to a balcony with a splendid view to the jungle.

"Doctor Frank, if there is anything I can do to enhance your stay with us, please call me," Carina told me, handing me her card.

I placed the card in my pocket and said, "thank you Carina, you are very kind indeed, thank you."

The shower was unbelievable. Water came out in volumes I had never seen before, from above and from the walls. What an experience! I washed my underwear and undershirt on the sink, hung them on the edge of the countertop, and got dressed for the day.

The first thing I like to do in the morning is to read a little. The Bible and A Course in Miracles are my favorites. Then I pray a little, or meditate, or both. Finally, I love to make notes in the morning. In this case, I mostly wrote about this unlikely journey, how I ended up here, and the actual trip on a first-class seat. Then I made some notes about the babies, whom I would not pick up on Monday morning.

Frank Baler Finds T.H.

As I got ready to go to the lobby and find Tonho, I reflexively reached into my pockets. I pulled out a card that said:

Carina Pereira

Head Concierge

On the flip side of the card, there was the Hotel Logo, name, address, a series of phone numbers, e-mails, fax, TELEX and Skype ID.

'Unreal!' I said to myself smiling. 'See?' I told myself, 'what you are looking for is always closer than you think. Sometimes it is right in your face… Open your eyes, Frankie!'

At a quiet corner in the massive lobby, I found a couch and a house phone. Perfect to call Carina!

"Carina, this is Frank…"

"Yes Doctor, is everything acceptable in your suite?"

"Oh yes, the suite is quite fine, thank you. Ahhh, Carina, do you know Tonho?"

There was a long pause on the other end of the line, but I could hear her breathing.

"Tonho will be here tomorrow morning. You can meet him at 8 by Sagi's cage."

Frank Baler Finds T.H.

"Do you know if I can talk to him today?"

"No, Tonho is not available today; but he will be available tomorrow morning at 8 sharp."

"Sure, thank you. Would you kindly tell me where Sagi's cage is?"

She laughed so beautifully and freely, a bit of a surprise, then explained: "Sagi is our eldest monkey…"

As I slipped into bed that night, I felt so grateful to life, to God, for the opportunity to be there and having lived that wonderful day. I was treated like royalty since the night before, all day, and I spent wonderful hours with an amazing woman. I had learned so much about the forest and the culture. Life is good, I thought as I dozed off.

I woke at 5, as usual. Had coffee, read a little, prayed, then made some notes starting with my dream. The dream called my attention because I had barely been dreaming since the breakdown over one year earlier.

In the dream I was watching Frank in that grotto in Corumbá, as he spoke about his demons. Then I wrote the journal entry:

'In the past feeling rejected, real or imaginary, triggered need to destroy. Now appreciate Carina, despite rejection. Solved. Dream confirmed.'

Frank Baler Finds T.H.

Many of my notes were a bit cryptic, sometimes abbreviated. Every important personal achievement of mine in the past had been punctuated by a confirmatory dream. I had noticed that I saw women differently since the experiences at the grotto, but it was not until the splendid time with Carina, and the dream that night, that I ratified the healing. I was beginning to feel like an adult, and a man, even though I did not have a woman in my life. In the past I thought I would never feel like an adult or as a man without a woman. This was impressive.

At about 7 o'clock in the morning, I went down to the restaurant, grabbed some fresh fruits and black coffee. After some time, I had some prunes and raw yogurt, with another cup of coffee. Then I rushed over to Sagi's cage.

Tonho was already by the cage, sitting on the ground. When I approached him, he looked up uninterested as I mentioned my name and asked his. I sat down next to him and told him a bit about my story, then I told him that I developed sophisticated ways of helping other men who no longer cared to live. I threw that last comment in there intentionally, thinking that we could save time and spare formalities.

Tonho stood up, I followed him. He was taller than I, black, round face, quite muscular, no belly, a full head of hair. He was clean shaved and had no dental plaque. Both his trousers and shirt were pressed. He seemed freshly showered and wore a pleasant cologne. His shoes were clean, and his belt did not indicate recent weight changes. He spoke in a deep, calm voice:

"I am sorry about your loss," he said.

There was nothing about Tonho that indicated the sort of abandonment Maharay had described, nothing. Still, I pressed on, thinking that I would break through a wall of denial.

"Tonho, have you ever felt broken, like you no longer cared about anything?"

"Broken yes, like I no longer care, no."

"Would you tell me about feeling broken?"

"Sure, but let's go to the waterfall. Give me the keys, I drive."

That was right, I remembered, spot number 7. Manuel handed me keys to a rental car when I checked in.

"Sure, let me get the keys in the room. Meet you at spot number 7?"

"Sounds good, he said and walked away."

When I got to the rental car I told Tonho that I would drive because I was the only insured driver for that rental car.

Frank Baler Finds T.H.

Furthermore, I told him, "I like to drive because I tend to get motion sick when I ride shotgun."

Tonho got a little agitated. He explained how the road to the waterfall was dangerous:

"It is a two-way highway, unlike your expressways in the first world," he said. Besides, he continued, "the road is littered with potholes."

Tonho cares about a lot of things, including my safety, for a man who unplugged from the world, I thought. But I was determined to make *Abuelita* proud and fix Tonho, even if he was not broken.

"Tonho, thank you for the concern, but please remember, I am Brazilian, just like you. Just tell me where to go."

I repeated those last words in my mind for a while as we got under way. I wondered what I meant by what I said, and what one thing had to do with the other. Tonho's concern was valid, and so was mine. I was not used to driving on narrow two-way highways filled with potholes. On the other hand, I was told that Tonho no longer cared to live, and that he was thinking of accidents. I would never get into the car if he drove.

While I drove, Tonho indicated where to turn, and where to go. Traffic through the city was absolutely brutal, but we eventually got on the road he had told me about.

Frank Baler Finds T.H.

Periodically I would ask a question, certain that I could break through his denial. Tonho's answers to all my questions were monosyllabic. He was clearly not interested in much conversation, but he was polite, frank and helpful. The journey took about 2 hours. Tonho had not exaggerated, the road was horrible and dangerous.

We arrived at a bend on the otherwise straight road deep in the Amazon Jungle. I thought it was a park, but there was no entrance, no gates, no park rangers, no formal parking lot, no entrance fee, and certainly no change room or bathrooms. Cars were parked on the dirt, among trees, on the sides of the road, and a few people walked around to and from their cars. I picked up my bag with a towel and a change of clothes, put on my hat, locked the car, and followed Tonho down the trail to the waterfalls.

"We hike this way, 1 kilometer to the waterfalls," Tonho informed me.

The hike was pleasant; an occasional person crossed our path on the way back from the falls. The hike down was not too steep, yet Tonho and I did not speak much.

We arrived at a beautiful bend on the river that looked like a small lake; the water was almost still. All around the bend, on the opposite margin of the river, almost like a

Frank Baler Finds T.H.

screen, or a curtain, in front of us, were the actual falls. Majestic, gorgeous, really impressive!

Tonho told me, more like an order than a suggestion, to enjoy the waterfalls as he sat under a tree, clearly not welcoming a conversation. I knew what to do, I would pretend to go swimming for a moment, give him some space, then I would come back and ask him a sharp question that would jolt him out of his denial. I would fix Tonho and make *Abuelita* proud, I thought again as I went into the river.

The water was surprisingly cold; it was dark brown, muddy river water. I stayed safely close to the margin, half walking, half swimming toward my right, until I reached the edge of the water fall. I went under the water, imagining how that water would purify me, cleanse me, renew me, heal me, and help me help Tonho.

When I came back to where Tonho was sitting, he handed me a small paper brown bag with a sandwich inside and a small pouch of water, one of those that comes with a small straw glued to the side. I have no idea where he got the food, but I did not ask because I was actually famished.

After he and I ate, I fired it off:

"Tonho, there is no shame in asking for help if you do not feel well. I am here to serve you… how about you tell me what's really going on with you?"

Frank Baler Finds T.H.

Tonho surprised me by telling me about his life. He is a civil engineer, currently in charge of building a large vacation resort on the edge of the Amazon forest. He is in a happy relationship with a woman he adores, has one son from a relationship he had out of high school. He is good friends with the young man's mother; both of his parents live, are married, and love him. Tonho said that he had no financial worries or complaints, and that he was in good health.

'Jesus,' I thought to myself, 'this guy is doing much better than I; what am I here to fix?' No question I asked brought out any hint of a crisis.

Then I felt a hint of anger lurking deep within my bowels. Maharay I thought! This was a joke she thought would be funny. She would force me into a luxury vacation I cannot afford. It all made sense now, Maharay knew that I love feeling needed and that I never enjoy myself. She made a few calls, asked a few favors, and I was having the time of my life; even feeling a bit like Tarzan swimming in the river in the middle of the Amazon Jungle. I was angry that she fooled me, but I began to accept that I was having a good time, and decided to relax.

Frank Baler Finds T.H.

Suddenly, Tonho became motionless; his eyes looked deep into the river in the distance, he seemed to be in a light trance. Tonho startled me by jumping up and saying:

"We leave NOW! Move it!"

When we got to the car it occurred to me that, as a man who grew up in Manaus, maybe the river 'spoke to him', and told him that a storm was approaching, or something like that.

We drove for a good 45 minutes before I felt sleepy. I looked around, hoping to find a coffee shop on the side of the road, but we were deep in the Amazon Jungle; nothing was available until we got back to town. Tonho was quiet, and a bit apprehensive I thought.

Then the traffic stopped. People in front of and behind us started turning their engines off and reclining their seats, as if this was a common occurrence on this road. The entire region around us turned quiet as all cars around us went dormant.

There is a road that connects south Florida to the Florida Keys, US1. It is a well-paved two-way highway. Sometimes a bad accident on that road requires blocking all traffic for a while, until emergency crews can open the road again. It should be the same here, I thought. It cannot be long until

Frank Baler Finds T.H.

emergency crews remove the vehicles from the road and traffic flows again. So, I reclined my seat a bit, and closed my eyes.

Closing my eyes felt good because actually I was really sleepy. Once my eyes were shut, in fact, I did not feel I could open them again. Then a wave of panic ran through me.

'He drugged me,' I thought. 'Tonho put something in the sandwich. But why?'

When I opened my eyes, Tonho was not in the car. There were several dozen people all around. By now most people had stepped out of their cars to cool off in the breeze. Some men were urinating deeper into the foliage, some people sat on the other side of the road, which carried no traffic at that point, and had full picnics. Nobody seemed agitated, surprised or concerned about the traffic holdup.

I decided to walk forward, toward the cause of hold up, which I assumed was an accident. For sure, I thought, someone tried to avoid a pothole, veered off to the left, and hit oncoming traffic. Head-on collisions are usually ugly, and occupants typically do not fare very well. Traffic here was relatively slow, however, so the people would be fine, I decided in my mind as I walked forward next to a line of parked cars to my right.

Frank Baler Finds T.H.

As I walked, the scene became more surreal. At one point, I felt like I was walking within clear gel, in a sort of slow motion. Then I started hearing people running in the opposite direction screaming:

"Tem corda? Tem corda?" They needed rope for some reason.

I kept walking and other people came toward me, then past me, screaming:

"Quem é médico? Tem mortos…" Who is a doctor? There are casualties…

Eventually I happened upon the scene of the accident. There was an orange pickup truck hit head-on on the left side. The truck had skidded and was resting across the road blocking both lanes of traffic. Skid markings told a chilling story.

My eyes followed the dark lines on the pavement; they ended at the edge of a precipice. The trees and shrubs there were broken. No wonder they needed ropes; perhaps they wanted to pull the car up.

I kept observing the scene from a position close to the pick-up truck where a woman cried unconsolably on the ground, while a man held her tightly. I assumed they had been in the truck at the time of the collision.

Frank Baler Finds T.H.

A man wearing no shirt and red shorts eventually emerged from the precipice with a motionless body on his back.

"Find a doctor," many people screamed.

She was about 30 years of age I estimated from a distance. Dark hair. Motionless. Blood had streamed from the corner of her mouth, but it seemed dry now.

The man who carried her up the precipice laid her body down on the tarmac, with her feet pointed in the direction of our rental car. Then he climbed down the precipice again; evidently there were more bodies down there.

Soon a man wearing a white t-shirt and blue bermuda shorts approached the scene speaking in a loud, authoritative voice:

"Excuse me, excuse me, I am a doctor, excuse me…"

The doctor examined her for a few minutes. At one point he brought each of his ears to her chest. Eventually the doctor pronounced the woman dead and asked the men around to give up their shirts to cover the body on the road. Before her torso and head were covered with shirts, however, everything changed.

"She is asleep!"

Frank Baler Finds T.H.

The voice, the power, the look, now in plain daylight, was unmistakable. It was him. We met in the desert in New Mexico, I saw and spoke with him in Florida after the Sweat Lodge, he delivered the lecture on Magic in California, he performed the exorcism in that grotto in Corumbá, and now he stood there.

"Step aside," he said in a firm but loving voice. "Clear the area," he now commanded.

Perhaps the people were mesmerized by his strange necklace, or intimidated by his presence, but the fact is that people obeyed him. Quite immediately, there was a circle about 3 meters in radius clear of any person, other than him and the body on the road. People watched speechless, as he knelt down above her head, karate style, looking in the direction of her feet.

The mysterious man extended his hands and began to do passes on her chest and abdomen. He inclined his body a little to reach all the way down to her pelvic region, and the passes continued for a while. Sometimes his hands moved from the center of her body toward the sides, other times from the sides through the center then up toward the head. His hands never quite touched her body; at times they were really close to the body, other times they jerked away, as if removing something from the body and throwing it far away.

Frank Baler Finds T.H.

Several people got on their knees and started praying. Other people stood motionless. Some children clung to their mothers. Nobody, however, interfered with what he was doing.

At some point, he placed both of his hands on the pit of her stomach and closed his eyes looking up, as if pleading with God. After what seemed like two or three minutes, he put his hands over her chest, where the heart would have been, and again kept them there for two or three minutes with his eyes closed, saying nothing. This time his hands were about 5 centimeters away from her body. He then put his hands on top of her face, again about 5 centimeters away, and held that position for a while longer.

Eventually he made the loudest sound, almost like a shriek, startling the crowd who soon started to scream. He pronounced sounds that I related to certain mystical mantras. He repeated the process several times, each mantra lasting about 40 to 45 seconds with his hands about 5 centimeters from the woman's face.

What happened next changed everyone on that road forever.

The woman coughed. Then she turned her head to the side and spit out blood. Then what seemed like blood clots came

Frank Baler Finds T.H.

out of her mouth. She began to contort herself a bit. She moved, then began to cry.

It was obvious that she was in pain, but she was moving, clearly breathing on her own, and her head would turn from side to side, occasionally spitting out blood. She moaned in pain, as people rushed over to cover her and bring water to her mouth.

Finally, there was full pandemonium on that road in the Amazon Jungle. Some people were prostrated; some begged Jesus for forgiveness, some just screamed randomly. Some people sat quietly observing, while others rushed down the precipice in search of survivors.

The strangest thing was that some people knelt at the strange man's feet. The crowd now closed in on him, and he was in a delicate situation.

Moments like these bring out strange behaviors and emotions out of people. While some people dropped to their knees, thinking of the man as some sort of messiah, others perhaps began to think of him as doing the work of the devil. Emotions ran really high, and there are always those who want to be the next hero by eliminating the devil amongst us.

"Quiet!" He said in a commanding voice. "All of you, sit down, now!"

Frank Baler Finds T.H.

Again, the crowd obeyed him, for the most part; enough for him to say a few words and make a safe exit.

"You are all blessed," he said when he could be heard. "The woman will be fine, thanks to your prayers." He actually credited the crowd and their prayers for her recovery.

"We all came together here today so that you would always know that nothing is impossible if you give thanks to the source of life and share what you have freely. Your lives will never be the same again, for you too will heal and do great good in the world. Please, just serve your brothers and sisters," he said, pleading.

"Master, can I follow you?" A woman asked. "No!" He said emphatically. "Follow only your heart, that is where you will find God."

"What is your name?" asked a man wearing a green shirt.

"Call me Shinhú."

Then he walked over and placed his hands on the doctor's shoulder. The doctor was sitting on the tarmac, head between his knees. He seemed to be crying. I could not imagine how he felt, pronouncing dead a woman who apparently was just asleep.

Frank Baler Finds T.H.

"You are a good doctor, and a good man. Go and heal the sick, care for the poor, and take care of your family." He said in a loving voice.

Then he turned back to crowd and said something that I believe few heard, for his voice was much softer now:

"I love all of you!"

As I walked back to where the rental car was, I could hear the divided opinions as people argued over what had just happened before their very eyes. True, the woman had been injured and was motionless when brought out of the precipice. Perhaps she had just fainted and the several minutes of rest laying down on the road were enough to naturally bring her back.

The doctor, however, examined her for several minutes and pronounced her dead on the scene. True, the doctor did not have any instruments with him, other than his senses.

As I sat on the driver seat, it took me a moment to notice that Tonho was already sitting there. I did not know where he had been, but when I looked at him more carefully, he was strangely relaxed. I asked Tonho whether he would mind driving the rest of the way. My belly hurt quite a bit. There was some blood on my hands; I must have caught blood in my hand when I coughed, perhaps after biting my tongue, I reasoned. I felt disoriented, but that was normal under the circumstances, I also concluded.

It took a while for traffic to flow and Tonho to drive at normal speeds. My seat was reclined, my eyes were closed, and deep inside I was rejoicing.

'His name is Shinhú, I thought.'

When we got into town, Tonho asked me if it would be okay to drop him off at home, since it was later than usual for him to get home.

"Absolutely," I said, thanking him for bringing me to the waterfall.

He stopped the car in front of a lovely wooden house and beeped the horn. For some reason Brazilians seem to love using their horns. I burst out laughing when Carina came outside to receive Tonho. They embraced and kissed, exchanged words I could not hear, then she asked if I would like to come in and have dinner with them.

"No thank you, thank you so much, though." I said, thinking that I had enough excitement for one day.

"I trust you had a great day?" She asked us both. "Oh yeah," I said as I got into the car. "Good night friends, thank you so much!" I said as I drove away.

Lola, the nickname one of my daughters gave to the voice on the GPS, showed me the way to the hotel. I parked the car

Frank Baler Finds T.H.

at about 7 in the evening and went straight to my room for a long shower.

My belly still hurt, but there was no blood in my mouth and my tongue did not seem bruised by a bite. I just washed my hands off and forgot about where the blood could have come from. After the shower I requested a full dinner in the room and called the spa. Fabiana would treat me with a full-body therapeutic massage and hot stones after dinner. While I waited for dinner to be delivered, I ran to the hot pool for a few minutes.

The massage was awesome, I was able to really relax. Fabiana did something that I really appreciated. Instead of showing me to a massage table and where to leave my clothes when I got to the spa, she showed me to a small, cozy room, with two small couches in it. I felt as if I was at the office, about to start a session. We chatted for a while, then she asked if I had specific concerns I wished her to address. The conversation, and the opportunity to speak freely and confidentially, made it possible for me to relax.

I told Fabiana that I felt I was being guided through a mystical journey. I felt elated to have this opportunity, I told her. I felt that a lifetime of hard work had paid off, but that I was sad that this discovery had cost me my family. Fabiana was very understanding and professional. She was also a wise woman. Fabiana said something that brought tears to my eyes:

"Doctor, what if your family was not taken from you? What if you had already learned your love lesson? What if you graduated and no longer needed to learn love through pain and disrespect? What if you are now ready to love and be loved with peace and respect?"

"Yah, maybe." That was all I could say at the time.

I left the spa really late. My body was free of tension, and most importantly, I felt jovial and humorous. Life was beginning to look good again.

In the morning I sat by the pool and wrote for a few hours. There were three deep concerns on my mind: the circumstances of my visit to Manaus; and the events on the way back from the waterfall. And then there was this thing about this guy who seemed to show up at the most impressive moments.

Asking Maharay whether she knew I would witness the accident or whether she meant for me to enjoy a nice vacation would not satisfy my true curiosity. I remembered Tonho's urgency to leave the waterfall at a certain moment, and realized that if we were much later or earlier we would have missed the events that followed the accident.

Frank Baler Finds T.H.

It was impossible not to relate the events of the day before to the biblical narratives of people coming back to life. In one passage, a blind's man sight was restored. When a disciple asked Jesus whether the man or his parents had sinned in order for him to be blind from birth, Jesus replied:

"The man chose to be born blind so that the glory of God would be manifested at this moment."

Could that accident have been 'staged' by the Cosmic in order for all those people to feel blessed as Shinhú said? I guess we will never know whether the woman was initially dead or not, but she certainly looked dead to all there, including the doctor who examined her. If she was dead, and came back to life, all those people witnessed something miraculous. Indeed, they are all blessed.

Finally, I learned something interesting about that mysterious figure who had been showing up more and more in my life at the most opportune moments. His name was curious to me, as a student of kabbalah.

I think I know where I can find him, I wrote right before closing my journal and going to have lunch.

Right after lunch I called Manuel and asked whether I should drive the rental car back to the airport or take a taxi. Manuel once again surprised me:

Frank Baler Finds T.H.

"Doctor Frank, if it would not be too much of an inconvenience, I would love to accompany you to the airport. My personal driver knows the safest route," he said.

"Manuel, that would be lovely, and I would welcome the opportunity to thank you for the wonderful stay at your hotel. I need to be at the airport at 18:00, what time should we leave here?"

"I will have someone pick up your luggage at 17:00 from your room and accompany you to the front lobby; we will leave then."

"Thank you, Sir," I said and hung up the phone.

The trip back was a bit anticlimactic and exhausting. I finally got home at midnight the next night.

The next morning, I had a ton of calls to answer. A bunch of late bills awaited payment, for which I had no money. I started getting desperate as I wondered what the total charges on my credit cards would be when they came in. Maharay had definitely gone all out for me, but I knew that stuff did not come cheap. For sure now all my credit cards would be way over their credit limits.

I had to lecture that evening, and now the babies were crying. They missed me, naturally, and insisted on going to the store to get one particular doll they had always wanted,

Frank Baler Finds T.H.

their whole lives wanting it; would I please just give them that one gift?

"Papi, we will never ask for another doll *ever* again, please…" my daughter Celeste said.

How could I say 'no' to that? I thought. I found another credit card in a box and strapped them to their car seats.

Frank Baler Finds T.H.

IT IS ALL OVER, FINALLY

———O———

A couple of weeks had passed since I returned from Manaus and no charges had appeared on my credit cards. Brazilian computer servers are slow, I thought initially. Then I remembered that the charges from the previous trip to Brazil appeared on my credit card statements the same day. Something was wrong, I concluded. I called Maharay.

"Maharay, I have to ask you something" I said when she picked up the phone.

"Frank… guess who says hi!"

"Let me guess: *Abuelita*?"

"She loves you; you know. She says you have a good heart. She says you are kind of crazy, and a jerk sometimes, but she says you have a heart of gold. She also told me something about you… I am jealous!"

Frank Baler Finds T.H.

"Let me guess, she has another wife lined up for me?"

"Ha ha ha, you joke around, but you do read minds."

"Well, I am calling you because I believe there has been a mistake regarding the…"

"Was the vacation not adequate?" She interrupted.

"Oh no, please, the vacation was exquisite, of course, it is just that…"

"Frank, *Abuelita* loves you," she interrupted again. "Think of it as a gift from the family. Listen, gotta go, talk later, okay?"

"Sure…" she had already hung up.

A gift from the family? This little vacation must have cost a small fortune; I feel a bit embarrassed, to be honest. But wait, I thought, if it was a gift, why did she ask me for a picture of my credit card? Both sides, no less.

Then it came to me. His voice loud and clear in my mind. It was as if I was sitting there in the Temple. The night sky clearly visible with an untold number of stars above. The wooden benches, the torches, and all the adepts listening to the Grand Master:

"Trust, absolute trust in divine providence is the magician's main tool. All magic comes from the Cosmic; what allows the magician to do magic is his absolute trust in the Cosmic to provide."

Frank Baler Finds T.H.

'Wow,' I thought, she asked me for my credit card knowing that I was tight on cash only to see if I would trust. She never mentioned a gift vacation, she said somebody needed my help. 'Glorious Egyptian days,' I thought… 'we learned so much there!'

Now it was time to get to work. No more trips, no more Initiations for a while. I had a lot of bills to pay and two babies to raise. I still had severe challenges with many aspects of daily life but honestly, I was doing much better. My life was taking a completely unexpected direction.

When I took stock of how broken I was in late 2018, soon after the NDE, I purchased a couple of notebooks and started journaling. I had never experienced such total devastation; I had never reached a point in my life from which I was certain there was no recovery. I figured at the time that, if I ever, by virtue of a miracle, recovered, it would be interesting to have a record of the recovery. Consequently, I developed the habit of taking detailed notes, as Montaigne[14] did, on everything that was happening in my life and around me.

The first few days of January 2020 I wrote extensively on the panoramic view of the last 13 months. Zero sleep, an

---

[14] Philosopher Michel de Montaigne, 1533-1592.

Frank Baler Finds T.H.

NDE, huge legal troubles, total financial ruin, the inability to work, the conference in May, the trips, and the pace at which things started happening after I met that strange man in New Mexico. The conclave on magic had been out of this world, and the two experiences in Brazil, particularly the last one, had been huge blessings in my life.

I was sleeping better, not well yet, but better. It still troubled me that I could not work as much as I used to. I could see a few clients a week, but I quickly developed extreme anxiety and had to run away from the office. I was still therefore disabled, in a sense, so the bills were piling up.

On one of the trips to Brazil I had met a man who was on a similar path to mine. He was a philosopher as well and had also been badly damaged by two horrible divorces. Unfortunately, he had lost contact with his children for the last 10 years, and now was trying to rekindle those relationships. We kept in touch through a voice application on the smart phone. I would not say that we were actual friends, but we offered each other an ear to listen, a shoulder to cry on if needed, and a strong voice if we lapsed on our recovery.

One early Sunday morning in January Luke called me and told me about a meeting he really thought I should attend in Scotland.

Frank Baler Finds T.H.

"Man, you gotta be there," he said enthusiastically. "There is a nonstop from MIA to Heathrow on Wednesday night, I already checked. We eat breakfast in London then we take a train to Edinburg. We will be there by nightfall. The meeting is on Friday afternoon. I will send you a link to sign up."

"Luke, thanks, man. Really, thank you so much; but I really cannot go. I have no money, no credit cards, plus I gotta a mess over here dude."

"Wait, wait, wait, man. Hold your horses," Luke said firmly. "Where is Mr. 'Trust divine providence' now?"

"I suppose he is talking on the phone with me from Geneva right now, right?" Luke laughed, he was doing much better, I could tell.

"Frank, you cannot let a few Dollars keep you from your destiny! Dude, I don't know what else to tell you, man. You simply have to be there." Then he simply said one more thing and hung up the phone.

"Text me later where and when we meet for breakfast. I want to ride up to EB with you, so we can catch up."

I did not think I could go, but it turned out that I did not have the babies that weekend. Humm, I thought, that could be an omen, perhaps I should go. Then I clicked on the link he sent me. The headline on the sales page read:

Frank Baler Finds T.H.

WHAT IF TODAY WAS YOUR LAST DAY

That was all I needed to read. I would be travelling to London in a few days. First of all, I really came to trust Luke when it came to resources on the Path, as we both called these experiences. Second, the description of the seminar was tiny. They were not trying to get people there; those to me, were the best events ever.

The sales page simply said that we must be prepared to depart this Earth at any time, since we never know when that time will come. I clicked on the button, signed up with a credit card I was sure was maxed out, and started shopping for flights.

My phone rung. I ignored it because I did not recognize the number. The phone rang again, and again, until I answered it. The lady told me that she was the best friend of a client who gave her my cell number. She told me that she was very upset over something and she wanted to come in and see me as quickly as possible.

The prospect and I made plans to meet at the office on Monday morning, soon after I dropped the babies off. She explained her situation and agreed to a discount on the fees in exchange for paying for a couple of months of sessions up

Frank Baler Finds T.H.

front. I had all the money I needed to be in Edinburg for the weekend; just like that!

Once I was done with the session, I quickly made plans to travel on Wednesday as Luke had suggested and texted him the message:

'Per your request: Kings Cross Tube Station, Thursday, 1/9/20 at 11:35AM local.' The reply was almost immediate.

'You the man; thank me later.'

There was nothing out of the ordinary with that trip. It was so ordinary and incident-free that it actually felt to me as if life was saying: 'you've had enough excitement lately; time for some ordinary moments'. I checked in, took my seat, the plane took off, landed, I took the train, the tube and met Luke.

The train ride from London to Edinburg takes a bit over five hours. Enough time to have a little of everything. Luke and I took a short nap, we talked, we ate, we read, and we browsed the internet. Nothing out of the ordinary.

Night came, we ate dinner, talked some more about the same things we had already talked about, I wrote on my journal, and we went to sleep. The next morning, we had breakfast and found the hotel to be filled to capacity. We later discovered that several hotels in the area were also

Frank Baler Finds T.H.

filled. This event was going to be bigger than we each thought and anticipated.

I remember as if it was yesterday, during my first year in college in 1983, having a conversation with Dr. Berger, my calculus professor, at his office. Once we were done discussing the homework, we got into a conversation about the country, and eventually about 4th of July celebrations. Authorities had published the actual attendance at the most recent 4th of July celebration around a public lake, not at a venue with numbered seats or ticket sales. I asked Dr. Berger how authorities know how many people are at an event where heads are not counted and there are no numbered seats.

Dr. Berger told me that authorities look at how close together a small group of people are; in essence, they count how many people are at a small area that they can measure. Then, they take that density and multiply by the total area occupied by the crowds, something that can easily be measured from maps.

I discovered that thinking of Dr. Berger and reminiscing about a conversation that took place almost 40 years earlier was not just about estimating that about 500 people were at a large warehouse in Edinburg; those memories were a harbinger of what was to come until the next day break.

Frank Baler Finds T.H.

The speaker was not introduced by anyone. There was no fanfare, no music, no dancing. A man came onto a simple stage and spoke plainly. There were several loudspeakers along the sides of the warehouse, but no video screens.

At about 6PM, with hundreds of us sitting around, some on blankets, others on the cement floor, he simply said:

"It is a fact: we will all die."

I was not surprised by the general gasp I heard from the crowd; I was surprised that I also gasped in disbelief. The veracity of the statement was beyond question; yet, the involuntary response we all exhibited demonstrated that this is not a fact our minds are trained to consider.

The man spoke about existential issues for about three hours. He was paused and somber at times. There were many stories and examples, but never laughter, from him or anyone else. The overall mood was that of a funeral. Many people were lying on the floor; the sound of people crying prevailed when the speaker was quiet, sometimes sipping on a cup of water.

At about nine o'clock in the evening Ron, the speaker, started explaining that we should go for a walk outside, alone with our memories and thoughts, in silence. A couple of assistants would lead the way with red flashlights. The walk

Frank Baler Finds T.H.

would be long, Ron said, but he never told us how long or where we were going.

That night was somewhat warm, considering that it was winter in Edinburg; I later found out, that it had been about 39 degrees for most of the night. There was no ice or snow on the ground. My Brazilian/Floridian blood protested against such a bad idea as walking outside in the middle of the winter in Scotland, but something within me told me that it would be all right, and that, in a sense, I did not consider the choice of not going.

I had only been to Edinburg once before, for a couple of days, many years earlier, so I was not familiar with the town at all. All I know is that hundreds of us walked together through streets that were sometimes narrow, sometimes wide. We went up small inclines a few times, but mostly the terrain was either flat or we walked downhill.

At one point, I could see both ahead of and behind me what seemed to be an infinite number of people walking, mostly looking down, and all in silence. A song came to my mind at that point. Roberto Carlos sings one of my favorite songs ever, called 'Jesus Cristo'. I felt that I was in that song, and that our Father above was guiding us somewhere.

The walk started off as the typical walk where modern people are in a hurry to get from point A to point B. I was

Frank Baler Finds T.H.

not sure that there was a point B; I felt that the walk itself was the point, not the destination. I turned out to be wrong, of course.

At some point, I lost awareness of time and distance. When I reconstructed the events of that night, I came to estimate that the walk lasted about four hours.

That initial sense of purpose and destination wore off the crowd as the leaders kept going and going, we were not arriving anywhere it seemed. People started relaxing, I felt, and introspecting more. I had been sobbing the whole time.

I had nearly died some 13 months earlier, spent most of the year before not wanting to live, and had just listened to Ron talk for hours about the meaninglessness of it all when we all must, at the end, let it all go. Yes, my relationship with life itself had changed after the TSL retreat, but now I felt that I had indeed died and was walking into some sort of afterworld.

Feelings that I had died indeed probably brought on early fantasies about death, probably instilled into the mind through religious indoctrination. In my case, I started seeing scenes of my life, moments, people, situations, interactions. In all cases that came to mind I saw how I could have been more loving and caring. All situations that came to mind had to do with people and interactions with them; I saw each of

Frank Baler Finds T.H.

those interactions as sacred opportunities to learn to love, and I felt I had missed the point on all of them. With each scene that came to mind my cry intensified.

A few times I collapsed on my knees in pain and sorrow. 'How could I have been so selfish?' I would ask myself, sometimes screaming aloud. The longer the walk proceeded the louder it got. Although other people were also screaming and crying violently in some cases, I could not discern any actual words from anyone else; in fact, all sounds seemed really distant to me, even when a person was screaming right next to me.

At one point I wondered whether to stop and help a person on the path. Then a voice within me told me not to; it was not my place at this point to help anyone, for I needed much help myself. Furthermore, I sort of understood, this process we were all going through was highly individual; we each needed to have our own experience with ourselves, within ourselves. As that thought waned, I noticed that some people dressed all in white were indeed caring for those who collapsed on the ground and could not go on. They would hug, hold one another and simply cry together in consolation.

I was tempted to turn back somehow; I wanted to run to each of the people I had hurt and fix it somehow. I looked

Frank Baler Finds T.H.

back often, thinking of how I could exit this walk and go back to fix my life. At one time I took a sharp turn to the left intent on exiting the crowd and go apologize to a girl I met when I was 13 and never saw again. As I made my move, a pair of very loving hands, a gentle lady, lovingly guided me back into the walk, as if reminding me that there was nowhere to go, other than forward.

My crying intensified to a point I did not think was possible, or healthy, which was a crazy thought, considering that I felt dead already. I kept collapsing on my knees, covering my face and crying violently, always asking God, I guess, how come I had been so small as a human being, so selfish, so uncapable of love. I could not bear the pain of having hurt others. I could see now how my words had caused a light in them to shrink, to collapse; I could see how each interaction had diminished them. Worse yet, in my mind at the time, I could see how people had come to me throughout my life hoping to be uplifted and reminded of their divinity, yet felt dejected and sorry they came to me.

At one point it occurred to me that the walk should end in hell, which was what I deserved. Then the thought changed into: please dear God spare those souls in hell of my presence there, I will hurt and offend them too. No, I didn't even

Frank Baler Finds T.H.

deserve hell either, I concluded. Then the strangest thing happened.

It occurred to me that I was indeed having a conversation with God in my mind. From the beginning of the walk the Jesus Cristo song had come to my mind. Then I had been wondering how come I was not more loving. Then I wondered whether I should stop and help others. I thought of going back to fix, to apologize, to make right, to correct past mistakes. Yes, I concluded, I was indeed having a conversation with God in my mind, and the only desire within my entire being was to be a better person for the benefit of others.

The complete self-loathing turned into a different question in my mind; with the new question came a huge amount of energy and the determination to keep on walking no matter what else happened. I would walk and never stop, I told myself.

Suddenly I wondered how come I had become so hurtful. I was sure I had not started out that way; 'What happened?' I asked.

Scenes from my very early childhood came to mind. Scenes in which I was victimized and hurt myself. I did not pay any attention to those, for I knew they were consequences of a deeper past, not causes of a hurtful present.

A few other people walked behind me at times with their hands on my shoulders. I was still crying, but it felt very different now. I had hurt many people, but those encounters never started with the intention to hurt them. The conversation in my mind about intentions was important to me, in light of the fact that I had been talking to God this whole time. There had to be a connection there, I thought, but I had to be careful, I also thought, for my mind was probably trying to get me to evade responsibility for my past hurtful behaviors.

The types of scenes that came to mind shifted completely; I was now re-visiting several past lives. I had caused much pain in the past as well, but I had also been deeply wounded by many. Feeling betrayed and devastated seemed to be a common occurrence in my past, as were the deaths of spouses and children.

There are no past lives, I concluded. What we call a 'past life' is simply a memory we had forgotten, but there is only one life. We wear many bodies throughout our lives, but it is only one continuous life. All those guys were me, and I am them, it is the same story over and over, it is one life, many bodies.

Frank Baler Finds T.H.

A thought popped into my mind. Of course, we must wear different bodies, I thought. The scenery has to change in order for us to continue learning the same lessons from every imaginable angle. If the scenery changes, the body has to change as well to correspond to the current situation we are learning in. The lesson is the same, but the setting changes so we can learn the lesson fully, and as the setting changes, the body changes. Then I concluded to myself: The body itself is a part of the setting that the part of us who learns is immersed in.

I eventually laid down on the floor of a warmer warehouse. I am not sure to this day if it was the same warehouse we started at, or another one. I do know that I was exhausted, not only physically, but also emotionally. This time, however, they had thin mats for us to lay down on, and a warm blanket to cover us.

As I closed my eyes in the darkness of the warehouse, soft, somber music played in the background. I concluded that the true origin of my problems cannot be in the past, as in a past life, because no matter how far I searched, every apparent cause was itself a consequence of a prior insulting event against me. I was hurt, so I hurt someone, so I was hurt. That formula seems to go back all the way, forever, therefore that analysis was fruitless, I concluded as I gave up and apparently dozed off.

The next thing I remember was a man and a woman lying right next to me, one on each side. They sort of embraced me lovingly. I cried softly for a while; I cried tears of total surrender. I was aware of what I had done, the effect that my words had on people for centuries; I was both a healer and someone very hurtful. I was aware of several betrayals against me; being betrayed hurt immensely, but I also inflicted immense pain onto others. I was aware that I sought God above else; my physical life, however, did not reflect my love for God.

Eventually the man lying on my left side asked me a question, while the woman just held me; all three of us laying on the floor, I on a thin mat, and them on the cement floor next to me.

"What was it all about?" He asked softly.

"Lots of pain," I responded.

"What is your desire now?"

"To go back and do better, I want to go back there and serve God by serving others." That was all I said.

The warehouse we were at had large windows all around. The first rays of sun hit my eyes and woke me up. I looked around, many people were still in deep sleep, while others sat up crying. Some paced the room aimlessly. Others were dancing in silence. Some seemed happy. Some seemed somber. I did not notice any of the leaders or organizers around, not that I could distinguish, so I figured the 'event' was over and walked out.

My first priority was to find a restroom. My bladder was painfully full. Thankfully, there were plastic temporary restrooms setup around the exit of the warehouse. I found an empty one and urinated. Then I stood there, in that green plastic bathroom, my penis hanging out of my trousers, my hands on my hips, in deep contemplation.

I noticed that something was radically different about me when I became aware of what I actually contemplated: there is something quite godly about the pleasure of voiding one's bladder when one really has to. Having our physical needs met just feels so good, I thought. So, why do we have so many and such complex needs? Could we have been designed with needs just so we could experience the pleasure of having them met?

I went to my hotel room, showered, picked up my backpack with my journal and went to find a quiet restaurant where I could eat something hot, have coffee, as hot as possible, and write in silence.

Frank Baler Finds T.H.

The first thing I wrote about was the dream I had the night before. I remembered getting to a warehouse after the long walk and finding a thin mat on the floor to lay down on. I remember thinking about my life for a while and surrendering into sleep. Then I remembered dreaming about a man and a woman, both dressed in white lying next to me. The detail that was now clearly present on my mind was that they were both dressed in very light white linen, and seemed to float slightly above the ground as they held me.

That morning, after sipping on good hot Scottish coffee, I wrote the last entry on my journal for that day. It was more poetic than usual:

'And when it was all over, finally, angels came to him and comforted him.'

Luke and I met for a late afternoon meal. We did not talk about the experience the night before. We were both quiet, mostly introspective, occasionally discussing future plans. Eventually Luke told me that he was taking a train to Ireland later, where he would visit a cathedral he always wanted to explore. I told him I had to get up really early to take the 4AM train to London, to make it to my flight to Miami on time.

Luke and I walked together, occasionally talking, to the train station. The train station was the same we had just been

Frank Baler Finds T.H.

in hours before when we got to Edinburg, but we both looked at one another, saying, in silence, 'we are not the same people at all.'

Finally, Luke broke the silence:

"We are fortunate to live another life in the same body."

"Yeap," I said, "fortunate indeed."

Luke pointed to the departure board and said:

"That's my ride."

We hugged in that train station as two souls who love one another profoundly would. Then we traded the mandatory hard slap in the back to remind ourselves that we are tough men and he walked away to the platform. I called him:

"Luke!" I shouted a little. He turned around.

"Thanks man."

Luke touched his heart, then a namaste salute and turned around. I stood there for a while longer. I felt like a baby just out of the womb, with my whole life ahead of me. My heart was filled with love, compassion and desire to serve. I felt light and ready to be useful to someone.

It was time to go home. It was time to get to work. It was time to live.

PART 3

ONENESS AT LAST

Frank Baler Finds T.H.

Frank Baler Finds T.H.

WAKING UP

The journey home was completely devoid of any adventures or excitement; not even some turbulence to write home about. I did not feel like talking to anyone.

I walked into the empty apartment just shy of noon. I was different, the world was different; life was different. I had been on the other side of life and came back more than once now. I was beginning to see this side of life differently somehow, but I was not sure of how.

I sat on the white couch at the apartment I was struggling to turn into a home and stared out the fifth-floor window.

I remembered walking into that apartment for the first time; the huge floor to ceiling windows and the fact it is a corner unit, makes it really bright during the day. The generous L-shaped balcony allows me to face each cardinal point. I would never have moved into such a nice place as that had it not been because I was so broken, too broken to make rational decisions at the time, and because my sister and oldest daughter helped me.

At that time, I would stare at the walls, ceiling, and specially out of the panoramic windows for extended periods of time. During those periods of apparent idleness, the weirdest thoughts and images would occur to me.

That afternoon I distinctly remembered the first time I passed out. I fell off a small cliff at school in fifth grade; no injuries. Later, during the summer between high school and college, I passed out again. I worked so many hours at three jobs during that summer that one night, talking to the restaurant manager after my shift, I passed out. They took me to the hospital, checked me out, I was fine. More recently, I had general anesthesia twice. Those two experiences were more interesting because I was able to bring back some awareness of the other side. 'I guess I have always been fascinated with the other side of this life,' I thought.

I must have dozed off for a moment, for I could see that I was back inside of the great pyramid of Egypt. Indeed, I had been there years earlier on occasion of an Initiation I cannot describe at this time. Suffice it to say that the sarcophagus,

Frank Baler Finds T.H.

which is the only object ever found within the King's Chamber of the pyramid, was used extensively.

Three years after the experience in Egypt I received that same Initiation at a Lodge in Florida, using a plywood sarcophagus. Three years after that, almost to the day, I delivered that same Initiation to a Worthy Seeker. I had become an official Teacher on the Path by then.

My Mentor told me in Egypt that the Initiation I had just received would be reactivated about 20 years later, signaling the beginning of a new phase of my life. I did have general anesthesia 20 years after Egypt, but it took another 5 years to have the near-death experience that completely changed my life. Just one year after the NDE I had just experienced death again and come back to this life in the same body.

'What a glorious experience in Edinburg,' I thought.

There was so much on my mind about the meaning of all these experiences, but at the same time my mind was still and calm. There was no need to think or do anything; everything was in profound Order as it was. It was a strange paradoxical feeling: a mixture of chaos and order...

When I thought of Frank as a person on this earth I would cry. I cried as if he had died; I missed him as I would miss a great friend from long ago. I could see his mistakes, his pain, the love in his heart, I could understand him so much, but he

Frank Baler Finds T.H.

was gone. He had died. Thinking of him, I would cry softly sometimes.

Other people validated the notion that the man I had been was no more. Students started telling me that the classes were totally different, right down to the tone of my voice and cadence of speech. Explanations were more direct, examples more explicit, ideas were expressed fully and unapologetically. The same change had occurred in the private sessions: clients were experiencing significant transformation in fewer sessions and finding much more joy than I had noticed before.

The paradoxical experience of chaos and order intensified to the point I questioned my sanity all over again. Could I really have gone too far with this idea of the mystical?

Three thoughts came to mind almost simultaneously. One was hearing from adults, when I was a child, that those who attempted to understand too much ended up crazy. I quickly identified that thought as coming from a small part of me that still feared myself, life itself, and ultimately God. Yes, it was almost as if that 'voice' within me, from a long-gone childhood, still feared that God would punish me for trying to understand this life as a reflection of the other world. As the Biblical story of the tower of Babel came to mind, I blamed myself for reading too many books, for intellectualizing my spiritual understanding of the Divine, and above all, for being too harsh on others whom I judged as not being sincere Seekers.

Another thought on my mind was a Biblical passage in which a student complains to Jesus that, despite doing as he was told, he had not felt illuminated.

"What else can I do to receive enlightenment," he asked Jesus.

The answer Jesus gave him is still debated among theologians to this very day.

"Sell everything you have, give the proceeds to the poor, and follow me." Jesus said.

Selling everything I had, and giving it to the poor, meant to me, sharing as much as possible with all those around me. 'The poor' can be anyone who has less than I in any domain in life, not just money. Knowledge, friendship, and service are examples of a type of wealth I definitely could share more of with others, if only I could stop feeling sorry for myself.

The third thought on my mind, almost simultaneous with the other two, was that the truth would set me free; another Biblical passage. I did not feel free from chaos, so I figured I still had not found a truth profound enough to set me free. That last thought, I recognized as the notion of a 'higher

Frank Baler Finds T.H.

truth', a central idea in a book I called 'The Philosophy of Therapy'[15].

There was one thing I had been good at, I decided; that was reading, and learning from other authors. So, I started reading again. If felt delightful to immerse myself in books because I had regained my ability to focus and concentrate. While I was focused on a topic, totally concentrated, I felt free and joyous. As soon as I allowed my awareness to return to 'my situation', 'my life' or the worst of all: 'what had happened to me' I would cringe and feel horrible all over again.

Books on dating and relationships kept showing up, somehow, and I kept reading them. These books were awesome, yet I felt horrible reading them. The more I read about what women 'really want', how to keep women excited in a relationship, and how to enjoy unending sex, the worse I felt. As I put one such book down and contemplated what I had learned, it occurred to me that I had never gotten one single thing right when it came to women and relationships. I had it all wrong and backwards all along…

---

[15] The Philosophy of Therapy, by Flavio Ballerini, Ph.D.

Frank Baler Finds T.H.

no wonder I felt so sad, I concluded as I put the book on the bottom shelf where all the read books were piling up.

Other teachers still came to my classes a couple of times each week. When this ordeal first started, I asked three experienced teachers, friends of mine, to attend my classes and monitor my performance. I was afraid of allowing my own personal turmoil to contaminate the mystical quality of the classes I taught, thus confusing students. I never, ever, received a complaint from a student or one of the other teachers though. Eventually, two of my friends declared me well enough to continue teaching, and stopped attending my classes. Michael continued attending; he later told me that he continued, not to monitor me, but because he was learning so much.

Michael and I would often chat on the parking lot after class. Michael always had an interesting follow up question about a point I had made, or a question about a particular pedagogical strategy I had used that night.

"Why did you introduce Hermetic Law with the Law of Polarity, as opposed to Mentalism?" Michael asked one night after class.

"Michael," I started, "the 7 laws described in the Kyballion are not necessarily all the laws that exist. Similarly, there is nothing sacred about the order in which

Frank Baler Finds T.H.

they are presented in the book. The important thing is that disciples learn to use them, and apply them to improve their lives and help others."

"I see," Michael said. "But why start with polarity then?"

"Over the years of sharing Hermetic Laws with students, I found that most people can relate more readily to the Law of Polarity. In a sense, it matches our experience, and the language used to describe it is much more colloquial than what I would use to describe Mentalism, for instance. I found that going from the more relatable to the more novel facilitates learning for students."

After some further follow up questions, we chatted about the School itself. Finally, Michael asked how I was doing, personally.

"I couldn't have gotten it more wrong all my life," I told my long-time friend.

"What do you mean?" He asked.

"The woman thing, man. I got it all wrong, I never understood them, I never treated them right, I was never generous enough… no wonder my romantic life is a mess, I said in a louder tone than was usual for our conversations."

"Frank, I am telling you," Michael said, "you have been through a lot these last couple of years, both mystically and personally. It is time to integrate all of these experiences; it

Frank Baler Finds T.H.

is time for you to digest and assimilate, it is time for you to extract meaning from these experiences."

I just looked at him and noted how wise this man really is.

"I am trying man; don't you think I am trying to understand it all?" I said beginning to show my frustration.

"Frank, there is nothing wrong with receiving help, you know?"

That last comment really bothered me. I had been helping people sort out their problems for years as a hypnotherapist and as a teacher. It never occurred to me to seek therapy for myself.

"Michael, I give help, I do not receive help. How long have you known me man? Frankly, I am a little surprised that you suggest I see a therapist."

"Nothing wrong with that, Frank." He said.

"Michael, you know that people who go see therapists end up worse off than they started. You know that better than anyone I know. Why would you send me right into the lion's den Michael? Have I hurt you in a past life?" I asked frantically.

"Do your clients end up more confused after seeing you? Have you ever lost a client to suicide? Frank, you are a therapist of last resort, as everyone sees you. You see people

Frank Baler Finds T.H.

no one else can help; you have the skill and the patience to enter their world and help them out of their chaos, don't you?"

No, I had never lost a client to suicide in almost 24 years of service. Yes, people thought of me as the last stop when nothing else would help. And yes, for the most part, people transformed their lives and solved their problems permanently when they came to see me. Why was I so anti-therapy? I wondered for the first time.

"I work a little differently Michael, you know that. I do not diagnose mental illness, I am not a therapist in the modern, medical sense of the word. I am a therapist in the mystical sense. I help people fill the void they feel within, from within. That is not the same thing as modern therapy."

"Yes, I know what you do Frank. You helped me when I was desperate, don't you remember?"

"That was a long time ago Michael. Besides, you are a wise man, very strong and capable. I didn't do much for you."

"Frank, tell me the truth!" Michael leaned in and said in a low, inquisitive voice. "Do you actually think you are the only one, or the best? The only person who actually helps others?"

Frank Baler Finds T.H.

Michael's question was tough; it cut deep into me. With one question Michael put me right in front of my own Shadow. Perhaps, I thought... perhaps he is right after all. Perhaps, hidden underneath my nice guy, mystical façade... perhaps... I could not say the words even in my thoughts.

I must have wondered longer than I was aware of, because Michael continued emphatically:

"Frank! Snap out of it! What is it? Do you?"

"Do I what?" I later realized that I was resisting the obvious conclusion.

"Do you think you are the only good therapist in town? The only one who can help others?"

"Fine. You win, I finally said trembling a little, as if confessing to a crime. Perhaps I am an arrogant bastard. Deep inside I guess I do think I am the best... no wonder I feel so devastated, so broken. Michael," I said slowly, "this is awful."

Michael did not skip a bit; he was not impressed by my confession either. He simply pressed on, the same way I would have, under the same circumstances, at the office.

"Now that you acknowledge that other therapists can help," he said suggesting, more than summarizing, "can we talk about you?"

"Me? What about?"

Frank Baler Finds T.H.

"Yes," Michael pressed, "are you ready to see a therapist? Can you accept help Frank? Would you please receive a little of what have given so much of, for so long, to so many?"

"Michael, the truth is that I am living a paradox. I live in heaven and hell simultaneously. I live the life of a mystic, and that of a miserable man at the same time. If I am not working, I think of my past and hurt Michael."

Michael seemed to feel triumphant. He looked as though he achieved his objectives; he got me to see that other therapists could help their clients, and that I should seek help from a good therapist. More importantly, Michael had skillfully broken through my wall of hidden arrogance.

"But hey, I am sleeping better," I said as if to justify myself.

"I know Frank. Listen, I really gotta go. Later?"

"Sure thing man, later." I said as he walked to his car on the now empty parking lot.

"Hey Mikey!" I think I shouted. He turned around while still walking. "Thanks man." Michael waived as he got into his car.

Frank Baler Finds T.H.

CLARITY

Michael had not known that during the last two years, I had seen a total of twelve therapists. Indeed, not one of them could help me, I thought. One was an obese man who sat on a higher chair while I sat on a couch that was artificially low to the ground. One day, I actually looked and saw that the couch legs had been cut off. This man just wants me to look up to him, I thought.

Another therapist claimed to be a hypnotherapist. When I asked for some serious hypnosis, he went through a simple relaxation routine. No good, I thought. One woman insisted on hypnotizing me but pulled out a laminated paper and read a script to me. "What is this?" I would ask the lady, who seemed oblivious to my existence, as she struggled to read the script. That did not work too well.

Frank Baler Finds T.H.

One REIKI therapist told me that I did not need therapy. According to her, I was experiencing male menopause, hence the crying. "Just wait it out," she would say. You will be fine in a couple of years. I had extensive blood testing done and discovered that I was quite jovial and healthy, at least biochemically speaking. That therapist was not right for me either, I decided.

An interesting experience happened with an acupuncturist who got angry at me when I told him that I was experiencing bouts of inner anger that troubled me. "Are you taking the herbs?" He would ask aggressively and accusatorily. "Most of the time, yes," I would say. "That is your problem…" The scolding would start again. The other therapists were similar, a few sessions and very little progress.

Only I knew the truth, however. I had not really been open to therapy in any of those twelve instances. Furthermore, I did know of a therapist who could help me, but I had not called him.

Santin Arellis was reputed to be best, but he charged a hefty fee. The biggest problem, I thought, about going to see Santin was his therapeutic style. Santin laid out his rules very clearly upfront. He knew what worked, and why it worked,

Frank Baler Finds T.H.

so he would not work with a person who would waste time justifying himself or questioning the process. He wanted to work only with those who were truly ready to heal, regardless of ability to pay, I later learned.

The waiting list to see Santin was over three years long, his web site said. In the email I sent his office asking for an exception to the wait due to my despair, I mentioned that I had attended several of his courses. Claudia, his secretary, claimed to remember me from a week-long course I had attended a couple of years earlier, she said when she called me back.

"What impressed everyone in the class," Claudia said, "was your answer to Santin when he asked you to demonstrate a hypnotic induction. You told him that you never hypnotized anyone without a therapeutic intention."

I remembered that class. "If the subject would care to share with us a therapeutic need," I told the Teacher in front of his packed class, "I would be happy to demonstrate the hypnotic technique, and reward him with therapeutic suggestions for his kindness in volunteering for this demonstration."

The class had gotten really quiet when I said that. As usual, I thought I was in trouble with the Teacher, and mentally prepared to be asked to leave. This was a very

Frank Baler Finds T.H.

advanced class; every student there was a teacher as well, and the one serving us as a Teacher now was seen by everyone as nothing short of a god. This god of a teacher called me forward and asked me to demonstrate a basic technique, and I had objected, possibly embarrassing the Teacher, I concluded.

Santin allowed the silence to linger for what seemed to be an eternity. Even feeling that I was in trouble, I was ready to take the heat because I had spoken my truth.

Finally, Santin spoke. "Did you all hear what Frank said?" He asked the class. "Listen to Frank," he continued as he started to repeat slowly what I said, as if driving the point in.

"Never hypnotize anyone without a therapeutic intent. We are not in the show business, we are healers. We do not hypnotize to show off our skills, we hypnotize to serve the person, and ultimately to serve God." He added to my words.

"You spoke well Frank, please proceed with the demonstration as you see fit." Santin said, as the class got even quieter.

Those days seemed so distant to me now, I thought as I read a follow up email from Claudia. I would have the required phone interview in a couple of weeks; if Santin chose to work with me, we would get started shortly

338

thereafter. The email ended with a link for payment and instructions.

'Santin requires a retainer prior to the phone interview. If Santin chooses to work with you, the entire retainer will be taken as the fee, regardless of the number of times we meet during a period of two months. There will be no refunds, in part or in whole. The fee is not transferable. The fee expires in two months from the first session, regardless of how many sessions occur. If Santin chooses not to work with you, the entire retainer will be promptly returned to you. If you miss three scheduled sessions, this agreement is terminated, and no refunds will be issued. If you really cannot afford the fee, call the office.'

Wow, I thought, even with an agreement like that, he still has a three-year long waiting list. This man must be good, I concluded what I already knew.

During the days that followed I imagined what the interview would be like. I had been a student of Santin and used a method similar to his at the office, but Santin was known to always surprise his clients.

I was indeed surprised when the phone rung that Tuesday exactly at 6:00PM as scheduled. The contact on my phone was recorded simply as "*Maestro*". Santin never asked me much. He spoke.

Frank Baler Finds T.H.

"You had a break down; best thing that ever happened to you. You are an intellectual, and intellectuals only receive Illumination after a breakdown. The mind does not break; your mind is fine. What breaks is the interface between your mind and external reality." Then he paused a little and said tentatively "the screen on your phone broke, but not the phone itself."

"No wonder I feel like a baby, not quite capable of carrying on with my life." I responded.

"Well yes," Santin said. "In many ways, you did die. It is as if you are a baby again. This is normal and necessary."

"Best thing that happened? Normal? Necessary? Jesus!" I said showing frustration.

"The part of your mind that broke is the part that prevented you from receiving more Light." He said trivially, then continued "you have also been through several important experiences in the last years… time to integrate it all and gain some clarity."

I had no idea how Santin knew so much about me until I remembered that I posted quite a few videos on social media about my life. I had also written articles in which I disclosed some of what had actually happened. In my own classes I told students about what felt to me at the time like 'intense attacks from the forces of darkness'. Some of my students

Frank Baler Finds T.H.

were also in Santin's tribe; there were plenty of ways Santin would have known so much about my life.

Santin jolted me out of my introspection with the only question he ever asked during the interview:

"What have you done in therapy?"

"You mean as a subject or operator?" I asked.

"Operator," he clarified.

"Somewhere north of 42 thousand sessions." I responded in a low voice.

"Up there with the most prolific," Santin said slowly. Then he continued, "Exorcisms?"

"Well," I said hesitantly "I stopped counting after 300."

"Yes," he said, "you certainly roughed some feathers in hell, but you also earned lots of points in heaven. With 42 thousand sessions and over 300 exorcisms you certainly helped some people. Remember that each person we help positively affects about 2000 people. You left your mark in the world Frank."

"What do you mean? I feel quite stressed," I said.

"We will take care of the stress with the integration and clarity you will gain." Then he continued, "but Frank, think about this: you have seen about 10 thousand people, who each affect 2000. That is 20 million people my friend. That is certainly world-class."

Frank Baler Finds T.H.

I did not know what to say to Santin. His math was correct, of course, and I had worked at the office with well over ten thousand people; but not only did I not feel accomplished and successful, I felt quite broken. Despite some really interesting experiences in the last years, I honestly still felt as if I had failed.

One thing excited me as I made quick notes during our phone conversation: I definitely heard Santin say that we would work together; that is all I cared about at the moment.

As usual, Santin was one step ahead of me:

"Can you be here tomorrow at 10AM?"

"Yes Sir," I said.

Despite taking many classes with Santin and being a huge fan of his, I had never been to his office. As usual, when it came to Santin, I was surprised when I got there.

The office was located at an outdoor mall, a couple of doors down from a coin laundry. The mall was clean and well kept, but absolutely spartan. The lobby to Santin's office was very small, with only four white plastic chairs in it. To my left, when I walked in, there was a brochure rack on the wall. I had seen all of those brochures over the years in classes and events where Santin either promoted or participated.

Frank Baler Finds T.H.

There was no secretary or receptionist, just a sign that asked me to sit and wait. At about 10:15 Santin himself walked out and greeted me warmly. There was no small talk beyond the warm greeting, just a sense of urgency, as if we had lots of important work to get done.

When I went through the door beyond the lobby into the office, I was even more surprised. There was a long and narrow hallway, narrower than building codes allowed, I thought. There was an open area to my right where a lady sat in front of a fancy computer with three large screens. On the wall opposite to the hallway there were a couple of shelves with books and more papers. The wall behind the lady was entirely covered with diplomas. I later stopped to look... Santin had diplomas in philosophy, engineering, medicine, theater, aviation, therapy, and others I could not see from the hallway. At the end of the hallway there were two small bathrooms, one of which was always locked. There were two small offices on either side of the hallway, and one larger office to the left. Santin explained that they ran group sessions and some advanced classes in there.

Interestingly, Santin gave me a little tour of the facility. I later learned that he did that often with his clients, and that there was a point to his method. The two offices on the right side of the hallway, as I walked in, were used by a

Frank Baler Finds T.H.

social worker and by Santin. The two small offices on the left were his paper office, and his 'assistant's'.

"I thought Claudia, in the front, was your assistant?" I said, asking.

"Claudia helps me with external communications, announcements, emails, client communications and appointments. She also processes payments, including my salary" he said, "and client's fees."

Then he knocked on the door of the last office on the left side of the hallway and, when invited, opened the door cautiously.

"Sorry to interrupt. Cassandra please meet Frank. We are starting today."

After the typical "hellos" he closed the door and explained to me:

"Cassandra is an investigator of sorts."

"Oh, you also have an investigation agency?" I asked puzzled.

"In a sense, but it is not a separate agency, it is part of therapy…" He must have realized how quizzical I looked, for he continued:

"Let's sit down, I will explain everything."

His office was very simple, no windows or bright lights. There were 3 chairs; I assumed the third was for a partner

Frank Baler Finds T.H.

when doing couple therapy. There was a small table by 'my' chair upon which there were plenty of sealed water bottles.

"We talk a lot in here, so we get thirsty... help yourself to the water" Santin said, then he got right into it.

"In the past, we sometimes call this ancient therapy, we allowed clients to talk endlessly about very little of true significance, presumably until they figured out what needed to change in their lives. We are much more sophisticated nowadays," He continued.

"We need to differentiate between a problem with your perception of reality from a problem with your ability to respond to your reality, as it is, and to create what you want."

"Wow," I said truly astonished. "I have struggled with that very issue often with clients. Sometimes we end up in a confrontation and derail the therapeutic bond when it seems that the client's perception of reality is not accurate."

"Yes, that is a big problem," Santin said, "Because we must treat each category of problem differently." Then he said: "We solved that problem here."

"Professor," I asked, "how do you differentiate a perceptual from a response-ability problem?"

"Simple," He answered plainly. "Cassandra investigates everything, I mean everything. We have an objective picture of the client's life that is based on facts. The extent to which his descriptions match the facts is the extent to which he does not have a perceptual problem. Now, if you think of a spectrum, with misperception of reality on one end, and inability to respond and create on the other, we all fall somewhere in between. What we have here, however, is a precise determination of where each client falls on that spectrum." Then he paused, as if waiting for me to 'get it' and continued: "then we target the intervention to the actual category of problem."

"Isn't this 'investigation' a bit too invasive, from a therapeutic point of view?" I asked.

"Frank, we stopped apologizing for the invasiveness of our processes a long time ago. People who come here want and expect results; they pay top money for a personal transformation…" Then he added, almost as an afterthought, perhaps trying to make it easier for me to understand:

"Physical surgery is highly invasive; surgeons cut into the person's body, inject chemicals into their blood, take out and put in parts… nothing could be more invasive, right? Yet people subject themselves to surgery, both for medical and for cosmetic reasons all the time. People get surgery because they want results; invasion is a part of the process." Then he paused for a while, looking down. Eventually he continued when I did not fill in the silence with another question.

Frank Baler Finds T.H.

"And as long as I am comparing therapy to surgery, let me tell you about side effects. Any surgery brings with it side-effects, pain, discomfort and even temporary incapacitation during recovery; right? I have no idea where this modern crop of therapists got the idea that therapy should be free of side effects or discomfort." He was a bit louder now, and somewhat inflamed.

"This is why people quit therapy and complain that it did not work. They go see therapists who do not understand the transformational process themselves. These therapists are really afraid of not securing the paying client, so they offer what people want to hear: comfort, and lack of pain. They cannot possibly deliver on that promise because there is no such a thing. So, when the client feels the pain of transformation, they assume they failed the process, which, after all was not supposed to hurt according to their therapist." He would not stop now, and I did not dare to interrupt him.

"The real tragedy here is that these folks quit the transformation process thinking that they failed, when in reality, their therapists failed them for lack of understanding, and to a certain extent, dishonesty." I inhaled as if to ask a question, but he continued talking.

Frank Baler Finds T.H.

"Frank, you have had surgeries, we know that. You had those surgeries because you needed changes. There was pain and discomfort, but you got great results eventually."

That was true. I had been very public about the two surgeries I had had: a bilateral inguinal hernia repair in 2013 and an appendectomy in 2015. Both conditions were very painful and were completely resolved through the surgical intervention.

He was on again. "Right now, you are in more pain than you were before those surgeries… and you are about to go through a process that may be very uncomfortable, but it will lead you to joy." Then he leaned out of his chair, got close to my face, and, looking deep into my soul, said:

"I do not promise comfort. I promise results. I will not hurt you, but you may hurt enormously during the process. There will be no stones left unturned, nothing is off the table… there will be no secrets left once we are done. And, as you already know, we do it my way." After what I thought was a strategic pause, he asked me: "Are you in or out?"

"All in Sir," I said firmly.

"Come back in the morning, 10 AM." He responded.

As was his style, Santin got right into it the next morning.

Frank Baler Finds T.H.

"Working with you is a bit different than with the typical person who comes here, because there is a ton of public information about you. We have a very good idea of your life and of how you see it. What we needed was a better understanding of Liaran's life, as it intersected with yours. Cassandra has been doing her magic, and by now we have a pretty clear idea of who that person is."

Santin made it obvious that it was not my turn to talk; he was laying out the foundation for what was about to come, which I had no idea of.

"Liaran has a strong background in black magic. We found evidence of their involvement in black magic going back three generations. We also found incontrovertible evidence that she meant for you to die." Finally, he asked me a question:

"Why do you think you did not die physically, when so much energy was invested in taking you out?"

"Gosh I do not know," I said. "I certainly felt like disappearing for a long time."

"That is because Liaran is nothing more than a peon in a much greater game, a game she does not know of, even though she is a player in it. That game is God's plan for your life."

Frank Baler Finds T.H.

By then in my journey, I had examined the events and symbolism so many times that I had learned to stay quiet when hearing these interpretations of my life. Suddenly I felt as though I was with John and his wife, only version 2.0 of that experience. Instead of crying and being irrational, however, this time I was introspective and reverent of a process that is much bigger than 'I' or 'my' life.

As Santin continued, giving me just enough time to digest what he was saying, but not enough to add my own inner chatter into the mix, I thought of how relentless and even voracious, he really was. 'Not one second is wasted here,' I noted to myself as I felt determined to be more like him in my own sessions with clients.

"Frank," he said, "we found videos of you and pieces written by you explaining how, since when you first met Liaran, you thought you were soul-mates for life. You have said that you never questioned that idea, even while she was beating you up and saying how much she hated you. Is this true?"

"Santin," I said slowly, "This was a long time ago. I have just had an exhausting and exhilarating year. I really do not remember much about that woman, other than that several experts who know her told me that she is a psychopath."

Frank Baler Finds T.H.

"Hold it," Santin said quite seriously. "Remember we agreed to do it my way… when I ask you a question, you do not dodge it… you focus on the question and give me your highest truth. Last time I ask you Frank, are you in or out?"

This man was not kidding! I thought of myself as a tough therapist who got great results with my clients, but this felt a little over the top. I never imagined that a therapeutic style which felt harsh and abrasive, almost confrontational, could possibly be effective. Just then I remembered that I had found a 'problem' with all my previous therapists, and that I knew this man was effective, even if his style felt harsh at times. I decided to yield to his firmness and focus on his question. I jumped right back in:

"That is right Santin, I first met Liaran when a trainer said that a new member would be joining the gym, and that she was pregnant. I had not seen Liaran at that point, but I got the distinct and strong impression that she and I would be together for life, as soulmates forever. Our relationship turned out to be horrible from day one, literally. Liaran lied, no exaggeration, about everything, all the time. At first, she was violent with herself, hitting herself, and hitting her head on the wall. I still have those videos… saddest thing I ever saw. Then she turned violent toward me, beating me up like a man, viciously, while saying she hated me. No matter what she did, though, it never occurred to me, not once, to leave her. So yes, I continued, I am an idiot, if that is what you are driving at."

"Save the drama for your books Frank. We need you to focus on this, for this is important. Notice that, according to you, no matter what she did, you did not feel broken. You have said publicly how, even after you left her, you were not broken, and you still thought she would get over her misunderstandings and you would be together forever. True?"

"Yes Sir." I was determined to let him lead even if I had no idea what he was doing.

"When did you feel broken Frank? At what point?"

How weird, I thought. All this time, all this analysis, and I never did with myself what I did with every client at the office: I had never pinpointed exactly the moment when something snapped within me. For the first time in our session, I realized that Santin might be on to something important; something which has nothing to do with that person. I asked for a moment to think back, but nothing came to mind. Santin asked me to close my eyes, imagine myself unbroken back then, then broken.

"Focus on a particular moment, a specific event, when you feel unbroken."

Frank Baler Finds T.H.

"Got it," I said, as I imagined myself reading a book at the office the night I left her house.

"Now focus on a moment, an event, when you do feel broken." That was easy, I thought as I imagined myself driving to the courthouse one of the several times I had to go there.

Santin then guided me through what we refer to as a pinpointing technique. We imagine a timeline bounded by the two specific events the client remembers: feeling not broken on the left, and feeling broken on the right. We then ask the client to imagine the next event they can remember, after the original when they did not feel broken yet. Once the client focuses on something, such as me going to sleep at the office that night, after reading a book, we ask them to focus on something prior to the event when they felt broken. In my case I remembered stopping at a coffee shop for coffee prior to driving to the courthouse that morning. We continue this process as many times as it takes until the client 'sees' exactly when the rupture occurred. Eventually I said:

"Yes, I have it." I said. "It was when I received a warrant for my arrest for not showing up to court. Liaran had concealed the court-appearance notice from me, which was mailed to her house, then told the Judge that I was skipping court."

Frank Baler Finds T.H.

"Let's see what is underneath that event" Santin said.

The student in me was fascinated with what Santin was doing. He was using the inciting event as a marker that told us where to dig; underneath that event there was an emotion, an interpretation. The event was only relevant to the extent that it pointed us to a location where to dig for the emotion. The emotion was not important either, I later learned. The emotion itself was a portal through which I would find joy eventually.

"What did you feel when you read the warrant?" Santin asked

"In one moment, I understood how she had meticulously planned my destruction. It was not that I was not a good man, as she said, who needed to improve. No, she actually meant to destroy me. She planned and executed a detailed plan with one focus only!" I was being a bit loud now.

"Yes, that is what you concluded, but what did you feel?" Santin never missed a beat. He was sharp, I could sense, even while going through my personal agony!

The corners of my mouth trembled. No tears, no emotion, really. The words just would not come out. Then Santin tapped on my forehead as he commanded "Talk!"

"You are the devil," I said softly as I imagined that person in front of me. "You are vile, putrid, malignant and

Frank Baler Finds T.H.

repulsive." I now recognized the veracity of that conclusion in a completely dispassionate way. It simply is the case that this person took the time and energy to plan and attempt my destruction, instead of breaking up with me if she was not happy. For the first time I felt a hint of compassion for a person who is profoundly damaged as Dr. Scott Peck says in his famous book 'People of the Lie'.

"That a boy!" Santin said almost shouting, and I thought, triumphantly. As usual he continued without missing a beat:

"And what was your life like the year prior to the separation?"

"At home?" I asked.

"All things considered," He clarified.

"At home it was terrible, I would stay late at the office to avoid being near her as much as possible, except for a very intense sexual relationship. At work, which includes my mystical life," I continued "I was at the top of my game. Classes were awesome, according to other teachers and to students, and the sessions were powerful. Demand for my services was at an all-time high, income was the highest ever, and results were extraordinary. I had requested a High Initiation and had received the first two installments of it already. I eagerly awaited the conclusion of that Initiation, as I feverishly prepared to receive it."

Frank Baler Finds T.H.

"So," Santin asked simply, "At the top of your game, in the midst of a High Initiation, you feel spiritually pulled toward the devil? Does this sum it up?" He insisted.

"I never thought of it that way…" I responded.

"Think now dam it!" He did shout. "I did not ask if you thought of it that way before, I am asking for you to think now and tell me if that sums it up!" Then he repeated his assertion that in the midst of a High Initiation I felt spiritually pulled toward the devil.

"I don't know Santin… it is almost…"

"Talk!" He shouted as he slapped my forehead again.

"Yes!" I now shouted. "But…"

"That is enough!" Santin said while tapping my hand, interrupting my explanation and justification. "Open your eyes and look at me!" He said in a firm yet loving voice.

We both had some water in silence. I had no idea what to do with what I had said. To a large extent, I felt somewhat induced to conclude what I had said. Most prominently, the whole thing embarrassed me for some reason I could not understand. As usual, Santin was one step ahead of me.

"Why the discomfort with your conclusion, you think?" This was how he broke the silence. By now I knew better than being evasive and unclear with Santin, so I blurted it out, unedited:

Frank Baler Finds T.H.

"I cannot help but to think of Jesus being led by the Spirit into the desert to face the devil after his baptism." I said referring to a Biblical passage. "And in this business of mysticism," I continued, "any allusion to Jesus, or comparison between us and Jesus seems so cliché to me... To be honest, I am a bit embarrassed to even have thought of this passage in this context."

"And what was the lesson you learned from John... what was he again? An astrologer?"

"That was a long time ago Santin, we discussed superpowers and lessons hidden in the stories of Biblical characters."

"Not what you discussed, or how long ago it was!" He said sternly again. "I asked what the lesson was."

"The lesson was that, within the stories in the Bible, there is a thread that runs from cover to cover, laying out the Mystical Path precisely. There are many other stories and themes in the Bible," I continued, "but if you read carefully, you will see the Mystical Path clearly spelled out, one Initiation at a time, from involution to evolution, with consequences both for passing and for failing each Initiation. Ultimately, the Bible is a love story, the story of God's love for humanity, and how we can receive that unending love."

"Well said professor!" Santin said with an air of satisfaction. Then he added: "Tomorrow, same time."

When I walked in the next day, Santin got straight into it:

"I spoke to John yesterday afternoon. He told me you guys discussed the Initiations you would receive leading up to, and preparing you for, the High Initiation. Also, Cassandra did her thing, and told me that you had quite a busy past several months. She told me about several trips. How many initiations did you have so far?"

"Well, we discussed how several characters in the Bible hid a lesson that we all needed to learn. John and Priscilla explained to me how learning each lesson viscerally, not just intellectually, was akin to awakening a superpower. I never understood that learning a lesson was the same thing as receiving an Initiation."

"That is because of how you define 'learning'" Santin interjected seamlessly. "There are several levels of learning, the highest is through an experience that impresses the lesson upon your Inner Self in such way that the idea becomes second nature to you. An Initiation is a lesson learned, but at a much deeper level than what would be possible through the intellectual awareness of an idea." Santin explained.

Frank Baler Finds T.H.

"Okay, I see that, I said. Based on this new understanding of 'learning', I know I received the first Initiation, the one where I had to choose what was most important to me. I knew that I could have preserved my family by giving up on the Path, but I chose the Path so I walked out on the woman."

"Nothing else is possible on the Path if God is not number one, viscerally, not just in words, for a person. That has to be tested and proven in the most dramatic way possible." Then he added "there can be no doubt about this prior to proceeding on the Path."

"I am quite clear on that point," I said plainly.

"You had an experience with the Assembly of Masters. What was important about that, in terms of the Path?"

"Well, up until then I had been convinced that I had failed out of the Path because of how devastated I had felt. A true mystic, I thought at the time, would not have been affected by whatever happened then." Santin did not interrupt me, so I continued. "Once I met with the Masters, I understood that the feeling of failure only reflected the incompletion of the story. I compared what I was going through to Joseph's life while he was in jail; that was not the end of the story. Understanding that I was experiencing a dark point along my journey, but that the journey had a Glorious end, not only made it clear to me that I had not failed out of the Path, but also that God's plan is always perfect, even if we do not understand it."

"What was the consequence of that understanding Frank?" He asked.

"Trust, absolute trust that our lives are being guided and provided for by an intelligence vastly superior to our own." That was all I said.

"Interesting," Santin said, "and I am sure you noticed that absolute trust in divine providence is what actually unleashes it upon you?" I was not sure if that had been a question or a statement, but I nodded. Later, when taking notes about that session I wrote about not always practicing that absolute trust in divine providence. 'I have a long way to go' I noted on my journal.

Santin continued asking me about other significant experiences I had since the encounter with the Masters. I mentioned meeting a strange man in the desert who seemed to know all about me.

"What was significant about that encounter?" Santin asked?

"That man taught me to rescue my true self from the oppression of my mental drama and programming. In many ways the outer shell had indeed to die in order to liberate the Inner Light within."

Frank Baler Finds T.H.

"Do you see now why the previous two Initiations are absolutely necessary before you can face this one?" He asked. "Not sure…" I answered.

"Frank, if God is not number one to a person, there will not be absolute trust in the perfection of God's plan or in divine providence. Without that absolute trust, when the outer shell is peeled off, we would fight to preserve it, instead of letting it go. Without the first two Initiations, we would become our own enemy during the third. Do you see that?"

"Our own enemy - as in fighting to prevent our progress on the Path – fighting to protect the outer shell…?"

"Yes," Santin said, "that is the only sense in which the concept of enemy exists… the enemy is that which opposes your progress."

Santin said that last sentence but kept a gaze of expectation upon me. I felt that he wanted me to make a logical leap forward and advance the dialogue toward a Higher Truth. I hesitated, not quite knowing if it was my turn to speak, but eventually said:

"It is paradoxical to think of that which opposes our progress as the enemy, since it is overcoming the enemy that we become stronger and better, thus actually advancing on the Path." He kept looking at me with the hint of a smile, I

Frank Baler Finds T.H.

thought, so I continued. "The worse the enemy, the more they help us, the more they serve us." Then I got a bit somber for the first time in a while, adding: "What a difficult job they do, the sons of darkness. They work hard to help us progress and are often despised and scorned by so many… how sad."

"Yes my friend, you are no longer a neophyte, you have earned your place among the Seekers. You overcame huge opposition to your progress, you literally brought yourself back from a very deep hole, and you came out feeling compassion and sympathy, not contempt, for the sons of darkness who, unbeknownst to them, work for you." Then he added unceremoniously:

"Come back in the morning, at 9."

When I arrived the next morning Claudia offered me Cuban coffee, an important tradition in Miami. Cuban coffee is an expresso, very concentrated coffee, with lots of sugar. Part of the tradition in Miami regarding the coffee ritual is that you always accept it from a friend when offered. When Claudia poured my tiny cup, it came with *espumita*, that all important froth that defines high quality Cuban coffee. "Delicious" I said as I thanked Claudia.

Frank Baler Finds T.H.

Soon Santin was in front of me, as intense as ever. This man seemed to have endless energy and enthusiasm. Santin started seeing clients at the office at 9AM and typically worked until midnight. None of us understood how this man could do what he did.

"Cassandra tells me that you had four trips soon after meeting the man in the desert. What was that about?"

I had to think about that for a moment. I had been on several trips after the New Mexico trip, but I needed a moment to bring the details of each to the forefront of my awareness. Eventually I started recalling:

"Yes, there was a strange seminar called TSL, short for 'Though Shall Live'. Everyone there had lost touch with life somehow. Then I participated in a Sweat Lodge ritual… both of those were in Florida. Soon after the Sweat Lodge I went to a Conclave on Magic in California, and finally a very strange ritual in the middle of a jungle in Brazil."

"And what did you get from those?" Santin asked.

"Each of those experiences was very complex. Do you want me to describe each?"

"No." Santin said. "You need to tell me what the 4 experiences meant on your Path, as a whole."

I was fascinated by every word this man uttered. It was difficult to take my student's hat off. I noted how I had asked him whether 'he wanted' me to describe the experiences and he did not reply with what 'he wanted'. Instead, he said what 'I needed' to do, not what he wanted me to do. Santin was impeccable.

"What they meant as a whole…" I uttered. "I suppose you mean for me to look at the four experiences together, as if the four of them produced one single effect within me?"

"Yes." He said economically.

"One way I can do that" I reasoned aloud, "is to look at my state prior to the four experiences in question, and after them." I thought about it for a moment, then continued the reasoning. "The major experience prior to the four trips was encountering that man in the desert. My task there was to liberate the Inner Self from the clutches of my own mental structures." Then I thought about the second trip to Brazil, right after the one when I was asked to fight that man. That was when the woman who had apparently died, came back to life.

At some point I closed my eyes and imagined both situations: feeling quite broken at the desert and meeting a man who began to teach me to find myself, and witnessing a woman apparently come back to life. I thought of those two points on my journey as points 'A' and 'B', then I imagined what it would take to get a man from one to the other.

Frank Baler Finds T.H.

"These two experiences are worlds apart," I said softly.

"They are." Santin said simply. Then he continued "In as few words as possible, tell me the net result of each of the four experiences... let's call them 'bridge Initiations'.

"Ahhh," I started slowly "I regained the will the live; let go of grudge; gave up the notion that I was good, and by extension, much of the illusion of duality dissolved; and found the fighting spirit within me... oh, and who the true enemy really is."

I opened my eyes and saw Santin smiling softly. Somehow, I felt approval from the teacher, but I was not sure what the merit was. Santin explained:

"The difference between man 'A' and man 'B' is what you said above: man 'B' wants to live, has no grudge, is not distracted by illusions of duality, and he is a warrior who knows his enemy."

"Of course," I just had a huge aha moment "that is why you lumped them together and called them 'bridge Initiations'... these smaller Initiations bridge the gap between the initial point, which is the famous mandate to 'know thyself' and the experience of life itself, such as what happened at that jungle in the Amazon."

Santin sat back on his chair, visibly relaxed and comfortable now. There was an air of triumph all over him.

I wanted to say something to him, but the words never came out.

"Santin, I…"

"Never mind that for now," He interrupted what was not coming out of my mouth, saving me the agony. Then he pressed forward "there is something else on your mind, much more technical… that is important. What is it?"

"Well" I said, mostly trying to focus on a question that felt hazy on my mind. "I can see how the process starts with the 'Know thyself' and culminates with the experience of life. I can see how these bridge Initiations close the gap between the two. But, are the bridge Initiations the same for everyone on the Path?"

The academic in Santin sat up and came forward.

"First of all," he started, "the experience of life, as you call it when the woman came back to life, is not the culmination of the Path. It is a very important milestone, but not the culmination. Having said that, the bridge Initiations are very similar for all those on a Path similar to the one you are on." Then he added "not everyone breaks down on their way to Illumination, and those who do not break down rarely lose the will to live, thus that Initiation would not make sense to them."

Frank Baler Finds T.H.

Santin said so much right there; I had so many questions, that I did not know where to start. I felt fortunate that Santin was conceding to a Q&A session with me, so I did my best to focus on what I remembered him saying. Then I started:

"Santin, did I hear you say that a woman coming back to life is not the culmination on the Path?"

"Apparently you heard it because you are asking the question," he said. "And yes, I did say that. Correct" He emphasized. I must have looked quite puzzled because he continued.

"Cassandra told me that you were at the event in Edinburg. What was that about?"

"The end, death," I said.

Santin's logic was simple yet irrefutable, I was noticing.

"Pay attention to the sequence of events Frank. You went to California to let go of the illusion of duality, right?"

"Right" I said. "Okay." He said, "Then you experienced life, true?" "True," I said. "Right after that you experienced death, ah?" "Yah," I said. "Life and death are polar opposites?" Not sure if that was a question or a statement, I simply nodded. "Experiencing polarity after learning that polarity itself is an illusion should indicate to you that neither pole can possibly be a culmination of the Path."

Frank Baler Finds T.H.

I was flabbergasted. My mind was racing. I was agitated. Fidgeting on the chair. Something was definitely brewing within me. By then I knew better than allowing the agitation to take a hold of me, though, so I took several deep full breaths, and drank some water. Then I leaned back on my chair and did my best to relax. Then images started flowing through my mind.

John and his wife were on my mind. I remembered the notion that Biblical stories reveal the Mystical Path; then I recalled several Biblical passages where Jesus brought back to life people who were apparently dead. Then Jesus supposedly died, then came back to life.

Many people, I thought, consider the resurrection to be the culmination of the story of Jesus, but clearly that cannot be the case. One man surviving death, then disappearing again, cannot be the great mystery behind that story. That much was clear. Then another question burned in my mind, so I asked before it would flee:

"Santin, we started off talking about bridge Initiations. I asked if they are the same for everyone, you said that they are very similar for all those on a Path similar to the one I am on. How many Paths are there to Illumination?"

Frank Baler Finds T.H.

"There are many Paths," He answered as naturally as if we had been talking about drinking a glass of water. "But they all fall into one of three categories."

He definitely had my attention at that point. I said nothing, so he continued.

"The intellectual, faith, and devotion, also known as service."

"Faith?" I was shocked, and the tone of my voice showed it. "You mean as in religion?" I must have grimaced when pronouncing the word 'religion', for Santin smiled.

"Most definitely, because the common denominator among all three main Pathways is sincerity, but a selfless sincerity."

At that point I remembered my Mentor on the Path always emphasizing the importance of being a sincere Seeker, not for oneself, but to share more Light with others. Wow, I thought, it was all making sense now. All dots were connecting.

"Are these three Paths equivalent?" I asked that question, but it felt as though one million other questions lurked in my mind at the same time.

"Those on each Path end up erecting temples that must be destroyed before Illumination can happen. Temples are

Frank Baler Finds T.H.

artificial constructs upon which we place our lives... for instance," - he must have noticed my confusion, - "the intellectual idolizes his mind. His mind becomes a god to him, a temple of sorts. Destroying the temple, since you seem to like Biblical metaphors, means to break down the mind. The side effect is the loss of will to live in this world. Do you recognize that?"

"Yeah... what about the religious and the devoted?" I asked trying to pick one question out of so many.

"They experience crisis as well, but slightly different ones. The religious will battle the devil, since, unbeknownst to him, the devil is at the forefront of the religious process."

"What?" I almost jumped.

"Isn't religiosity about overcoming darkness or the devil? Didn't your Jesus fight the devil?"

"Well, now that you say that... but I never thought of him as 'my' Jesus." I was not sure if I was becoming more clear, or more confused, but there were more questions on my mind. Santin, again, jumped right in:

"And since you asked, the devoted to service, to himself or to others, will have to battle disillusionment. They will inevitably arrive at the idea that 'it was all for nothing', the sacrifice was 'not worth it', they will feel, in a sense, broken hearted."

Frank Baler Finds T.H.

"Going back then, life cannot be the culmination to the Path, just as death cannot be either, because they are polar opposites, and polarity is an illusion of perception?"

"Yes," Santin concurred. "We perceive reality through the lens of duality, notice we have two eyes, two ears, two nostrils, two hands and two main regions on the tongue. But Frank, do not confuse your perception of reality, with reality itself."

"So, reality is unipolar, or singular, while the perception of reality is dual?" I was either getting it or thinking that I was getting it.

"Yes, ultimate reality is singular. In religion they say there is one God; God being the ultimate reality. In kabballah they also show the top sefirot as singular."

I was mesmerized, I suppose. I had learned these ideas over the years, but I had never connected the dots. Now it was all making sense to me at a much higher level. Santin seemed to always be one step ahead of me; at least it felt that way to me when he suggested:

"How about you answer your true question now…"

"About the culmination?" I said tentatively.

"Yes, what must the culmination on the path look like? What obvious element must be present?"

"Well… singularity, in some way?"

Frank Baler Finds T.H.

"Come back in three days, 9AM."

That was the unceremonial end to an extremely intense, I would say extraordinary, session. Just like that. I was beginning to see a pattern in Santin's work style. The sessions did not seem to be timed, he did not wear a watch, and there was no clock that I could see in his office. Whenever he felt that a major point had been made, he would interrupt the session and tell me when to come back... he never asked.

When I left Santin's office I realized I was late for a session at my office. On my way to the office, I called the answering service to listen to messages. Except for when I went to the radio or television as a guest, and offered a gift to callers, we would average between seven and nine calls a day at the office. There were three types of calls: someone just asking questions about therapy, someone ready to start therapy, or a client in need of changing an appointment. The urgent type of call was the third, because, if a client was not coming to a session, I had some extra time to get ready for the following session, or I could offer someone else the time.

That morning I had no change of appointment calls, so I called the first client of the day and warned him that I was running a few minutes late. The second client was already waiting for me when I finished the first session, but I had 15

Frank Baler Finds T.H.

minutes before starting the third session of the day. With a full 15 minutes to spare, my priority was to have some Cuban coffee, frothy, but no sugar. Then I went back to the office and took cryptic notes for a few minutes.

It was not until after my last class that night that I sat down, relaxed, to take some detailed notes on the session with Santin that morning. By then it was about 11:30PM, but the morning notes, and a whole day hypnotizing clients, made it easy to fill in details.

When I sat in front of Santin next, he surprised me yet again. I was sure the session would be about Jesus or about Illumination. Instead, he asked me to describe what surprised me the most about the end of the relationship with Liaran.

I was taken aback by the question, and the change of pace from the previous session. Furthermore, to be frank, by then, I hardly thought of that woman. Of course, because of her crimes, I had detailed notes on what she did, but just as several people had told me the year before, she passed into oblivion and became irrelevant to me.

"Santin, I am surprised that I can hardly find memories of her within me… she is gone." I said.

"Not what surprises you now. I asked you what surprised you about the breakup then." The student in me could not

Frank Baler Finds T.H.

help but to notice how often we respond to a question without answering it. But Santin was patient and loving, he simply clarified and repeated the question.

I had to close my eyes and think back for a moment. Then I remembered:

"Santin, what surprised me at the time was how surprised I felt. We never said goodbye, there was no breakup talk. She refused to talk to me on Thanksgiving Day, as she did often and particularly on thanksgiving holidays. I went to sleep at the office, as I often did when she gave me the silent treatment. After I left, she called the police and accused me of violence, as she had done about a dozen times before, unbeknownst to me at the time. Dozens of cops had been to the house, they took pictures and videos, and not one shred of evidence that I ever touched her inappropriately was ever found. All the pictures the cops ever took were of my wounds and bruises when she would assault me violently, objects she broke, and my clothes thrown on the front yard by Liaran. She filed twelve false police reports. Yet, the cops never arrested her."

"Frank, the ineptitude of the police to deal with domestic issues was not what surprised you," Santin tried to interrupt my rant.

Frank Baler Finds T.H.

"Yes, they are inept at domestic issues for sure. I later learned that most cops who get hurt do so during domestic calls. Clearly, they are not trained to handle domestic issues."

"Frank," Santin said, "What really surprised you?" He refocused me a second time.

"Yes, of course," I said. "What surprised me was that we made passionate love the morning I went to sleep at the office. It surprised me that she was so verbal and caloric in our daily love-making sessions. It surprised me that she would ask me to make sure we were together the following lifetime... all that crap while planning my destruction and building a relationship with someone else. That really surprised me."

"Did you ever think of leaving her?" Santin asked.

"Santin, this woman is crazy. Yes... No..." About now I was feeling a bit crazy myself. "Well, I left her twelve times following epic fights that made no sense to me. But she would ask me back and offer lots of great sex, nothing else. I thought we were soulmates and interpreted the sexual activity to mean love... Santin, that was the worst period of my life... she was crazy." I was agitated all over again. After a few deep breaths and some water, I recognized the PTSD signs and made a mental note to myself. "It was horrible man; you have no idea." Is all I could conclude.

"Remember the conversation about perception of reality being possibly broken?" Santin asked me referring to the first time I came to his office. "Cassandra is good at what she does. Your perception is not faulty on this. We found evidence that Liaran is a malignant narcissist, most likely a psychopath, the kind that gets away with murder for a while because they are experts at feigning victimhood, they modulate their behavior in order to appear calm and rational, they are definitely intelligent and typically successful at work. The term people are using nowadays is 'integrated psychopath' referring to their ability to integrate successfully into our society while doing atrocious things under the radar. Cassandra also found records of several cancer surgeries, abortions, and cosmetic surgeries. Liaran definitely uses her version of black magic, participates in such rituals, and even posts pictures of herself in social media sporting ritualistic regalia. We have plenty of evidence for all of that, so we know your perception is not faulty. But notice" He continued pressing "that you have not told me what surprised you about the breakup."

"That!" I blurted out loudly. "The breakup itself, I had no idea she wanted out, I had no idea she was with someone

Frank Baler Finds T.H.

else, I had no idea she was planning my destruction. She kept blaming me for little details, so I was busy and caught up in trying to fix little details while she blindsided me with the breakup. I was working hard so she could stop working and raise the baby, that was our plan. Meanwhile, I later learned, she was working on a promotion at work. It was all a lie man; you have no idea…" I was getting agitated again.

"And the breakup was not a simple, 'please leave, I no longer wish to be with you'" I was all over the place, ideas flowing in a disorganized way, as they often flow when a person is expressing emotions without the filter of reason, without editing them, without self-censorship.

"No," I continued. "The breakup was a full assault on my life, including almost running me over with her car, and accusing me of crimes I did not commit." I would not stop… "We discussed her intense hatred toward me, but you know my view on hatred as form of mental illness. I guess I really thought I could cure her!"

"Okay," Santin summed it up for me with no emotions, "the breakup surprised you because you had an intense love life filled with promises of love forever more, then you learned that she had been secretly planning your destruction with the police and dating someone else. Right?"

Frank Baler Finds T.H.

"Right?" Now it was my turn, I was not sure if I was agreeing with Santin or asking him a question.

"Wrong." He said that with a fierce intensity, then he added "You have to dig deeper… Now!" That was a shout. He said 'now' loudly as he approached me, and tapped on my forehead, this time whispering softly "Let go and sleep, deep relax, now… that is right, let go… deep sleep… deeper even… ten times deeper than ever before… that is right…"

Again, I was flying like an eagle well above the turbulence of daily living. It was quiet and peaceful up there. I felt safe… and I felt something else… something that I always felt when in deep hypnosis or meditation… something powerful and gratifying, yet something that I could not put my finger on. This time I found out what it was.

"How does it feel?" Santin asked.

"Awesome, safe, quiet, peaceful… but there is something else… awesome, but I do not know what it is."

"An image forms… See the something else… tell me what the something else is." Santin's voice was quiet and soft. I couldn't help but to notice how awesome he was as a hypnotist… the suggestions were simple, short, non-intrusive… easy somehow, I felt. Suddenly an image formed in my mind, then I got it!

Frank Baler Finds T.H.

The image was that of the god personified in the fresco at the Sistine Chapel's ceiling, essentially a large healthy man, with a long white beard. He stood behind me, encouraged me to go on with my life, explore and experience whatever I wanted to, and stood in the near background ready to take care of any problems I created… as a loving father would for a son he loves.

"I feel absolutely provided for!" I said triumphantly. "Now I get the divine providence thing. God provides me with whatever experience I need or want and takes care of my mistakes… always pushing me forward lovingly. No judgements, just pure love, acceptance, and total providence. Like a loving father…"

I felt soft tears of joy running down my cheeks, but I was too enthralled by the feeling to care about wiping my face. Santin, as usual pushed forward relentlessly.

"Bask in that feeling… stay with it. From within that feeling of total providence recognize that you have felt such deep joy and Light before, in relation to the surprise we were just talking about."

The thing with proper hypnosis is that the subconscious mind of the operator melds with that of the subject. At some point, in true mystical hypnotherapy, it becomes impossible to know whether the subject is responding to the operator's

Frank Baler Finds T.H.

suggestions, or if the operator is responding to the images formed in the subject's mind with suggestions to express them.

As I was listening to Santin's voice in the distance, two images were forming on my mind. One image was of me, at my praying table, with two candles and a mirror, sometimes tarot cards in hand, for I did that each time Liaran and I had a problem, which was often.

I would attempt to merge with her soul, mystically speaking, almost as if to 'explain to her' our troubles away. I would seek God's intervention and help, for I really wanted to have a good marriage and family. I also incessantly inquired of myself on my errors during those 'sessions'. What 'corrections' must I make, I would ask of myself. I always found plenty of behaviors and sentiments that needed to improve or to be completely changed, but one answer would jump at me, each time: *forgive.*

Those 'sessions' always ended with the experience of pure Light and love. When we met, Liaran had told me that she was the reincarnation of Blavatsky. I would never joke with something like that, and I would never say something like that unless I were totally certain of it. So, I believed her. Then she told me that my Master, who had just left the physical realm, appeared to her in a dream and told her to

Frank Baler Finds T.H.

marry me. I had not yet been in contact with my Master, and she had! I was enthralled and mystified by her. I experienced Light during my moments of deep inquiry, coupled with her assertion that she was the reincarnation of a notorious mystic, and she was in psychic contact with my Mentor! I concluded that the Light I experienced during those deep meditations emanated from her; or that it was about her somehow.

"Yah," I said, "what she did during and after our relationship is the opposite of the Light I experienced during those sessions. You are right," I continued, "what really surprised me was how wrong I had been about who she really is."

"Relax deeper..." Santin said. "It is common for therapists to want to heal their significant others... that is how they express their love, toward their mates and clients. But the desire to heal, itself, what we call *furor curandi*, is the key we were looking for. The presence of *furor curandi* within you toward a psychopath... what does it tell you, about you?"

What happened next amazed me. I cannot tell if my mind was responding to some hypnotic suggestion I had consciously missed, or if my being was answering the question in the most impressive of ways. I experienced the same Light I frequently did at my praying table when inquiring about Liaran, except that this time, the existence of the mirror, which was an integral part of the experience, came to mind. I had been looking into the mirror all that time, thinking that I had been looking at someone else.

Soft tears, with no crying, were flooding my closed eyes. Santin spoke again, in such a loving voice…

"It is common to repudiate psychopaths. When we see them with love, compassion and even feel like helping them, however, we are experiencing who we are at a deep, fundamental level." Then he continued. "Speaking of who you are, another image formed in your mind… what is it?"

The way in which Santin was offering my hypnotized mind suggestions with questions, or possibly experiencing the activity within my mind, was another example of that mind-meld experience common in deep hypnosis. This was important to me because it confirmed to me the depth of trance.

I saw Liaran and I sitting in the living room of our home weeks after she gave me a severe beating, while telling me she hated me, with the baby watching. I still have trouble 'seeing' that baby's eyes, watching her mother absolutely beat up a man while screaming wildly. That man, I, only pleaded with her to stop, nothing else. Liaran then called the

Frank Baler Finds T.H.

police and told them that I had hit her. The police photographed me covered in bruises, cuts, and beads of blood. My eyeglasses were broken. The police asked me what 'really happened' and I classically said I had slipped in the bathroom. They left. I left. Liaran drove 34 miles each way two days later to the Court House to get a restraining order against me. I never reached out or called her; never came by the house. So, one week later she came to get me, and asked me to come back, offering to remove the restraining order.

A few days after I came back to the house, we were sitting in the living room late one evening. The situation was eerie; I loved Liaran very much, but for the first time I recognized that she was profoundly mentally ill. Her mother and her childhood friend, also a coworker, Mavis, spoke to Liaran and encouraged her to seek professional help. Liaran talked that night with a coldness that was absolutely eerie.

At some point, I decided to ask Liaran for a few minutes in silence. Sitting right there at the living room, I inquired of my unconscious what was happening with her, and with us. Suddenly I felt the deepest pain I had ever known, I started panting heavily and eventually gasping for air. Sometimes we call that experience 'abreaction'. I had never known such intense pain before. When the emotions began to wane, the aftertaste was very clear: the feeling was of intense betrayal.

I assumed I had tapped into Liaran's past and discovered that she had been betrayed in the most horrible of ways. I felt deep compassion for her and asked her about that when I was able to talk, which took several minutes. Liaran told me that she felt betrayed by her first husband, but she said that in a very casual way. Furthermore, she and I had talked at length about that relationship, and, according to her, she had betrayed him. In fact, Liaran always expressed pride in telling me that Lesser, her first husband, was absolutely destroyed for three years after she had left him unexpectedly.

"Yes," Santin said. "Now you know… Did you tap into her past?"

"No," I said, "Not her past… my future."

"You are in good company," Santin said, "Other mystics have sweat blood when seeing their future. You are fine now, relax deeper and rest."

Somehow that last suggestion to 'rest' sunk deep into my subconscious mind. I really had never rested since my first daughter was born. I worked all the time, and I took care of so many people… I was always 'on', at night, weekends, and even during vacations.

Frank Baler Finds T.H.

I took Santin's suggestion to rest as permission to do so. Eventually I imagined that I was laying down on a cloud, high above the trials and tribulations of daily living. Above me, to my right, an image of my Mentor on the Path formed. He was smiling, as if saying 'well done... you are done for now'.

Santin asked me to take my time and come back to room awareness whenever I felt ready, then open my eyes. He offered me some water then said:

"Call me if you need anything else."

"Thank you so much," I said. Then I added "Blessings..." he walked out of the room, leaving the door open.

Frank Baler Finds T.H.

THE MOUNTAINTOP

---o---

The hours after I came back from Edinburg quickly turned into days, weeks and perhaps months; I am not sure. I lost awareness of time, or perhaps I no longer cared to pay attention to time, since I now knew it does not exist. Paradoxically, and mysteriously, without any effort or intention from me, I solved a long-standing problem I struggled with my whole life: punctuality.

I noticed that I spoke less, but that when I spoke people listened more. I did fewer therapy sessions, but they were more effective than ever before. Sleep continued to improve, and I started to dream again. Certainly, the highlight of that period had been the sessions with Santin, after which I

Frank Baler Finds T.H.

gained profound clarity on the purpose for the experiences of the past several years.

Eventually it happened. It was sudden and unexpected, yet certain and irretrievable. It was as if a contract had expired, it was time to let go of my position teaching mystical philosophy. I had been associated with the school for 29 years, about to turn 30, and a volunteer teacher there for 25 years. Suddenly it was all over. I was out of what was, to me, my life. Again.

A few days after leaving the School, I received an invitation by physical mail to attend a small conference in Colorado. In this conference they would honor authors who had made a contribution to other men.

Although I was honored to have been invited to speak at the Colorado conference for men, I really did not think I belonged on stage next to the other authors being honored who were true giants in the industry. There was no false humility there, I simply still felt only half alive, and not very productive.

When it was my turn to speak there were no notes or visual aids. I did not mention my name or discuss any of what I had done in the past. I simply told the attendants of the conference what I saw.

Frank Baler Finds T.H.

'The thing with broken bones, I said, is that you get a white cast. Everyone sees that you have a broken bone, and everyone helps you along. People treat you differently when you have a cast on your body. You have a broken bone, there is a white cast on it, and you deserve sympathy and special treatment while the bone heals.

There is no white cast for a broken heart though. Nobody sees that your heart is broken, therefore you get no special treatment or sympathy from anyone, anywhere. There is no disability payments and no insurance coverage for a broken heart.

If you announce to others how broken you feel, how devastated you are, people tell you either to get over it already, or to give it time. The truth is that the other person is equally or more hurt than you; they just learned to cover it up more effectively.

Most people walk around with a broken heart. Most human lives are about ways of medicating their hearts and numbing their minds to avoid embracing the devastating pain of a broken heart. Some people give it time and discover that time does not heal at all. Other people move on, only to discover that they bring their pain with them, which has a

Frank Baler Finds T.H.

nasty way of showing up in their future lives when it is least convenient.

When you hear of a major accident or illness right before an awesome vacation, the demise of a marriage to an affair right before the baby was born, or perhaps the scandal at the firm right before a major promotion, you are witnessing pain that was stored away in the unconscious mind coming back.

Other diseases, like diabetes, do not require a white cast, so no one would know if a person has it. There is a blood test for diabetes though. At least a person knows they have the condition and a treatment for it has been formulated.

There is no blood test or imaging study for a broken heart. We call it a broken heart, but we don't know what it is, how to identify it, and much less how to cure it. Yet, most people die of a broken heart, whether by deliberate choice or by a slow process characterized by self-neglect.

Deep pain that cannot be properly identified and that does not elicit sympathy from others causes us to feel that we have literally lost our minds. Those with a broken heart feel that they have gone mad, or that they have lost their minds.

In some ways, embracing the loss of the mind is the best way to heal a broken heart. When a person embraces the idea that their heart was broken because their minds ruled their

Frank Baler Finds T.H.

lives before, they can begin to take steps to build a new life; not to rebuild the old one, but to build a new life.

Tonight, my dear brothers and sisters, I invite you to look into your hearts. Leave your minds out of this conversation; scrap the logic, forget about time. Look into your heart and acknowledge to yourselves what it really feels like to be you right here and right now. Never mind what people would think if you totally bared your heart open; tell yourself what you would say if you dug deep into your heart and exposed all of it.'

I finished the talk describing a simple breathing exercise I used to expose my heart to myself. Then I got off the stage. There was total and complete silence in the room, only interrupted by quiet sobbing. Then I went to my hotel room.

"Is this Dr. Frank?" The man on the phone asked.
"Yes Sir it is, who is this please?"
"This is Dr. Woo. Am I disturbing you? "
"Dr. Woo, what a surprise… no this is no bother at all."
Dr. Woo was the event promoter, a full professor of robotics and engineering, and a man who enjoyed the highest respect and admiration from all he interacted with. I thought I was in trouble, of course. I felt like the principal was calling

me to announce my punishment. I figured we would get through this ordeal as quickly as possible, so I asked:

"How may I help, Dr. Woo?"

"Could you have an early dinner at my house tomorrow night?"

"Dr. Woo I would be most delighted, thank you so much... but my flight..."

I was embarrassed to tell Dr. Woo that I had a coach fare already paid to return home in the morning, and that I had no money to get another plane ticket. As luck would have it, Dr. Woo saved the moment:

"I will have Alice make sure your airline and the hotel know about the change in schedule. I will have a town car pick you up at 4. Is that all right?"

"Yes sir, thank you," I said.

"You are at the Four Seasons, right?" He asked.

"No sir, actually I am staying close by..."

"Don't worry, just text me the address. Good night Dr. Frank."

Well, I probably was not in trouble, I concluded, or else he would not have invited me to his home.

I pulled out my journal and took notes for a long time, including what I remembered having said at the conference. That night my last entry read:

Frank Baler Finds T.H.

'First reaction was still shame and fear, but I faced it quickly, head-on.'

Dr. Woo's house was gorgeous. One floor, circular driveway with a beautiful water fountain at the center of the circle. The double glass front door allowed unobstructed view to the pool in the back.

Once inside I was surprised. The huge living room was covered in a celestial blue thick carpet but had absolutely no furniture whatsoever. Dr. Woo said that they used that room for meditation and motioned me to a dining room to the left.

Standing by their chairs, as if waiting for me, were two women. When the four of us sat down, Dr. Woo introduced me to his wife, sitting across from me, and her mother sitting to her right and across from Dr. Woo who sat to my left. Food was already served at the center of the table.

Dr. Woo started telling me about his life:

"When I turned 40," he said, "I went to my country, we are from Laos, and presented myself to my guru. I had never had a girlfriend up until then, despite having come to America in my early 20's. My guru introduced me to my wife after analyzing all of our past lives and determining we are compatible."

"Wow," I said, "that is so inspiring!"

Frank Baler Finds T.H.

"My wife can talk to the guru without the telephone. They communicate by mind every night."

We ate mostly in silence after that. The food was vegan. There was no desert.

When we were all done eating, his wife invited me to follow her. I looked at Dr. Woo, as if asking for his approval.

"Go, go," he said.

The wife, whose name I never learned, led me to a bedroom in their house. This bedroom had wood floor and no furniture. The wife asked me to sit in front of the closet door, which was closed. She leaned on the wall toward my right and told me that it was possible to communicate mentally if you practiced meditation.

"Meditation, however," she said, "is hard. It takes many lifetimes to learn to meditate." I listened in silence, while she proceeded.

"You have meditated in your past life," she said. "You can communicate."

Then she opened the closet door.

Inside there was a small statue that I thought was of the buddha. I looked at it for a while. I must have entered a deep trance, I may have fallen asleep, or maybe I was unconscious for a moment, but eventually I had a strong feeling, a strong sensation, so strong it was that it felt as though someone was talking to me.

The sensation surprised me. The voice I heard was definitely that of a man, but it did not sound as Dr. Woo.

"Welcome home. Well done."

Then I sobbed soft tears. I was not hurting; I don't recall joy. I just shed tears, soft tears for a while; a long while with my eyes open staring nowhere in particular. Somehow, I knew what the voice meant: the search was over.

"Please join us for lunch tomorrow," Dr. Woo said. I had not noticed when he walked into the room or when his wife walked out. "The car will pick you up at 10, if that is okay with you."

"Thank you so much Dr. Woo," I said while I risked a small hug.

When the driver dropped me off at the motel I went for a long walk. There were no emotions, no human emotions within me, I just felt an infinite amount of energy in my body. It felt as though I could have walked around the entire earth without tiring. Something incredible had happened.

The fog in my brain, the most uncomfortable feeling I have ever experienced had lifted; just like that, it was gone. I was able to think clearly now. I saw how everything made sense in my life, how everything had gotten me to this

Frank Baler Finds T.H.

moment. More importantly, given who I was before, I cannot think of a better way to get me from who I was to who I had become.

I got back to the motel by about 9 that evening. I was not hungry. I just wanted to write. I wrote as much as I could about my life. I wrote as though I was writing a college paper on a fictional character. I felt that I needed to preserve memories from a life that was no longer my own. I wrote for hours, until I fell asleep.

When I got to Dr. Woo's house the next morning, at about 10:35, there were about twelve people or so sitting in a lotus position on his living room, apparently in deep meditation. Dr. Woo's wife seemed to be directing the meditation, because she sat in the front, facing the other twelve, all in deep silence. The entire house was completely quiet.

Dr. Woo's mother in law showed me to the same bedroom I had been in the day before and motioned me to sit down in front of the closet again. This time, however, there was a small cushion there.

The closet door was closed, as it had been the day before when I had come into the room. No big deal, I thought, I already knew what was in there; a small statue. I eventually relaxed and started thinking of my life. Somehow, I

Frank Baler Finds T.H.

remembered being given a book on mysticism at the age of eleven and having lived an entire life with a single focus of finding God somehow.

I thought of how unlikely so many events in my life were. I thought of the many people who had helped, intervened, and collaborated so well and perfectly for me to end up in this bedroom. The Cosmic, I thought, spent a lot of energy, used a lot of intelligence, to get me here. The plan was perfect, I concluded.

Just when I was about to see how the plan itself, with its perfection, is God, the door opened softly behind me. Dr. Woo's wife walked in as if she floated just above the floor. She knelt behind me, placed both hands on my shoulders softly, then asked:

"Are you ready?"

"I am." I said, knowing that I was, but having no idea for what.

She blindfolded me. Then I heard the closet door being opened. Then I heard her say:

"When I leave, you look."

I heard the bedroom door close behind me, so I removed the blindfold from my face. The closet door was now open.

Inside of the closet there was a mirror. Just a mirror.

Frank Baler Finds T.H.

At first, I smiled, then I thought of the movie *Circle of Iron*, then I thought of all the years meditating in front of a mirror, not quite understanding what I was doing.

Then my gaze became foggy. It seemed to me that I was seeing something else on the mirror; clearly, I was just imagining them. Many scenes of my life came to mind, or showed up on the mirror, particularly scenes I was extremely ashamed of.

After each scene I felt ashamed of, I remembered, or thought of, or saw, Shinhú on the mirror. It was as if Shinhú was there, with me, while those events were happening. It felt like he was not only watching, I felt as though he was protecting me and teaching me a lesson each time.

Scene after scene showed up on the mirror, always followed by Shinhú's loving eyes. Finally, I simply saw myself, broken, defeated, done. Shinhú showed up again, triumphant and glorious. Then I was back on the mirror. Then... the two images merged.

I almost jumped up startled. I felt a sudden ray of Light come into me and emanate from me at the same time. The sensation was of incredible expansion and connection with everyone and everything. My life had been perfect, just as it was, I concluded, because God's hand was always guiding it and protecting it.

Frank Baler Finds T.H.

I felt like screaming, like jumping, maybe even and this was really strange – maybe even dancing.

Dr. Woo's wife was the first into the room, followed by Dr. Woo himself. They each embraced me from one side, such a loving and soft embrace...

Then one by one, all twelve of the people who had been meditating came into the bedroom. They formed a circle around us, and a soft song started playing.

'Love finds the way through...[16]' the lovely, angelical voice sung away.

I felt so much love and joy that it seemed my heart was about to burst like a star. There was an incredible energy running through me, something I had never felt, experienced, or even imagined.

Somehow, in that small room in Colorado, I had been fundamentally transformed.

When the song was finished, Dr. Woo offered me a small sword with a metal sheath.

The sword's handle was resting on his open left palm, I noted, while the tip rested on his open right palm. There was

---

[16] I later looked up the song: 'Love finds the way through,' by Tarisha.

Frank Baler Finds T.H.

no expression on his face, as he looked deep into my eyes. I looked down at the sword, knowing what it meant, but never too sure that I deserved it.

Both the sheath and the handle are engraved with symbols and figures that I had seen at one time or another in some book. I picked up the sword with my left hand off of his left hand, according to Tradition. I showed him the sword, handle on my open left palm, tip on my open right palm.

As I flipped the sword around, I read the engraving on the other side. I was mesmerized as I read the words:

Theophilus Humanini

"That is the name of the sword's rightful owner," Dr. Woo said. "This is your sword, you earned it." He said plainly, still looking into my eyes. I bowed my head down slightly, then said: "I swear to use it only to transfer Light."

Everyone stood motionless and quiet, as if waiting for the solemn vow to be spoken, according to Tradition. I said:

"I will use this sword for the benefit of All, and for the Glory of God. I will seek and share the truth, love, kindness, and

Frank Baler Finds T.H.

forgiveness. I will bless all. I will seek and live the will of God, not mine." Then I added, "so help me God."

To my surprise, everyone in the room said in unison:

"So help you God!"

I looped the sword under my belt, on my left side, still locking eyes with Dr. Woo who stood firmly in front of me. Nobody moved or spoke until Dr. Woo stepped forward and embraced me as an Adept would.

Once Dr. Woo walked out of the ample bedroom, his wife approached and embraced me softly. She walked out as I stood there. Each person then faced me, saluted me in the same way: with their palms touching in front of their chests, lowering their heads slightly, taking one step forward, embracing me softly, then turning around and walking out of the bedroom.

Finally, I was alone in that Colorado bedroom. I looked at the mirror again, feeling quite joyous, I have to admit. After mentally thanking all my Teachers on the Path, and blessing all I could think of, I turned around and walked out slowly.

There was a feast awaiting us in the living room. The table was twice as large as the one we had eaten on the day before;

Frank Baler Finds T.H.

it was packed with all kinds of foods. Soft Asian music played in the background, and people danced softly on the living room. Nobody wore shoes.

After we all ate and celebrated, Dr. Woo handed me an envelope and introduced me to a young woman.

"This is Alice," he said as he handed me the envelope, "she is my personal assistant. She will accompany you to the airport. Here is your ticket."

"Dr. Woo, I have no words to thank you…"

"Don't thank me," he said, "do it for someone else."

With that non-ceremonial goodbye, I was shown to the car. We stopped at the motel to pick up my backpack in the second-floor bedroom. When I dropped the backpack off in the car, I was about to tell the driver that I had to stop at the office to make sure they had charged me for the extra nights. Just then Alice was coming from the motel's office:

"You are all set," she said. I simply brought my hand to my heart and bowed to her slightly, there was nothing to say.

Alice congratulated me sincerely when I got off the car at the Denver airport. I wanted so much to say 'thank you', but not with words, with my soul. I looked at her and tried to speak, my lips were trembling a little.

Alice put her right index finger on my lips; it was an interesting moment of not quite knowing which way this was

Frank Baler Finds T.H.

going. I guess she meant that no words were necessary, then she turned around to get into the car. She shut the door of the shiny sedan and rolled down the window. I looked at her, and she said:

"Frank, true gratitude is about service to others." Then the driver pulled out, and she was gone.

When I got to the airline counter, I handed the lady the envelope Dr. Woo had given me. I never even bothered to check the time of the flight. Freda checked me in and wished me a good flight:

You are all set Doctor. Your seat is 2A. Enjoy your flight home.

Dr. Woo had actually done this; seat 2A was definitely in the front of the aircraft, one of the nice seats.

PART 4

WHAT NOW?

Frank Baler Finds T.H.

Frank Baler Finds T.H.

THE AFTERMATH

Once again, I sat on the white couch at the apartment after a trip that, had it not been for my copious journal notes, I would have no words to describe.

So much had happened in such a short period of time, I thought. I just felt like relaxing for a moment before jumping into action and starting a new life.

Looking out of the panoramic windows, a white truck driving on a road about one third of a mile away from the fifth-floor apartment building where I lived, caught my attention. The driver had been going east, but pulled into the yard across from the building and stopped the truck.

The driver climbed down from the cab and paced back and forth next to the truck. I felt drawn toward him. Quite suddenly, I found myself standing next to the African American man who a moment ago was driving the truck. No physical words were possible, and he did not seem to perceive my presence. Still, words were not needed, for I understood him.

Frank Baler Finds T.H.

This man was about 63 years of age. He was hungry, but he only had five dollars in his wallet. He was not mad or angry, but he felt very sad. I walked up to him, very close, and talked to him, as I would talk to a client in hypnosis at the office. I turned around, took a few steps, then turned back to him and said: I am impressed by you driving that huge truck around town.

As soon as said that last phrase I found myself back on the white couch, still looking out of the panoramic windows, at a white truck on the lot across from the building.

I could see that same driver now running back into the truck with a spring in his step and driving away.

I smiled quietly, knowing what so many before me had discovered. My awareness was no longer limited to the immediacy of my physical body. A sense of relaxed freedom filled me with joy.

As long as I was on the subject of freedom and joy, I thought of a past life in France. I knew intuitively that something which bothered me in my present had something to do with that time. I had already visited a few key events in that life-time, but this time I wondered what that man, I after all, felt as he was dying; what the end was like that time around.

Frank Baler Finds T.H.

My belly was huge. I laid on a small bed by myself. A friend sat close by, we periodically talked. I was sad. My wife had died several years earlier alone in a different country. I was a doctor and had immigrated to work with the understanding that I would hurry back to her. I got caught up in one issue after another, and by the time I came home it was to dispose of her assets. She had already been dead. I felt sad that I never enjoyed her or the marriage; work was all I ever thought about because my work was always tied to my spiritual life. Spiritual life, I thought, is a 24-hour thing.

Back on the white couch I confirmed what I had suspected: my ability to travel in time was also expanded and enhanced, just as my ability to translate into space was. Not only could I reach other times faster and with less ritualistic effort, but also, I was able to get into more detailed emotions and feelings than ever before.

Finally, I wanted to test my ability to reach higher dimensions, but that would wait until nighttime, I thought.

I pulled out my journal and wrote a few notes about the experiments I had just performed. Then I wrote something interesting:

'Just as a baby who is just born needs to develop his body, anguage, and thoughts, I needed to build a new life, almost

Frank Baler Finds T.H.

from scratch. I needed to learn to eat better, make a home, sleep, speak coherently, make a living, organize my bills, and hopefully have some fun. Eventually I will have a woman in my life, with whom I can grow even more. For now, I need to begin to serve others right from where I am at. I can do that because I am really not a baby; a baby would not be able to serve anyone until much later, after much preparation. I can prepare and serve at the same time.'

That is the advantage of living another life in the same body; uninterrupted service even while one builds a life. What is the flip side? What is the disadvantage of starting fresh on the same body?

As I asked the question soft tears filled my eyes… the sort of tears that I came to identify as a connection with my Higher Self. Then I understood and noted on my journal:

'Physical death and reincarnation produce amnesia. Forgetting the past lightens the load in the present. That seems like a good thing, as it is an expression of God's compassion towards us.

'Without memory of our own past, however, life does feel quite unjust. When good things happen, we feel lucky; but when bad things happen, we feel that an injustice has taken place, for we cannot find a cause for our misfortune. The amnesia, therefore, which was meant to lighten the load as an expression of compassion from God, may lock us into the feeling of being a victim of an unfair life. Once a person feels like a victim of an unfair life, they easily quit trying to learn and evolve. 'What for?' They frequently ask in therapy.

'In coming back to life in the same body, and remembering the past, we must go on in service knowing what we have done. At first, it appears that the retrieval of unconscious memories from long ago violates the God-made amnesia that was meant as a form of compassion toward us.

'The disadvantage of starting fresh on the same body, therefore, is that we must often experience the same pain we have inflicted upon others in the past; not as punishment, but as a lesson to be learned of what not to do again.

'If you can endure the pain you inflicted on others – I wrote to myself on my journal – and commit to not doing it again, then you deserve three gifts.

'The first gift is an elimination of the feeling of victimhood, which brings back your will power as a consequence. Now you have something to work for… life is fair, and you will now work to be a better person, to experience more joy, and to restore joy in those from whom you took it.

Frank Baler Finds T.H.

'The second gift is the realization that, despite what you have done, you are alive and well. This means that you were not condemned, there is no hell; instead, you have been forgiven.

'The third gift is the privilege to forgive others. This is a big deal, for doing what God does, consciously and intentionally, even when others hurt us, makes us similar in nature.

To be continued…

Frank Baler Finds T.H.

NOW I NEED A FAVOR FROM YOU

I hope that reading about how I found T.H. has been a good experience for you. I hope you now feel inspired, joyous, and free.

I would love it if you would kindly write a useful review of this book and post it on Amazon. Your sincere review will be very useful in helping others find this book and benefit from this Journey.

Thank you and Blessings,
Frank Baler

UPCOMING BOOKS BY FRANK BALER

———○———

Frank Baler Finds T.H. The Complete Mystical Novel

Living with T.H., by Frank Baler

Made in United States
Orlando, FL
14 May 2024